I AM
UNWORTHY

ANGELA MACK

For all the everyday heroes that have made a difference to someone else's life, no matter how small. Thank you.

Here I am in wave form
Crashing down on you,
The unaware tourist with so much to learn
Drowning your expectations until you learn
to not stereotype.
I am unstoppable.
I am brave.
I am me.

Georgia Richardson

Chapter 1

Isabel

You can do this. You can do this. You can *do* this.

I leaned closer to the bathroom mirror, scrutinizing my reflection through narrowed eyes. I tilted my head left and right, checking my makeup at different angles. If you looked close enough, you could still see the puffiness under my eyes, but it was passable. I didn't usually wear much but I had barely slept the past couple of days. Well, the past week really. The bags under my eyes had been so dark that it looked like I had dirt smeared underneath them. I had probably used half my concealer just to look semi-presentable, but it was important that I felt good today. That I felt confident. I wanted today to go well. Really well. I wanted to get off to a good start. No, I *needed* to get off to a good start.

I looked down and saw that my knuckles were white

from gripping the edges of the sink so fiercely. Shit, I was nervous. I couldn't have another two years like the last couple. I could feel the panic building, clawing at my throat and restricting my oxygen. *Deep breaths, deep breaths.* I closed my eyes and tried to imagine what my perfect day would be like. I would walk through those doors with my head held high. I would have a smile on my face and look carefree. Almost happy to be there. No one would be able to ruin my good mood, because I didn't give a shit about what anyone else thought. I. Didn't. Give. A. Shit. That was my new mantra.

The last couple of years at school hadn't exactly been enjoyable. OK, they'd been hideous. I'd made the mistake of trying to do a good deed and it had come back to bite me on the arse.

I had been friends with a group of girls and honestly, I'm uncertain how I became friends with them in the first place. I never quite felt like I fit in with them. But they were nice enough and I had most of my classes with them, so I kind of fell into their friendship group. Most of them had grown up together and had been friends since primary school. My family and I had moved into the area right before I started at Gilleford Secondary School, so naturally, I hadn't bonded with them in quite the same way.

The whole group was pretty popular, not *Mean Girls* popular, but everyone knew their names and wanted to hang out with them. Ellie Sparks was the most charismatic of the bunch. She was short, a little over five feet, and very curvy. She wasn't the skinny, supermodel type you see in American high school TV shows, but she was still beautiful. She had a round symmetrical face, big blue eyes, and long blonde hair almost to her waist. She had developed early, which the boys loved, and had a great smile. I didn't have a lot in common with her, but it was easy enough to have a superficial conversation with her.

Ellie liked to be bold and stand out from the crowd. Two years ago, she entered into a 'grunge phase,' which was unusual considering the school was dominated by chavs wearing designer labels. Ellie bucked the trend, started wearing heavy eyeliner and listening to Linkin Park and Blink 182. Obviously, everyone in the group started doing the same thing (I'm ashamed to admit that I was also a sheep) and soon she set her sights on a guy with a skinhead and several body piercings.

Jonny was unusual too in the sense that he was charming and likeable. Most of the grungers at school were grumpy, introverted and didn't mix with non-grungers. Jonny, on the other hand, could get along with almost anyone. He was tall, had well-defined arms and shoulders but wasn't overly stocky. He was attractive, for a grunger. Even with the ear stretchers, nose and lip piercings and shaved head.

I think Ellie surprised herself by how hard she fell for him. They were together for about six months, when I overheard a girl gossiping at the back of class one day. She was bragging about how intimate she and Jonny had been at a party over the weekend. And by intimate, I mean that she described in detail a certain sexual act that she had performed. She was another grunger, with black hair and dark brown eyes and pale skin. She was the complete opposite of Ellie.

I struggled, not knowing whether I should say something or keep it to myself. Eventually the guilt I felt for *not* saying anything was too much. Before biology one day, I pulled Ellie aside in a quiet corridor and explained what I had heard. She had cried, flung her arms around me and thanked me for telling her. I had floated home that day, feeling as light as a feather. Little did I realise how pivotal that moment in my school life had been.

The next day I had come to school and strolled over to the benches where our group always sat. There were boys hanging around nearby as per usual and in fact, most of the girls in the group were coupled up. As I approached, the couples had all stopped chatting and turned to stare at me. I felt like I was a caged animal in a zoo. And that's when the bullying started.

"Lying bitch."

"Sneaky little shit."

"She just wanted him for herself…"

Apparently, Ellie had confronted Jonny and he had denied the whole thing. For good measure, he had told her that I was often flirting with him behind her back and he thought I was trying to split them up on purpose. Even though it was obviously, completely untrue, the whole group had turned on me in an instant. The boys ignored me from then on out, as if I didn't exist. The girls, however, were vicious. They made up rumours about my sex life (which was non-existent), shouted out disgusting and embarrassing things in the middle of classes (I still cringed when I thought back to the shouts of "Isabel has a fishy fanny" part-way through English class) and went out of their way to be spiteful. Ellie was the ring-leader, but it seemed like there was no end to the amount of girls that would happily join in on her taunts.

The teachers were useless, pretending they didn't hear the vulgar shouts. I tried so hard to tune it all out, ignoring them and praying they'd get bored after enough time. I even started wearing one headphone during classes, listening to music to block out the background noise, but still being able to hear my teachers. After a couple of unrelenting weeks, I gave up on that tactic and put both my headphones in. I slumped down at the back of class, turning my music up as loud as it could go before the teachers would notice. I didn't care that I was missing out on what was being taught. I just didn't want to hear them anymore.

I had always had reasonably good grades, but my As and Bs soon started dropping to Cs and Ds. Some weeks were so unbearably humiliating that I began faking illnesses and skipping lessons. I prayed to a God that I didn't believe in that they would stop sooner or later. Surely, someone else would unwittingly stumble into their firing line? I was a terrible human being really, hoping that some other poor soul would swap places with me and bear the brunt of their bullying. But I'd take all the bad karma in the world if it meant they would stop. They didn't though. Two years later and I was still cowering in the school bathroom before classes.

I opened my eyes and glared. I was sure the mirror was going to shatter under the force of my stare. I gritted my teeth, grinding them from side to side. It wasn't going to be like that anymore. This was the first day of sixth form and it was going to be completely different. I didn't give a shit, remember? I was a new person with new confidence and nothing bothered me. It was all like water off a duck's back. Yep, that was me. Couldn't care less what anyone thought. And besides, I wouldn't be alone anymore and the bullies wouldn't be here anyway.

My reflection shrugged nonchalantly in the mirror as I tried to get into character. If I acted like I didn't care, eventually it would be true. Right? I pulled my shoulders back and strode confidently from the bathroom. I wouldn't waste any more time hiding in there, no siree. It was like I had tunnel vision. I was going to get to that sixth form common room and I was going to get there without incident. But even if someone did shout something at me, it wouldn't matter. I. Didn't. Give. A. Shit. I just hoped that no one noticed the tremble in my legs, the beads of sweat gathering at my brow, or that I was practically running. Kind of ruined the self-assured facade I was going for, really.

I hesitated for a split second before I pushed open the double doors of the common room in front of me. I scanned the room. *Please be here, please be here*. My persona started to falter even more as each second ticked by that I couldn't see them. I was about to turn and bolt when I caught someone waving at me out of the corner of my eye. My smile slipped back into place as I relaxed, sauntering over as if I wasn't the most terrified person in the world and about to have a meltdown.

"Hey Izzy. Didn't think we'd abandoned you, did ya?" Sophie smiled as I sat down.

"And even if we had, it wouldn't have mattered. Right?" Jess winked.

"Because I don't give a shit!" The three of us chorused together, making me laugh. Jess had been the one to come up with that particular chant, encouraging me to use it every time I felt even slightly anxious.

I had befriended Jess and Sophie over the summer break. They both lived in Woodley End too, a little village on the very outskirts of Gilleford, Suffolk. Originally a small, lazy village set in the middle of rolling hills and vast farmland, a couple of developers had purchased some of the arable terrain about ten years ago. New build housing estates had started popping up all over ever since. My house was at the start of one of these estates, down a quiet street with a forest at the end of it. I absolutely loved where we lived and this increased even more when the bullying started; few people from school lived anywhere near us. It was a good twenty-minute bus journey from central Gilleford, where most other students lived. At least I'd had a reprieve at weekends and didn't have to worry much about bumping into anyone.

This was true even though I worked every Saturday at a florist in town, *Buttercups.* It was amongst a little parade of shops near the high street, but teenagers don't tend to visit florists. Most of the kids I knew didn't work at all and wouldn't be awake any earlier than 10 a.m. on a Saturday. This meant that even my bus journey into work was mostly uneventful. Occasionally I'd come across someone whilst waiting at the bus stop to go home, but even if someone did screech obscenities at me, it didn't bother me as much. I would soon be home and away from them.

Don't get me wrong, my parents were financially stable and always gave me money when I asked for it. But they had wanted me to learn the value of money early on. I had started working at the florist almost a year ago when I turned sixteen and was pleasantly surprised by how independent I felt. It was only minimum wage, but that was a fair bit of money for someone who didn't have any friends to go out with. Still, if I wanted to buy a new book or some new clothes, I could make most of the purchases myself without asking my parents for money. It was very self-gratifying. In fact, it felt like the only positive thing in my life. I always counted down the days of the week until Saturday.

One afternoon, two girls had walked into the florist. I recognized them and knew that they attended my school. I had seen them around and they had never said anything untoward to me, but I felt the familiar pang of anxiety swirl through my stomach. You never knew when someone would have the sudden urge to be unkind.

The shop owner, a gentle middle-aged lady called Mary, was currently in the back room checking a delivery. She would be out there for at least another ten minutes, making sure the delivery driver was being careful with the flowers and ensuring all the stock had arrived. I knew I was going to have to serve them. There was no chance of me hiding in the back room. I plastered on my fake 'customer smile,' took a deep breath, and asked how I could help.

"Hey. It's Isabel, right?" the brunette asked. She was short, pale with freckles and had mousy brown hair. She was pretty in a very natural way, despite the layers of makeup she had caked on. I nodded at her.

"I'm Jess and this is Sophie," she said, gesturing to the girl next to her. Sophie was a similar height but where Jess was skinny, Sophie had a very athletic build. She was probably the same dress size as Jess (they were both easily an eight) but her arms were toned and she had shapely legs. Her long, blonde hair was wavy and thick and she was very tanned, as if she spent a long time outside in the sun. Sophie smiled and I could feel relief begin to creep up on me, albeit reluctantly. They seemed harmless enough. I hoped.

"It's my mum's birthday today and we're having some family and friends over. I wanna surprise her with a bunch of flowers, around twenty quid please," Jess said. I was grateful to be able to turn away and break eye contact. I appraised our flower display, plucking a selection of my favourite seasonal blossoms. I soon had a bright bunch ready, filled with yellow gerbera daisies, yellow roses and a couple of sunflowers. She paid, smiled her thanks and both girls turned to leave. Jess hesitated as she reached the door, turning back to me. My heart leapt into my throat, certain she was about to fling out a parting snide comment.

"Are you doing anything tonight?" she asked

instead. I shook my head, wary of where this was going.

"Would you like to come? To my mum's birthday get-together, I mean? You only live a few streets over from me and my dad keeps telling me 'the more the merrier.' So you should come, if you want to...?" Was this a trick? Why was she asking me? Would there be other girls from school going and she only wanted to lure me over for some more humiliation? I could hear my pulse roaring in my ears.

"I'm the only other person from school going. The rest are Jess's mum's friends or close family. But it should still be cool," Sophie chimed in, as if reading my mind. To this day, I'm not sure what made Jess ask me and I have no idea what possessed me to agree, but it was the start of a great friendship between the three of us. We were inseparable all summer after that. My parents were so relieved when my disposition improved. I had never confided in them what was happening at school, so my drop in grades and mood swings had confused them. They suspected something was going on when I stopped socializing and buried myself in books. I was doing anything I could to escape reality. My mum often tried to coax it out of me, but I knew she wouldn't understand. The bullying was never physical and I thought I would sound weak that I couldn't handle some name-calling. I also didn't want her intervening in any way. She was fiercely protective of me, both my parents were as I was their only child, but they would only make things worse.

Still, none of that mattered now. Sixth form was a fresh start. As Jess and Sophie chatted about the latest series on Netflix that they were binge watching, I coolly glanced around. The three of us were grouped together near the entrance doors, our plastic chairs pulled together. My gaze flitted across the faces of the other students in the room, being careful not to make eye contact. I didn't want to draw attention to myself.

"She's not here, Iz. I already told you. I even double-checked Facebook this morning in case there were any last-minute changes. But there weren't." Jess had a glimmer of pity in her eyes as she reassured me, yet again, that Ellie wouldn't be here.

I had deleted my Facebook account last year when Ellie and her friends had started up cyber-bullying. It clearly wasn't good enough to just do it face to face. Jess knew how nervous I was about coming back, so had kept tabs on everyone. She happily informed me every time someone posted an excited update, confirming that they were doing something other than attending Gilleford Sixth Form after summer. Crucially, Ellie was not returning this year as she had chosen an apprenticeship in hairdressing instead.

Jess and Sophie had never witnessed Ellie's cruelty towards me. Gilleford Secondary School had hundreds of kids attending, so it wasn't surprising that we hadn't had any classes together previously, or seen each other in the canteen at lunchtime. However, everyone had heard of Isabel Johnson, the jealous, lanky girl who tried to steal Ellie Sparks' boyfriend, and who deserved everything she got.

But this year I was going to be Isabel Johnson, the girl who, yep you guessed it, didn't give a shit.

Chapter 2

Joshua

"Fuck off and stare at someone else or I'll rip your fucking head off."

I watched the skinny, little runt duck his head and run off, desperate to escape my wrath. I looked around and glared at the other students in the corridor, daring them to continue staring. I smirked when I saw them all avert their eyes and scurry away or busy themselves. I knew why they were looking at me. I had a black eye, a busted lip and my eyebrow was split open. I was always getting into fights and to be fair, most of the students and teachers didn't bat an eyelid anymore. But it was the beginning of a new year and the new students always stared. Until they learned the hard way that I didn't like being gawked at.

The good thing about now being in sixth form was

that I didn't have to wear that godawful uniform. We were told to dress smart and that was it. For the first time, I wasn't tugging at my tie and loosening my top button to breathe. I was kind of stretching the definition of 'smart' though, choosing to wear black jeans, a black polo top and some black trainers. I wasn't going to waste money buying poncey trousers or shirts. They didn't fit me properly half the time anyway. The trousers were always too tight in the leg, and the shirts too tight across the chest or arms. I was pretty muscly for a sixteen-year-old, with thick thighs, broad shoulders and decent sized biceps. I worked out a lot. I had to be able to defend myself.

I had fifteen minutes before classes were due to start, so I strolled towards the sixth form common room. It was at the very back of Gilleford Secondary School, in a separate demountable building and away from the younger students. Although Gilleford Sixth Form was part of the same campus, the sixth formers had their own designated areas. Apparently, we were morphing into adults now, so we were allowed the illusion of superiority; we didn't have to mingle with the uniform dwellers.

The common room was a large, white, square block of a building. Single storey, with small square windows evenly spread out along all sides. It was nothing particularly inspiring. It was like they wanted to spend as little money as possible, so constructed the most basic building they could. There was a ramp to the left, winding up towards the central double doors, with steps on the right for a more direct route. Not in any hurry, I ambled up the ramp, letting my fingertips trail along the steel railing that ran alongside it. I caught glimpses of students as I passed the windows. They were sitting in groups and gossiping, no doubt exchanging stories about all the thrilling things they had been up to over the summer. Most of them looked happy to be back. Excited even. I couldn't care less. I was just biding my time until I was eighteen and old enough to be legally considered an adult. Adults could make their own decisions without being judged. Adults didn't have to answer to anyone.

I pushed open the doors and gave the equally dull and unimpressive interior a once-over. It was one open room with some navy-blue lockers lining the front wall. There were random clusters of furniture spread throughout, with mismatched chairs, sofas and tables. It was like a dumping ground for unwanted furniture. The floor was dark grey carpet, with sporadic thread-bare patches and colourful stains that I didn't look too closely at. It was dimly lit, as if the person who designed the space knew that they wouldn't want you scrutinizing the room too much.

"Fuck, you look like shit, mate. Who did you piss off this time?" My one and only pal scrunched up his nose as he looked at my face. Ollie Boon was a fucking funny guy. He was quick-witted with a fucked-up sense of humour that always seemed to get him into trouble. He, like me, got into plenty of fights. He was always goading people and winding them up, knowing exactly what to say to get a rise out of them. He loved it and got a kick out of pissing people off. The bigger the reaction they gave him, the bigger he smiled.

Ollie was quite short for a bloke at about five foot eight inches, considerably shorter than my six foot two frame. But he could still hold his own. He was a quick motherfucker with an impressive right-hook. Together we had taken on people older and bigger and still managed to come out on top. He always had my back and I always had his.

"Who don't I piss off, mate? You know me, I irritate the fuck out of people just by breathing," I shrugged.

"Big Mike then?" Ollie asked me, giving me a knowing look. Big Mike was the one guy I could never beat in a fight. It wasn't for lack of trying, trust me. But he wasn't called Big Mike for nothing. I shrugged again, not wanting to talk about it.

"I tell you what, I am loving the whole 'no uniform' thing. Look at Lucy over there, her tits look amazing," Ollie said. He gestured towards a petite brunette wearing a very tight, low-cut white blouse. She was sitting with around ten other students at the far back right of the common room. I shook my head at him, laughing. Ollie knew not to push me to talk about something I didn't want to and was always good at changing the subject. More often than not, changing the subject always involved talking about girls.

Lucy clearly heard Ollie's remark, he hadn't exactly whispered it, as she turned and gave him the middle finger. Ollie blew her a kiss, causing her to frown, flick her hair over her shoulder and turn back to her conversation. Some other students had obviously overheard their exchange, glancing at us and smirking or rolling their eyes. They were used to Ollie's antics and loud opinions.

Whilst looking our way, I saw a few of them notice my face, their eyes widening. Most turned away pretty quickly, a few others shook their heads in disgust. I was used to being judged. Most people thought I started fights on purpose and that I enjoyed making trouble. And they were right most of the time. Big Mike had been particularly aggressive this last time though and I had a banging headache. Normally he avoided hitting me anywhere that would be visible to other people. Didn't want to get into trouble, I 'spose. For whatever reason, I had annoyed him enough for him to forgo his usual rule.

I spied an empty wooden bench, the kind that you would usually expect to see outside in a park, and made my way over to it. I dumped my black backpack on top, unzipping it and starting to rifle through it. I always kept a pack of paracetamol in there. Ollie followed me over, sitting on the tabletop and letting his feet rest on the part you would usually sit on.

"What A Levels did you sign up to?" he asked, watching me rifle through my bag.

"P.E., business studies and art," I replied. I had picked the easiest subjects I could. I wasn't planning on using them for any kind of career. I didn't kid myself. I knew I wasn't going to university and I wouldn't have some highly paid, hotshot job waiting for me afterwards. I wouldn't have even bothered coming back to sixth form if I didn't have to, but someone would notice if I wasn't continuing my education in any way at all. I couldn't afford to draw attention to myself like that.

I knew Ollie was going to sixth form and if I was going to be stuck in education, might as well be with my mate. Unlike me, Ollie was intelligent and had big plans for going to university and escaping this shithole town.

Back in the early days of secondary school, our teachers had been surprised that Ollie was so clever. It wasn't typical for a boy from our neighbourhood with a penchant for violence to actually have half a brain. But no matter how many lessons he skipped or how often he ended up in detention, he usually achieved As. Especially maths. He was a whizz kid when it came to numbers. He had signed up for A Levels as soon as possible, whereas I had only applied last week. I had somehow convinced the Head to allow me to come back on short notice and with my mediocre GCSE grades.

"What about you?" I asked, finally locating the pack of painkillers.

"Maths, business studies and…"

"Ah fuck…" I interrupted him. "Fucking packet is empty." I massaged my forehead, cursing myself for not thinking to put a new pack in my bag after using the last one up. I didn't think I'd make it through the whole day without some kind of pain relief.

"You got any paracetamol or ibuprofen on you?" I asked Ollie, even though I knew what the answer would be.

"You know I'm not a pussy like you, I never need that crap," Ollie grinned at me. *Cheeky shit*. I growled, frustrated with myself. I really did not fancy going to classes with the pain throbbing through my head right now. I contemplated skipping my first class to go to the shop down the road from school. I worked there part-time and Tracy, the assistant manager and Ollie's mum, would likely give me a couple of boxes for free. I could get there and back in twenty minutes, so I wouldn't miss much.

"Here, I've got some." I heard a chair scrape back as a girl balanced her chair on its back legs. She stretched over towards me, holding out a box of paracetamol. She and her friends were sitting in a selection of random chairs not far from where Ollie and I were sitting. I hadn't paid them any attention when I walked over and they hadn't seemed to notice us either. Now though, her friends had both stopped talking, waiting to see how I would react. I didn't exactly have a reputation for being friendly and often snapped at people for no reason. The girl sitting next to her was shocked, her eyes so wide I thought they might pop out of their sockets.

"Well, do you want some?" the girl said, shaking the box at me when I didn't respond straight away. I looked at her and she gave me a small smile. *Isabel Johnson*. Her name flicked into my brain. We had been at the same school for years, but I had never been in any classes with her. I'm pretty sure this was the first time she'd ever spoken to me, even though I knew she worked in the florist next door to the shop I worked in. I'd seen her enter the florist early every Saturday morning as I walked to work. She had never once made any effort to even look at me, let alone say hello. She seemed rather stuck up, if I'm honest. I had no interest in talking to her. We had absolutely zero in common and I knew she came from a well-off part of town. That didn't mean I couldn't admire her from a distance though.

She had long reddish-brown hair that was dead straight, falling to the middle of her back. She was slim but not skinny. Her tits were probably a B or C cup. She peered up at me now, her bright green eyes staring at me expectantly. She was pretty stunning really. But it fucked me off that she had always acted as if I was invisible and now all of a sudden, she wanted to chat? Yeah, alright. She could do one.

The bell rang, signifying five minutes until classes started. Everyone around us started standing up and grabbing their things, including Isabel's friends. I still hadn't given her an answer and her friends called her name, turning towards the door to go. She let her chair fall back down flat on the ground with a thump and stood up. *Woah, she's tall for a girl.* I hadn't noticed before, but she was only a few inches shorter than me. I could appreciate her figure even more now up close too. Her long legs were squeezed into black skinny jeans and she wore a plain black, long-sleeved t-shirt. Her outfit was nothing special, but on her, it looked great. Effortless. She clearly wasn't particularly bothered about dressing smartly either.

Isabel opened the box of painkillers, took a packet out and slid it across the bench to me.

"You look like you need these more than me," she smiled again, bending down to pick up her belongings. I scowled at her and her smile slipped a little. She placed the now half-empty box back in her black leather handbag and slung it over her shoulder. I watched as she walked out the doors of the common room, joining her friends that were hovering outside.

"Why the fuck didn't you say something to her, you arsehole? Someone was actually being nice to you for a change and you looked at her as if she was a piece of shit." Ollie punched me in the shoulder, shaking his head at me. I shrugged again.

"Just playing the part, dickhead. Can't have people thinking I'm suddenly a nice guy," I replied. I snatched the paracetamol Isabel left behind, popping three in my mouth. I swallowed them down dry, grateful that I didn't have to walk to the shop after all.

"You're a knob. Come on, I don't want to be late for my first maths lesson." Ollie jumped off the table, making the nearby windows shudder as he thumped down. This 'building' really was a cheap pile of shit.

"And you're such a nerd. *I don't want to be late for maths*," I mimicked in a high-pitched voice. Ollie grinned at me as he skipped towards the exit. He was an oddball. I smiled to myself as I followed him. Despite having a shitty summer and an even shittier weekend, I found my mood improving. Besides, it was better being here than being stuck at home.

Chapter 3

Isabel

I don't know what I was thinking. Why, oh why, did I think it was a good idea to try and talk to Joshua Bugg? I didn't really know him, but I knew of his reputation. He certainly wasn't someone to mess with.

"Izzy, have you gone completely mad? What the fuck was that?" Jess asked me as we hurried down the common room steps towards one of the main buildings. I didn't know how to respond. I guess I got caught up in playing my new 'character.' When I'd overheard someone complaining about not having any paracetamol, instead of ignoring them and trying to stay invisible, I thought *sod it* and reached for my own supply. I always kept some on me, having frequently suffered with migraines and headaches. My doctor said they were stress related.

When I stretched back to offer the box, I had no idea it was Joshua that had been talking. I had kind of frozen, smiling a little awkwardly to try and break the tension. Predictably, he had given me a thunderous look. But then again, anyone that had taken that kind of beating would likely be super cranky too. His left eye was almost swollen shut and there was some dried blood in his eyebrow above it. I bet it hurt like a bitch. His lip looked terrible too. It was as if someone had given him a huge dose of Botox.

I decided to give him the benefit of the doubt, something new I was also trying out this year, and give him half of the paracetamol anyway. I then scurried away as quickly as possible, my earlier bravery completely dissipating after he didn't even say thank you.

"I didn't realise it was him. I was trying to be helpful," I said sheepishly.

"I know you're trying to come out of your shell more this year but jeez, talking to Joshua is an easy way to attract trouble." Jess' high heels clacked on the polished wooden floor as we entered the humanities building. She wanted to study fashion at university and definitely looked the part today. She was wearing a tight black skirt, white frilly blouse and very high, black shiny shoes. Being so tall, I never wore heels. Ever. I had noticed that quite a few of the boys had caught up to my five foot eleven inches over the summer (some even over-taking me, to my great delight). Unsurprisingly, most of the girls were still way off and I knew it would stay that way. I often felt like a giant next to Jess and

Sophie and loved it when Jess wore heels. She was still only up to my shoulders wearing them, but it made me feel a little better.

"Well, I think it was nice of her. I'd have definitely been too scared to do it myself, but his face looked awful. No wonder he needed some pain relief,' Sophie said, smiling reassuringly at me.

"Woah, woah, woah, hang on. His face did not look awful. If anything, the bruising just added to the whole 'bad boy' image he's got going on. He still looked gorgeous," Jess said, as Sophie and I rolled our eyes at each other. Jess loved boys. She was a big flirt and with her looks, she got a lot of attention.

Not that I disagreed with her. Joshua was definitely hot. He was taller than me, which was a big plus in my book, and had an incredible body. You could tell he lived in the gym; I don't think there was an ounce of fat on him. His hair was so dark it was almost black. It was short on the sides and back but longer and mussed on top, as if he was forever running his fingers through it. He had a very chiselled jawline and I hadn't noticed before today, but he had coffee brown eyes. If he wasn't carrying such a chip on his shoulder and he wasn't always scowling, he would be even better looking.

"I don't know what all the fuss is about. He doesn't look like anything special to me." A boy fell into step next to Jess, bumping her shoulder fondly.

"Hi Ed," she smiled up at him. I was pretty sure Sophie had mentioned a guy in their classes last year called Ed, who had a big crush on Jess. Although he was trying to appear playful, you could still see the jealous glint in his eye.

I was the only one that had a class in the humanities building, but you could get to almost every other building by cutting through it. This building was a lot older than the rest of the school, being the first one erected when it opened in the 1950s. It had large arched windows, high ceilings and ornate brickwork. The library was in the very heart of the building and was my favourite place to be when at school. I had spent many lunch times alone in there, seeking safety and isolation. This building felt comforting to me. The other buildings had been added as the number of pupils expanded over time. The campus now consisted of five different buildings, but the others were all square and boxy. Nothing as architecturally interesting as this one.

"See you at break?" Sophie said as I arrived outside of my history class. I had chosen mostly the same A Levels as Sophie, so I knew I'd have at least one friend in the majority of my classes. She had chosen biology, chemistry and maths. She regularly helped out on her family's farm and was dead set on becoming a vet. I, on the other hand, had no idea what I wanted to do for a career. It had been hard enough thinking about enduring the rest of school, let alone what to do after it. I enjoyed science so I felt comfortable choosing biology and chemistry too. However, I hated maths with a passion, so my third choice was history. I was anxious about not knowing who else was in the class, but I was feeling cautiously optimistic. I was just grateful that they had let me in the Sixth Form in the first place; I had barely made the minimum entry requirements. And even then, I think they would have happily booted me out if they hadn't been so under-subscribed. Luckily for me, they needed as many students as possible to maximise their government funding.

"Sure thing," I smiled as my friends walked off towards their classes, Ed following like a lost puppy. Watching them leave, I felt like pinching myself. I actually had friends again.

~

So far, my first week back had gone brilliantly. My timetable was pretty decent, with various 'free periods' spread out between my usual classes. I had never had a free period before, but I was quickly learning to love them. Jess, Sophie and I had fallen into the routine of meeting up in the library and studying together. We were trying to get a head-start on the mountain of coursework we had already been set. Towards the end of the week, Ed started joining us along with his best friend Jack. I felt a little sorry for Ed as he was doing his best to capture Jess' affections, but she was adamant he wasn't her type. He had a warm smile and kind eyes with a smattering of freckles across his nose. He was tanned, lean and broadcasted 'nice guy' vibes. But that wasn't enough for Jess, apparently.

Instead of studying in silence like I usually did, the group was relatively chatty, even though the library was supposed to be a 'quiet zone.' I found out that Jack and Ed were pretty funny and often had all three of us girls in fits of giggles, earning us stern glances from the librarian. This of course made us laugh harder and it was a miracle that we didn't get kicked out all week. I can't remember the last time I laughed at school so much.

It was Thursday afternoon and I was walking towards the bus stop by myself. For once, I didn't feel scared or anxious, my spirits lifted after such a positive week. Sophie, Jess and I had been travelling together on the bus since the beginning of term, but not today. They had both joined the girls' netball team and had training after classes every Thursday. Nothing could convince me to do sports of any kind. I was ridiculously uncoordinated, often resembling a newborn foal trying to walk for the first time. And even when I was cold, I struggled with sweating. I had tried every type of deodorant available and even though I never smelled, I always struggled with dark patches under my arms. This was the reason I rarely wore coloured clothing; sweat patches didn't show up as much on black or white clothes. Ellie and her gang had taken great pleasure pointing one out whenever they could, so now I was super self-conscious of them.

This is why even when Sophie and Jess begged me to join the team (apparently, with my height, I would be a great goalkeeper), I refused. My face also has an annoying habit of going red within minutes of me doing any kind of exercise. I had no desire to look like a sweaty beetroot. Nope, this year I would only do things that I wanted to do. I was not going to be pressured into situations that made me feel uncomfortable. Not even by my friends, who only had good intentions.

As I neared the bus stop, which was the same bus stop I used to get to and from the florist, I thought about stopping in to say hi to Mary. She was a sweet lady and *Buttercups* was her pride and joy. When she'd put the ad up in her window for help on a Saturday, I had instantly been drawn to it. The florist was full of bright colours and had a modern yet comforting feel. The sign above the door was lime green on a neon pink background and the arrangements in the window were always over-the-top and eye-catching. Definitely not traditional in any way.

Mary had taught me the basics of flower arranging, so I could put together a simple bunch of flowers using complimentary colours. I left the bolder and more outlandish things to her. Her latest window display was very restrained compared to usual though. The centrepiece was a black wire-framed mannequin. It was the type that had no head or limbs, only the torso. She had constructed a dress made solely out of red roses. The bodice was made of rose petals with little jewels in the centre and the skirt was made of full-stemmed roses. They were layered over the top of each other and fanned outwards. It was amazing. I was desperate to ask her to show me how she did it when I went into work tomorrow.

As I was nearing the doorway, I noticed two young boys standing at the fish and chip shop next door. There were only four shops along the little parade: the chip shop, then *Buttercups*, the convenience store called *Martins*, and then a hardware store. The two lads didn't look very old. I looked around but didn't see any adults nearby. One of them was in the Gilleford navy blazer, pale blue shirt and navy tie, so he must be a little older than he looked. No more than twelve years old though. The other boy was even younger and was in the St. James Primary School dark green and grey uniform. St James' was across the road from Gilleford Secondary School. There was a strong resemblance between the two boys, presumably brothers. They both had dark hair and dark eyes and they were currently staring longingly in the fish and chip shop window. The younger one's nose was almost touching the glass.

"I can't remember the last time we had fish and chips," the oldest one murmured.

"Can we get some, pleeeeaaase?" the younger one said, bouncing on the balls of his feet in excitement at the idea of it.

"Don't be fucking stupid Georgie, you know we don't have the money for that. We're going to wait here for the food shopping, take it home and then I'll make you something to eat." The little one, Georgie, turned away from the window, his eyes shining.

"I don't want Pot Noodle again, Ryan," he said to his older brother, pouting. "It never fills me up."

"Yeah, well, it's cheap," Ryan muttered, crossing his arms. This little exchange was pulling at my heartstrings. They both looked underweight, with their uniforms hanging off of their thin frames. I fingered the ten pound note I had in my pocket, wondering if they'd accept the money from me. There was something about the older one, Ryan, that made me think not. He looked like the sort to get offended if anyone tried to help him.

I started feeling uncomfortable just at the idea of a possible confrontation, but I desperately wanted to put a smile back on Georgie's face. He was a cute little thing. I don't know why, but it bothered me that someone so young looked like he had the weight of the world on his shoulders.

An idea popped into my head. I strolled past them both into the chip shop. If they were still here when I came back outside, then I had made up my mind that I would do something to help.

Ten minutes later, I came out holding two portions of fish and chips. The boys were still standing outside, talking quietly to each other. I took a deep breath and headed towards them. I could feel my hands starting to tremble. *Don't be ridiculous, Isabel. Get a hold of yourself. They're only young, nothing to be scared of.*

"Would either of you like some fish and chips? I think they must have gotten my order wrong and given me an extra portion by mistake," I said, holding one of the wrapped bundles out towards them. Georgie instantly broke into a smile but Ryan frowned, looking suspicious.

"We can't give you any money for it," he said, eyeing up my outstretched hand.

"That's OK, they didn't charge me for it anyway. Like I said, I think they made a mistake," I rambled, praying that they didn't hear my voice crack. I was lying through my teeth, but I was determined to see my good deed through (I clearly hadn't learned my lesson when it came to those). Georgie peeked sideways up at his brother, waiting for his reaction. After a second or two, he quickly lunged at the food and grabbed it out of my hands, before turning and running.

"Georgie! Wait! Where the fuck are you going?" Ryan shouted after him. I smothered a laugh as he ran after his little brother, throwing evil eyes at me over his shoulder. I saw my bus pull up and hopped aboard, feeling pretty happy with myself. I placed the spare portion of fish and chips on my lap, wondering how I would explain it to my parents when I got home.

As the bus travelled down the road a few minutes later, I could see Georgie and Ryan huddled together on a bench, stuffing their faces with chips. I smiled again, proud of myself for not letting my nerves get the better of me and for bringing a little bit of happiness to two little boys. It felt good to not be afraid of people anymore.

Chapter 4

Joshua

WTF? Where are you?

I sent the text and waited impatiently, standing outside with two bags of shopping at my feet and my arms crossed. I started my shift at *Martins* fifteen minutes ago and DeeDee, the miserable old bat that was supervising today, would get the right ump if I didn't go back inside soon.

It was early September and unusually warm for the UK at this time of year. Usually overcast, wet and chilly, the past week had been clear, blue skies with lots of sunshine. It wasn't quite shorts and t-shirt weather, but you didn't have to wear a jumper much either. There seemed to be fewer cars on the road today, with people choosing to walk outside in the warmth instead.

I was about to turn back inside and leave the bags in

the staff room, when I noticed my brothers running towards me. You would know the three of us were related within seconds of seeing us near each other. They were like little mini versions of me, with the same hair and eye colour. However, they were both small for their age and definitely hadn't inherited the same height genes as me.

Ryan in particular was very skinny these days, and I looked at him with dismay as I saw how big his blazer looked on him. He was in his second year at Gilleford Secondary School and even though he'd be a teenager next year, he could easily pass for ten years old. Georgie was all skin and bones and his eyes were a little bigger, making his face appear even more gaunt. It really wasn't a good look for a nine-year-old.

I made a mental note to try and stock up on some more carbs for the next week's lot of shopping. I replenished our food stock from *Martins* every week and I couldn't help but feel guilty over the crappy job I was doing. The boys looked hungry and thin and it was my fault.

"Hey you two, where ya been? You know you're supposed to come and collect the shopping from me on your way home every Thursday," I said. I stretched a smile across my face and tried to appear more upbeat than I felt.

"Blame Georgie," Ryan responded, rolling his eyes at our younger brother. He had a smile on his face though, as if he couldn't quite be annoyed at Georgie. I looked at the little monster, waiting for an explanation.

"A girl offered us some fish and chips for free

because they messed her order up and it smelled so good and I didn't think Ryan would let us have it so I snatched it and ran away and we ate it all…" Georgie rushed in one breath, turning a little red with the effort. He looked down at his feet, worried about my reaction.

"And who was this girl?" I asked after I had a moment to digest what he'd told me. I raised my eyebrows at him, not quite sure whether to believe his story or not.

"I don't know, never seen her before," he mumbled. I looked over at Ryan for confirmation, but he shrugged at me.

"Well, accepting food from strangers probably isn't the best idea, but we deserve a little bit of good luck for a change," I said, ruffling Georgie's hair. He looked up at me in relief.

"Thanks for saving me some too, shitheads," I joked with them. Ryan knew I was winding them up, I'd never make them share food with me, but Georgie looked horrified.

"I'm so sorry, we should have…"

"Hey, I'm just messing around, you tit, don't worry about it," I laughed and Georgie relaxed again.

"OK, here ya go," I said, as I handed them a bag of shopping each. "Don't forget to hide the extras…"

"…In the den. Yeah, yeah, we know…" Ryan interrupted.

"Don't give me attitude, boy," I teased and he huffed in response. "There's a surprise in there too," I gestured to the bag Georgie was holding. He started rifling around in the bag, scrunching up his nose as he moved several Pot Noodles out of the way (I made another mental note to swap these for something else next week). He finally located what I'd hidden at the bottom.

"A twin pack of Oreos!" He exclaimed, joy spreading across his face. Ryan rolled his eyes at him, but I knew they were his favourite too.

"They were reduced to less than a quid but make sure you make them last. I don't know when they will be on offer again," I warned. He nodded enthusiastically before ripping the pack open, shoving two in his face. He handed two to Ryan too, who also jammed them in his mouth, before offering me two. I shook my head.

"You both eat them, but once they're gone, they're gone," I said. Georgie and Ryan split my two biscuits between them before Georgie scrunched the packaging closed again, replacing them in the shopping bag.

"I'll be home around nine but come get me straight away if you have any trouble," I said and they both nodded.

"Thanks, Joshy. You're the best." Georgie threw his arms around me unexpectedly. Ryan snickered as he knew I hated Georgie's pet name for me, but I always let it slide.

"You're welcome. Now off you go, see you soon." I waved them off, watching them until they completely disappeared from view, before turning to go back inside.

"You've been out there twenty minutes! If you don't want your pay docked, you can stay later tonight to make up the time," DeeDee raged as soon as I walked through the door. I sighed. I couldn't be arsed to deal with her right now. I glanced sideways at her as I walked past, working my way towards the back room where I had been putting away the latest delivery.

DeeDee was in her early forties but from looking at her, you'd think she was sixty. Years of chain smoking had left her face etched with deep wrinkles and yellowish skin. Her grey hair was pulled back into a severe bun and she had so much eyeliner on, she resembled a panda. She was close friends with the wife of the owner of *Martins*, an independent convenience store. This was how despite her poor customer service and complete disregard for the staff, she had worked her way up to supervisor. To her dismay, Ollie's mum Tracy was friends with the owner himself (a guy called Martin, funnily enough) and had been offered the promotion to assistant manager over DeeDee. DeeDee had been furious, even more so when Tracy's first act was to hire me as a part-time store assistant. That was a little over two years ago now and DeeDee still hated my guts.

I was lucky that Tracy had taken pity on me and convinced Martin to hire a young lad to help in his store. Ollie and I had been best friends for as long as I could remember, so she was very familiar with me and my family. She looked out for us when she could and her getting me this job was the best thing that could have happened to me.

Martin pays me cash at the end of each week because I'm still at school and work more hours than I am legally supposed to. Unfortunately, cash can be easily snatched away and is difficult to hide. That's why I keep most of my wages in my locker in the staff room, careful of how much I keep on me at once. I was lucky Martin was willing to bend the rules a bit for me.

I work 3.30 p.m. 'til 9 p.m. on a Monday, Wednesday and Thursday and then 9 a.m. 'til 9 p.m. on a Saturday. It's minimum wage so it only works out to about a hundred and twenty pounds a week, but it's enough to keep my brothers clothed and fed and the bills paid. Mostly.

"Oi! I'm talking to you. Are you going to stay late and make up the time tonight, or what?" DeeDee screeched at me as I pushed through the doors to the back storeroom.

"No, you can dock my pay," I mumbled. What I actually wanted to say was *go fuck yourself*, but I couldn't do anything to risk being fired. Plus, Tracy was in charge of submitting payroll at the end of each month. I knew she'd ignore it if my hours looked weird on DeeDee's shifts.

Tracy was an angel. A single mum to Ollie who knew exactly what it was like to not have anyone to help you raise a family. She knew how unbearable DeeDee could be and tried to put me on as few of her shifts as possible. Still, it wasn't completely unavoidable considering there were only seven members of staff in total, including Martin.

Not getting the reaction she wanted, DeeDee huffed and walked away, leaving me to it. I rolled my eyes. *Only five more hours to go.*

~

"Hey buddy, how was your evening?" I whispered to Ryan as I shuffled into our bedroom. I flopped down on my bed, turning to look across at him. Our room was small and unremarkable, with a set of bunk beds on the right hand-side. My single bed was pushed up against the wall opposite, leaving about a metre of floor space between them. Ryan was watching a film on a small television mounted on the wall at the end of his bed, the volume turned down low so as not to wake Georgie. Ryan always slept on the bottom bunk and Georgie on the top one.

There were no other pieces of furniture in the pale grey room. We only had as much as we did because I had managed to scrounge it for free from either Gumtree or Facebook selling sites. It was amazing what people decided to give away when they were moving house, or bored of something. Or they couldn't be bothered with the hassle of selling something. I mean, who gives a set of bunk beds away for free? Sure, I had to do some repair work and it had been a bitch to get home (Ollie and I had done six trips of walking the various parts back here from a house a few streets over), but it was free!

There wasn't enough room for a wardrobe, so the three of us used an airing cupboard just outside the bedroom. We had a couple of stacked plastic boxes for items like underwear and socks, and the rest we hung up using a rail I had fitted. We lived in a three-bedroom house, so there was actually enough space for me to have a bedroom to myself, but I preferred to sleep in the same room as the boys. I could keep an eye on them and make sure they were safe. I eyed the three deadbolts I had fitted on the inside of our door. No, they wouldn't really do much, but it put Ryan and Georgie at ease a little all the same.

"Fine," Ryan said, eyes glued to *Batman Begins* on the TV. We didn't have an aerial so no TV channels, but I had managed to purchase an old DVD player from a charity shop for a fiver. All three of us adored movies and we often hung out together, watching our favourites over and over again. If I wasn't working out in the den (a.k.a. the third bedroom), or hanging out with Ollie, I was with my brothers watching films.

"Big Mike come home at all?" I asked.

"Nope, still not back from work." I sighed in relief and closed my eyes. I was hungry but couldn't be bothered to move, and I definitely didn't want to go all the way back downstairs to the kitchen. I heard Ryan's bed squeak and opened one eye, peeking over at him. The light was off in the room so I could only make him out by the glow of the TV. He shuffled to the edge of his bed and reached his arm underneath, searching for something. A minute later, he pulled out a plate with a cheese sandwich on and a slice of malt loaf, along with a mug of water.

"Here, I brought some food up for you," he said, stretching over to hold the plate out to me. I smiled at him, my heart squeezing at how thoughtful he could be.

"Cheers mate." I swung up into a sitting position, sitting cross-legged whilst chewing.

"What did you two have for dinner?" I asked around a mouthful of sandwich.

"We weren't that hungry after the fish and chips, so just had some peanut butter on toast," Ryan said, back to staring at the TV screen. I knew they must have still been hungry, they were always hungry, but they were both good at rationing our food well so it lasted the full week. We'd had a couple of instances in the past where the food hadn't quite lasted, and none of us wanted to experience that again.

I put my empty plate on the floor, stripped off down to my boxers and crawled into bed.

"Don't stay up too late," I said, turning over so my back was to the TV.

"Mmmhmmm," he muttered.

A little while later, I was not far from dozing off completely when I heard the front door slam. The force of the motion vibrated through the walls and I cursed inwardly.

I watched Ryan launch himself over to the TV, switch it off and jump back into bed, pulling the duvet up to his chin. We could hear crashing around downstairs, Big Mike not making any effort to keep quiet.

"Josh?" Ryan whispered.

"Yeah?" I whispered back, keeping my voice as quiet as possible.

"I think I forgot to put the Oreos in the den." Aw shit. They definitely weren't going to be there in the morning. The den was where we hid extra food so that Big Mike wouldn't come across it and eat it all. I had a couple of gym mats in there, some random dumbbells, a skipping rope (all free from Gumtree again) and I'd fixed a metal bar to the ceiling so I could do pull-ups. I had also put a desk against one wall for Ryan and Georgie to do their homework at, as they got too distracted by the TV in our room. In the far left, back corner, there was a tall, narrow cupboard where we kept the boys' spare school uniforms hanging. We were careful to keep them separate from their other clothes, so they stayed as neat and crease-free as possible. There was nothing worse than a nosy teacher becoming 'concerned' if they didn't keep up appearances.

At the bottom of the makeshift wardrobe, I'd pulled up the carpet and tugged loose one of the floorboards. We hid the extra food we wanted to make last there. Things like biscuits, an extra loaf of bread, a box of cereal, a couple cans of soup etc. Often Big Mike would come back from the pub with the munchies and could demolish half a week's worth of shopping in one hit. So we made sure we kept spare food hidden away, just in case.

"That's OK. I have another pack in my locker at work. I'll bring it home tomorrow," I lied. I would have to buy a replacement pack tomorrow. Georgie would be heartbroken in the morning when he realised Big Mike had eaten them all.

"I'm sorry. I should have remembered…" he berated himself.

"Hey. It's fine. Promise."

Loud footsteps began thumping up the stairs, heading our way. I could feel my heart pounding against my ribs. The footsteps stopped outside our room and I held my breath, waiting to see if he'd try to come in. It felt like an hour, but probably not even a second or two had passed when the footsteps continued and I heard a door slam elsewhere. I released a breath and heard Ryan do the same. Thankfully Georgie seemed to have slept through it. We'd have some peace for tonight at least.

~

The shrill ringing of my alarm pierced my ears, waking me from my slumber. I groaned. I still felt exhausted and I desperately wanted to ignore my alarm and go back to sleep.

"Josh! Josh!" Ryan shouted at me.

"Yeah, yeah, I'm getting up," I muttered, rubbing the sleep from my eyes with one hand whilst the other rifled under my pillow for my phone.

"No, no. It's the phone, the phone!" Ryan sounded panicked. I blinked rapidly, trying to wake up faster. I located my phone: 6 a.m. I stared at it, confused by its silence. I looked over at Ryan and he was staring at me, terrified. Georgie was also awake and he was frozen in fear, eyes wide as he looked at me from his top bunk. The ringing continued and my brain clicked into gear. It was the landline phone ringing. *Oh shit.*

I scrambled out of bed, pulling on a nearby discarded pair of joggers from the floor as I raced downstairs to the kitchen. *Please don't wake up, please don't wake up.* I launched myself at the phone.

"Hello?" I asked breathlessly.

"I need to speak with your dad," a gruff voice responded.

"He's still sleeping," I said. I hoped.

"Well, wake him up and tell him Bob has called in sick, so I need him to cover his shift. He needs to get here in half an hour or he's fired." And with that, the caller hung up. *Shit, shit, shit.*

"WHY THE FUCK ARE YOU MAKING SO MUCH NOISE?" I heard Big Mike roar from upstairs, followed by thuds and the sound of glass breaking. I lurched back to the stairs, jumping two at a time. As I reached the top, I could see Big Mike standing in his bedroom doorway, fists clenched by his sides and jaw twitching as he ground his teeth. He was hunched over, his giant figure completely filling the doorway. He was shirtless, his gut hanging out over the top of his tracksuit bottoms. I could see the veins bulging in his thick neck as his face gradually started to turn a shade of crimson.

"You need to go into work," I said, concentrating on keeping my voice low and even.

"What the fuck did you say to me, boy?" He squinted his eyes and took a couple of steps towards me. I could feel the adrenaline start to kick in.

"Someone from your work called. A guy called Bob is off sick and whoever called wants you to be at work in half an hour or you'll be fired." I sounded calm, but I felt anything but. There were a few seconds of silence. My pulse roared in my ears as I waited in anticipation.

Big Mike suddenly let out an almighty growl, something you'd expect to hear from an agitated bear trying to mark its territory. He began moving towards me, slowly at first but soon picking up momentum. He weighed at least thirty pounds more than me and although I was fit and well-practiced at brawling, I knew from experience that the likelihood of me winning this fight was slim to none.

Ryan chose that moment to poke his head out of our bedroom, glancing around to see what was going on. As Big Mike moved past him, he threw his hand out and slapped Ryan's chest, propelling him backwards. There was a loud crash as Ryan broke his fall on something.

"DON'T YOU TOUCH HIM. DON'T YOU DARE FUCKING TOUCH THEM!" I thundered. Rage consumed me, dampening down the fear. Every encounter with this motherfucker was painful, sometimes excruciatingly so, but it was all worth it to protect my brothers. They had mostly escaped his wrath and I did my very best to put myself in the firing line, praying that he'd one day forget they even existed. As he neared me, I could smell the beer on his breath, and I smiled. Alcohol slowed him down and made him sloppy. Something I could take advantage of. I bent my knees, widening my stance and preparing to fight.

"You need to remember your place, you worthless piece of shit!" He swung a fist at my face and I ducked, side-stepping him as he barrelled past me and almost threw himself down the stairs. *Wishful thinking.* He turned with more speed and grace than a man of his size and inebriation should be able to. He used his momentum to hunker down and charge at me again, wrapping his arms around my waist and lifting me into the air. There was a fleeting feeling of weightlessness before I crashed down to the ground. He reared a fist back, straddling my waist and pinning me to the floor. I struggled, but it was like trying to shift an elephant whilst laying on your back.

His fists started flying and I raised my elbows up, curling my hands around the back of my neck. I turned and twisted, trying to deflect his punches and keep him at a distance, something I'd learned to do from watching hours of YouTube self-defence videos in the library at lunch.

I felt one of his punches bounce off my ear and another hit my shoulder, dull pain radiating down from the top of my arm. He was panting heavily and when he paused briefly, I lifted upwards to bear-hug him under his armpits. I yanked him back down with me so his head hit the floor behind us, raising my right knee to try and regain my footing. I pushed up off my foot as hard as I could, feeling my hip protest with the effort. I was trying to flip him over so I would end up on top, but the narrow hallway and his awkward, heavy bulk meant that I only managed to twist out a little from underneath him. I knew I couldn't beat him from the floor. I had to get up.

I scrambled to a sitting position, kicking my legs out to try and improve my angle. One of my kicks caught him in the side, pushing him off of me further until I had the space to stand. I rose to my knees and swung a punch, landing it solidly on his cheek. His head snapped back and he snarled, twisting to face me. I was back on my feet and this time it was my turn to launch myself at him. I darted a glance into the bedroom and saw

Georgie and Ryan huddled on my bed, holding each other. Ryan had a streak of blood down the side of his face.

"School! Now! Run!" I screamed at them. They disappeared from view again as I impacted with Big Mike. I rammed him into the far wall, throwing my shoulder into his chest. I stood over him and kicked him as hard as I could in the stomach. *Stupid.* He was too dense and flabby there for it to have an effect and he grabbed at my foot, shoving me backwards. Ryan and Georgie squeezed past me, their uniforms from yesterday hastily shoved on in disarray. I could hear them running down the stairs before the front door slammed. I exhaled a deep, slow breath. They were safe.

"You are going to regret starting with me this morning, you stupid shit!" Big Mike stood, laughing at me with a wild look in his eyes.

"Fuck off!" I shouted back. He ran at me and this time I didn't quite manage to get out of his way. He shoved me hard, and once again I defied gravity. This time though, I didn't land when I expected to. I fell backwards down the stairs, my legs going over my head, causing me to roll several times. My face cracked on one of the wooden banisters as I tumbled, my cheek burning. I landed hard on my left shoulder, my head spinning. The pain in my shoulder was instant and took my breath away. I could just about make out the kitchen in front of me, everything swimming in and out of focus. I willed myself to get up as I heard Big Mike thunder down the stairs behind me. The last thing I remember was seeing the empty Oreo packet on the kitchen table flutter to the floor. Then it all went black.

Chapter 5

Isabel

"Do you fancy going to the cinema tonight?" Jess asked as we made our way to the bus stop after school. It was a Friday night; I had officially finished my first week and it had been a complete success. I definitely felt like celebrating.

"Sure, what's on?" Sophie replied as I nodded my agreement.

"There's that romantic drama *Pulse*?" Jess responded, waggling her eyebrows.

"I thought you said that was basically porn 'cos there were so many sex scenes in it?" I laughed.

"And? That's exactly why we should see it! The critics said it was perfect for horny teenagers and *hello*, that's exactly what we are," she said, gesturing to us all with a flick of her wrist. I laughed again, shaking my head.

"We're not all sex-obsessed like you, you slut," Sophie ribbed good naturedly. Jess was definitely experienced in *that* department, although she wasn't quite a slut. Not really. She'd just had a lot more sexual partners than me, and I suspected more than Sophie too.

"Come on, maybe you two can get some tips as you haven't actually put it into practice yet." Jess looked pointedly at the pair of us. Sophie laughed it off whilst I went a little red in embarrassment. OK, so I'd had zero sexual partners.

We reached the bus stop and I was about to change the subject and suggest an action movie instead, when I noticed the little boy from yesterday standing outside *Martins.* He was on his own this time and he had his back against the shop window, his eyes puffy and red from crying. I tuned out Jess and Sophie's banter, watching him to see if anyone else would turn up. A couple minutes ticked by and I could see our bus approaching. Jess and Sophie started to move towards it as the doors hissed open.

"Izzy? You coming?" Sophie asked, turning back to see why I hadn't moved. I hesitated, torn between going home or going over to check on him.

"I'll catch the next one. Just need to grab some things from the shop," I replied. "Text me if you decide on a film." Sophie nodded and I watched her climb in and take a seat next to Jess, waving as the bus left me behind. I turned and approached the boy.

"Georgie? It's Georgie, right?" I asked cautiously, trying not to spook him. He looked up, suddenly resembling a deer in headlights. He didn't respond.

"I'm Izzy. We met yesterday," I reminded him. He paused, unsure.

"You gave us fish and chips," he whispered.

"Yeah." I gave him a broad smile, trying to appear as friendly as possible. "Where's your brother today? Ryan?" I asked. A sob escaped him as he shrugged.

"I don't know. He was supposed to meet me after school like always, but he didn't show up." A tear slid out and he roughly palmed it away.

"OK, so what are you going to do now?"

"My other brother works in there," he gestured with his head behind him to the shop. "But I forgot he doesn't work Fridays." More tears were coming now.

"Hey, hey, it's OK. What about your parents? I can call someone for you?" I asked, concerned. He shook his head.

"Do you live close by? I can walk you there. I'm sure your brothers are both at home waiting for you and this is some big misunderstanding," I said, not confident at all in my rationalisation. I had an uneasy feeling in the pit of my stomach.

"Are you sure? They're OK? And you don't mind walking me home?" Georgie looked at me hopefully, eyes shining.

"I bet they are absolutely fine, and I definitely don't mind keeping you company on the way home. You know how to get there?" I asked and he nodded. I had no idea what had happened to his brothers, but I knew for sure that I couldn't leave him on his own. It just didn't sit right with me. He pushed off of the wall and started to head towards a traffic light crossing at the top of the street.

"Hey, would you like some sweets before we go? My treat?" Once again, I found myself desperate to erase the sadness from his eyes. He brightened instantly, a slight skip in his step as we headed inside the shop.

It had taken longer than I anticipated but several minutes later we emerged, Georgie carrying a bag bursting with sweets. It had been heart-breaking watching him agonise over what sweets to choose. You'd have thought we were in Willy Wonka's chocolate factory, the way he was staring at all the shelves in awe. I ended up getting him near enough everything he looked at, even though I knew that much sugar in a boy of his size was asking for trouble.

We crossed the road and turned down a little side street, making our way down a steep hill. The houses were packed in tight next to each other, row after row of identical, square, red brick terraced houses. As we reached the bottom of the hill, Georgie veered left down a little alleyway and we came out next to a playground. It was overgrown with weeds, the pavement loose and cracked in many places. Groups of teenagers loitered close by, some on bikes and most with a cigarette dangling from their lips. Judging by the smell, I didn't think they were your typical Marlboroughs.

There was a swing set with only one swing, the second swing missing, with only two chains dangling in its place. A slide perched nearby, every inch of it scrawled in graffiti. There were several round holes dotting the ground, as if there had once been more apparatus present but they had been ripped from the earth.

Someone wolf whistled as we went past and I sped up a little, keeping Georgie very close. I was definitely not familiar with this part of town.

"How much further?" I asked, wary of the teenagers watching us as we went past.

"About ten minutes. Hi Ben!" Georgie said, waving to one of the youths on a bike. The boy raised his chin in a greeting, but then winked at me when he noticed I was looking over. I shuddered a little, uncomfortable in these hostile surroundings. Georgie turned down another alleyway and when we emerged, we were surrounded by more terraced houses. I had thought the other ones looked a little sad, but these houses were in a much poorer state of disrepair.

Instead of brick, these houses were clad in white wooden planks. Well, I assumed they were once white, but now they were greyish with peeling paint and patches of greenish-black grime. They were very small, about half the size of the other ones, and the front doors opened directly onto the uneven pavement.

Georgie's pace was getting slower and slower, as if he didn't want us to reach our destination.

"Everything OK, buddy?" I asked. He smiled up at me.

"My brother calls me buddy too sometimes," he answered instead. We turned down *West View* and Georgie stopped on the corner.

"I can get home from here," he said, looking down at his feet.

"No, I've come all this way, so I might as well make sure you get in OK," I said, frowning. This boy certainly didn't seem to want to go home. He hesitated and I could see him battling with himself, unsure what to do. Eventually he started moving and walked up to the door of number seventy-two. He stared at it for a minute or so.

"Do you have a key?" I asked and he shook his head.

"I forgot my keys and phone this morning," he sighed. He looked a bit young for a phone but hey, what do I know?

"When will your parents be home?" I asked and he shrugged. "OK, well let's see if your brothers are home." I knocked on the front door, listening out for noises inside. A minute passed with no answer.

"What's your other brother's name?"

"Josh." I tapped harder on the door and bent down to peer through the letterbox.

"Ryan? Josh? It's er...Izzy. I have your brother Georgie with me. Can you let him in please?" I called out. I felt a little awkward. I didn't actually know this little boy, or his family, and my parents didn't know where I was. Not my smartest idea.

I was about to give up when I heard something move inside. I straightened up, waiting side by side with Georgie for someone to answer. It must have been at least five minutes before whoever it was made their way to the front door. The door swung inwards and I was not prepared for who was in front of me. When Georgie had said his brother's name was Josh, I had not expected to see morose Joshua Bugg from school. He had on a pair of jeans and that was it. Boy, he was ripped. Although slim with narrow hips, the outline of his abs was prominent. His chest was broad and toned and his shoulders rounded with muscle. I could feel myself getting a little flustered until I noticed the bruises. He had a nasty looking purple bruise on his side, spreading up under his armpit. His left shoulder was smothered in bruises too, leaving a trail of glorious technicolour. *Ouch*.

"Shit. Your face…" I trailed off, not knowing how to finish. His left cheek was so dark it was almost black and there was a split in the centre, a trail of dried blood streaked down to his chin. His nose also looked swollen with dried blood around his nostrils. He was swaying on his feet, leaning heavily on the door frame. I was frozen, not knowing quite what to do. He was looking at me, but it was if he was staring straight through me, not registering that I was actually there.

The next thing I knew, he started sliding down towards the floor. I jumped over the threshold and grabbed his arm, slinging it around my shoulders in a desperate attempt to keep him upright.

"Josh!" Georgie cried, tears streaming down his face. I could feel the beads of sweat forming on my forehead with the effort of holding Josh up.

"Georgie, can you show me to your brother's room please?" I asked through gritted teeth. "He needs to rest." Georgie darted past us both, through a tiny kitchen and towards a narrow staircase. I knew my prayers for a downstairs bedroom were going to go unanswered. Georgie turned at the bottom of the stairs, waiting for me to follow.

"OK Josh, I know you're out of it, but I need you to do your best to help me help you. You're heavy and I can't get you to your room without help," I said. He grunted in response and together we shuffled over to the stairs. The ascent was slow, painfully so. By the time we reached the top, we were both sweating and my legs were shaking with the exertion.

Josh suddenly collapsed onto all fours and threw up on the floor in front of him. I noticed then a nasty looking wound on the back of his head, blood matted in his hair. Boy, I was way out of my depth here.

"We should call an ambulance, you need to see a doctor…"

"NO!" It was the only thing he'd said since he answered the door and he screamed it, turning abruptly to look at me with pleading eyes. It was heart-wrenching.

"Come on, almost there." I bent down and wrapped his arm around my shoulder again. I took shallow breaths through my mouth, praying that the smell of vomit wouldn't make me heave too.

"Georgie, do you think you can help us a little bit?" I asked. The tears were still streaming but he nodded, trying to lift Josh from the other side. I don't know if he genuinely helped or if just his presence spurred Josh on, but it was easier than I thought to get him back to a standing position. We all lurched forward, having to stay close and at a slight angle in order to fit through the slender hallway. We finally slipped through a doorway and Josh stumbled onto a small, single bed. He was panting with his eyes closed and his entire body was covered in a thin sheet of sweat.

"I think you have a concussion and probably need some stitches..." I trailed off as he opened his eyes to glare at me.

"No. Doctors." He was panting, face screwed up in pain. I was torn. Should I call an ambulance anyway? He was watching me through narrowed eyes, as if he knew what I was contemplating. *I'm going to give it one hour and if he hasn't improved, I'm calling for help.* I nodded to myself, feeling better now I had a plan.

"Georgie, can you get your brother an empty bag or a bowl, and a big glass of water?" I asked. He nodded and returned moments later with a big plastic bowl and a large mug. I set the bowl on the floor next to Josh's bed, in case he needed to throw up again.

"I need you to sit up a little. You need to stay hydrated." I moved closer, holding the mug of water out to him. He inched upwards, wincing with the movement. I lifted the mug to his lips, tipping it slowly so the liquid trickled into his mouth. I concentrated on keeping the mug steady, but my eyes flicked upwards, connecting with his. They were shining and the depth of despair there hit me like a train. I had no idea who this boy was or what demons he was fighting, but I was overwhelmed with the urge to help him and his family. An intense burning of concern bubbled up, lodging in my throat as if I was choking.

I heard the front door slam downstairs and Georgie yelped in surprise. Josh sat bolt upright, clutching his head and crying out at the sudden movement. Someone began climbing the stairs and Georgie started shaking. He looked completely terrified. *What the hell is going on?*

I turned to the doorway as Ryan strolled in, freezing in his tracks when he saw all of us.

"What the fuck...?" He whispered.

"Where were you?" Georgie barrelled over to his brother, shoving his shoulders. Ryan looked bewildered. He kept looking from me, to Josh, to Georgie and back.

"I had detention. I text you," he said, frowning at Georgie.

"I forgot my phone and keys when we... left so quickly..." Georgie said, darting a look back at me. Ryan sighed.

"Sorry, little man. I forgot to tell you yesterday that I had detention and didn't realise you didn't have your phone," Ryan said. "Why are *you* here?" he directed at me, his brow furrowed and his face riddled with suspicion. I noticed he had a small cut above his right eye, surrounded by a pale green bruise.

"I saw your brother on my way home. He looked upset and didn't know where either of you were," I shrugged.

"So you walked him back home out of the goodness of your heart?" he replied, eyebrows raised and voice dripping with sarcasm.

"Pretty much," I said, folding my arms and staring him down.

"Stop being mean to Izzy. She bought me sweets and she carried Josh up here by herself," Georgie said, voice rising. Ryan looked over to Josh, getting a proper look at him for the first time since he entered the room.

"Shit, bro." He rushed past me and stood by the side of Josh's bed. Josh gave him a weak smile.

"Looks worse than it is," he winked.

"Yeah right…" Ryan muttered, eyes going glassy.

"OK, who's hungry?" I asked after a moment of tense silence. "Because I am starving." Georgie nodded eagerly.

"Er…there's probably not much in the cupboards…" Ryan said, avoiding my eyes.

"That's OK, I'm a terrible cook. I was going to order pizza in?" Ryan's eyes widened and Georgie started jumping up and down on the spot. I looked over to Josh, but his eyes were closed and I could see his chest rising evenly.

"I'm going to order pizza, you two are going to keep an eye on Josh. If he starts looking worse, you tell me straight away, OK?" I asked. They both nodded. "When will your parents be back? Shall I order some for them too?" Ryan and Georgie looked at each other, silently communicating something.

"Mum's not around and Big…dad's working late at the factory," Ryan muttered.

"OK, no problem, I'll go order it now. Any requests?" I asked, smiling in what I hoped was a reassuring way.

"Stuffed crust and lots of pepperoni?" Georgie asked, grinning. I laughed and nodded. I looked to Ryan but he shrugged, as if he didn't quite believe I was going to order it. I walked out the room and back downstairs to the kitchen, dialling the pizza place as I went. Once I had placed an order for three large pizzas, garlic bread and a bottle of diet coke and paid over the phone, I started sifting through the kitchen cupboards for some bleach and a cloth. To be honest, I'm not sure you could call it a kitchen. There were only five or six cupboards lined up against one wall, a sink and an oven. Most of the doors were hanging off their hinges or missing altogether, and you probably couldn't fit more than two people in here at once.

I didn't find any bleach but did locate some washing up liquid and a dented plastic bucket. I loaded it up with warm soapy water and grabbed a clean(ish) sponge, heading upstairs to where Josh had thrown up. I scrubbed it clean, trying my best to ignore the smell. Now there was a very clean patch on the carpet and the rest of it looked terrible. I frowned at it, not really wanting to spend more time cleaning but at the same time, not feeling good about leaving it in such a state. *Sod it.* I spent the next twenty minutes or so cleaning the rest of the carpet until I had built up a sweat again. As I neared the end of the hallway, one of the bedroom doors was ajar. I peeked in and saw a very unkempt double bed, with clothing strewn everywhere. There was also a broken beer bottle on the floor, dirty plates and food wrappers scattered all over the place, as well as an ashtray spilling over with cigarette butts. I pulled the door closed quietly until it clicked. There was something about the room that gave me the creeps. In fact, the whole house made me feel...uncomfortable. I was extremely appreciative for the spacious living my parents' house afforded me, practically palatial compared to this place, and how clean they kept it.

Josh's house screamed neglect and poverty and although I'm sure Josh would be mortified if he knew, I felt a deep pang of pity and sadness for him and his brothers. I mean, they had three beds crammed into one bedroom for Christ's sake, and barely any room to move.

My thoughts were interrupted by my phone vibrating in my pocket. *Meet you at 7 p.m. for 8 p.m. showing of Pulse?* It was a text from Sophie and I noticed that it was 5 p.m. already. I didn't know how long I'd be here, but I definitely didn't feel like going to the cinema anymore. *Sorry not feeling too good. Do you mind if I give it a miss tonight?* Sophie replied within seconds. *No course not! Everything OK? Let me know if you need anything.* I smiled. I still couldn't believe that I had a genuine friend that cared about me. *Just a bit overtired I think. Speak to you tomorrow. Have fun xxx*

I saw I had two texts from my mum too, asking if I was alright as I was late home. *Sorry forgot to text you. Lost track of time in the library and am going to stop by Sophie's on the way home for some help with Biology xx* I didn't feel comfortable lying to her. Sure, I had lied by omission before, but purposely not telling the truth was different. I'm not sure why I lied but my instinct told me to keep my mouth shut. For now.

OK sweetheart. Try and remember to let me know next time, I was worried! Let me know if you want picking up xx

Sorry! Thanks. Love you :) xx

Love you too :) xx

There was a knock at the door and Georgie came running past me.

"Wow, that was quick!" he said, desperate to get to the door. I dumped the murky water (which I had to change three times whilst I was cleaning) down the kitchen sink and put everything back where I found it. Georgie balanced the food in his arms and carried it all up the stairs and into the bedroom. I laughed as he struggled to keep a hold of it all, helping him with the pizza boxes and handing one to Ryan. Josh looked like he was still soundly sleeping.

"This has pineapple on…" Ryan said, raising his eyebrows in disgust at the open box in his hand.

"Yup, I love ham and pineapple pizza," I said, grabbing the box from him and switching it for the BBQ chicken pizza instead. He opened the box, licked his lips and started shovelling the pizza into his mouth immediately. Georgie was doing the same, pizza sauce dripping down his chin.

"Hey, hey, make sure you save your brother some!" I gestured to Josh with my chin. They both murmured their agreement, not slowing down even a little. I sat quietly, eating my own pizza. *God, this is surreal.* A few hours ago, I had only spoken to Josh once, which hadn't gone particularly well, and now I was sitting in his bedroom eating pizza with his brothers. I looked over at him and watched him rest peacefully. What had he gotten himself into? I ran through the possible scenarios in my head. Owed his drug dealer money? Owed money to a loan shark? Joined a gang and this was some kind of weird initiation? I couldn't make sense of any of it; the squalid living conditions, the bare cupboards, the bruises and the tears. And where the hell were their parents? What had I gotten myself into?

Chapter 6

Joshua

Fuck. My. Life.

There was a family of goblins wearing steel toe capped boots jumping around in my skull. I fluttered open my eyes, groaning at the pounding in my head as I tried to roll over. My cheek was throbbing and my ribs ached something awful. My nose started twitching. What was that smell?

"Morning," Ryan called softly from his bed. I blinked rapidly, willing my vision to focus.

"Hey," I smiled. Ryan's eyes were red and he looked shattered. "Did you sleep OK? You don't look great."

"Ha! Look who's talking! You look like shit," he laughed, but then his face grew serious for a moment. "Seriously, we're worried about you. We took turns watching you all night. Georgie wouldn't sleep unless I promised to regularly check you were still breathing." Tears sprung to my eyes and it took several seconds of looking up at the ceiling to pull myself together.

"I'm not going anywhere, little bro," I said, knowing it was a promise I might not be able to keep. I looked up at Georgie's bunk, watching the peaceful expression on his sleeping face. They needed me to survive. I *would* survive.

I spied some pizza boxes stacked up in the corner and my nose twitched again.

"Don't worry we saved you some. There's about half a pepperoni left and same again of that weird pizza with pineapple on that Izzy had." Shit. *Isabel.* I vaguely remembered her helping me up to the bedroom but that was it. What was she doing here?

"How did a girl from my sixth form, who I have barely spoken to, end up over here?" I frowned at Ryan.

"Hey, don't blame me! Georgie is the one who befriended her and convinced a pretty girl to walk him home. He's got more game than you!" He chuckled.

"It's not funny, Ryan. How much does she know? Can she keep her mouth shut? Do you want to end up in care and the three of us separated?" I winced as I became more animated, the pain ramping up as I grew more alert. It wasn't fair to burden him with my worries, but he needed to know how serious our situation was.

"I don't know! I was just relieved you were still alive when I got home and that I didn't go to sleep starving for once!" He was sitting up now, chest rising rapidly and angry tears filling his eyes. I closed my eyes and took a deep breath. I didn't want to fight with him and it hurt that I knew he meant every word. I was doing a shit job of looking after the pair of them.

"Why are you shouting so early in the morning?" Georgie stirred, yawning and stretching. Neither of us answered him.

"Shit, is that the time?" I asked as I caught sight of the time on my phone. "I'm going to be late for work." I didn't have a fucking clue how I was going to make it through the day. Just the idea of standing up on my feet all day made me feel nauseous, but we needed the money.

"I called Tracy last night and told her you wouldn't be in, that you were sick." Ryan glared at me, daring me to argue.

"You *know* we rely on that money, Ryan."

"Yeah well, we need *you* more. Izzy thinks you have a concussion and you need to rest."

"I didn't realise she was a fucking doctor as well as a saint," I grumbled.

"Hey, she's my friend. Be nice!" Georgie piped up, suddenly more awake than he was five seconds ago.

"She is *not* your friend, Georgie. I don't know what she is, or why she is sticking her nose in our business, but teenage girls don't befriend nine-year olds." I rolled my eyes at him.

"Yes she is! She told me so last night. She said she was a friend and to call her if I ever needed something." The kid actually stuck his tongue out at me.

"Oh yeah? And how are you supposed to call her?"

"Err, with my phone dummy..." I'd given both of them a phone as soon as they were old enough to use one. They had a tiny screen and an old-fashioned keypad, but they'd be able to call if they ever needed help.

"You don't have her number."

"Yes I do."

"No, you don't."

"Yes I DO! She gave it to me before she left yesterday," he smiled triumphantly.

"Me too…" Ryan muttered.

"What the fuck?!" This was ridiculous.

"And you too! Look," Georgie pointed to a note on the floor next to my bed. I slowly reached for it, careful to minimize the pain from moving.

Josh,
Here's my number. If you or your brothers need anything,
please let me know.
Izzy

Who the fuck was this girl? I didn't understand her actions at all. We barely knew each other! Someone started knocking on the front door. *Oh Christ, what now?*

"I'll get it." Ryan went to move.

"No, no. You know I don't like you answering the door. I'll do it." I knew it was silly, but it was rare for someone to knock and I was paranoid it would one day be a social worker or something. And if one of the boys answered the door, they'd be able to just grab them and run, stealing them away from me.

"But you need to rest. Izzy said…"

"Will you shut up about Izzy!" I snapped. I stood up

gradually, testing to see how it would feel. Fucking awful, was the answer. But I didn't feel nauseous at least. And I really needed to pee anyway. I sluggishly made my way to the tiny, grubby bathroom and after a couple of minutes, headed to the stairs. I stopped before descending, thinking the landing looked different but couldn't quite put my finger on it. I squinted, looking around. *Holy shit, has the carpet always been cream?* Our once grey carpet was the cleanest it had ever been. It looked completely out of place. I don't know how I didn't notice straight away. The person at the door started knocking again, growing impatient.

"I'm coming," I growled. I gingerly opened the door, relieved when I saw Ollie standing there.

"What are you…?"

"I knew it!" he shouted, interrupting me and barging past.

"Knew what?" I closed my eyes and massaged my forehead, my headache taking on a new lease of life. The blood pulsing in my head reminded me of a timer on a bomb ticking down, waiting to explode.

"I knew when your brother called Mum last night that you being 'sick' was actually code for 'he's beaten to a pulp.' Especially after you didn't turn up for classes. Why the fuck didn't you call me?" Ollie was fuming. He shoved me into a chair at the small kitchen table, slammed the front door shut and started pacing. I grimaced in discomfort. He hadn't exactly been gentle.

"What good is it having a mate who always has your back if you never let them help?!" He slammed his fist on the table in front of me.

"I was pretty out of it yesterday, mate. Don't remember much of it."

"Yeah well, you could have gotten Ryan or Georgie to call me. And don't give me that bullshit excuse anyway. You never let anyone help you." He crossed his arms, staring me down. I shrugged.

"No, don't you shrug at me. How long are you going to keep this up? What if Big Mike starts hitting Ryan? Or Georgie? What are going to do then? You can't watch them 24/7."

"He hasn't touched them. I make sure I'm the one that gets the blame for everything." My temper was starting to kick in. It was far too early in the morning for this conversation and I really wasn't feeling up to it.

"Yeah, and what if that changes? What if he beats you up so bad it kills you? Who is going to look out for them then? Maybe Ryan will just take your spot and Big Mike will pick up where he left off, as if nothing happened…" he smirked, knowing full well he was goading me.

"Don't you think I worry about that too?!" I roared at him, my ears ringing and my vision starting to sway. "What do you want me to do?"

"You need to tell someone."

"Like who?"

"The police."

"Oh, fuck off. You know I can't do that. They'd chuck all of us in care and we'd be separated and stuck with some random families. You've heard the same horror stories I have. I'm not having either of my brothers being molested by a paedophile! And who's to say the police would even believe me in the first place?!" I couldn't believe Ollie was even suggesting I call the police. There was a kid a few streets over from here that committed suicide last year, hung himself in his room. He'd been taken away from his family, put into foster care and the foster dad had been hurting him in the worst possible way. Ollie knew this, and yet he was still suggesting I follow the same path. He was really fucking me off.

"Why wouldn't the police believe you?" he asked, completely ignoring the rest of what I'd said.

"Oh, come on. I've spent my entire life starting fights and even purposely letting people get a few punches in, just so no one would suspect my old man was doing it. And so far, it has worked a fucking treat."

"Well, he's getting worse. He used to show some kind of restraint and try not to hit your face much or do a lot of damage. Now he doesn't seem to care. He's getting worse," he repeated. I couldn't argue with that. He had been hitting harder and more frequently recently.

"I think it's something to do with his work. I overheard a couple guys in *Martins* the other week, saying there's rumours about the factory closing down and people losing their jobs." That was how this whole mess had started in the first place. Believe it or not, Big Mike used to be pretty decent. He had a temper, sure, and he'd shout like you wouldn't believe sometimes, but he'd never hurt us. And Mum, well she actually stuck around for one. She was a stay-at-home mum and although she didn't seem to have a great interest in what was going on in our lives, she did her best. But I *despised* her. How could a mother who spent years raising her children just abandon them? And leave us with that monster?

Big Mike used to own a car repair garage a few years ago. He'd trained up as a mechanic when he was a teenager and then decided to open his own place. For a long while, Big Mike's Motors was the main garage in Gilleford and almost everyone took their cars to him for repair work. We had a nice house and lived comfortably. But then Big Mike started getting greedy. He began hiking his prices up so he could take Mum out to nice restaurants, buy a flashy car and generally show off. Although customers weren't happy, there wasn't anywhere else credible to go to. That was until A1 Autocentres opened a branch nearby. They were a big chain with garages all over the country. Within a few months of their opening, Big Mike had lost pretty much all his customers and soon we started receiving final reminder letters and bailiffs began knocking. Turns out the business hadn't been doing quite as well as he had led us to believe anyway. He had taken a big loan out against the house for his fucking BMW and to keep the garage afloat too.

Within a year, the bank had repossessed the house, the car and most of our possessions. We'd been forced into a council house and Big Mike struggled to find work. Mum hadn't had a job for almost fifteen years and so she was practically unemployable. Eventually, Big Mike was offered a job on a production line in a pharmaceutical packaging factory. But his ego and pride were badly wounded. He started drinking regularly and stopping by the betting shop on the way home from work. *That* was when he started getting violent. He'd lose a good chunk of his wages betting on horses, drink a ton of beer and come home in a foul mood. First, it was Mum he hit.

"Why isn't dinner on the table, you stupid bitch?"

"This place is a shit hole, what have you been doing all day?"

On and on he'd criticise, no matter how many hours Mum had spent cooking or cleaning. Initially he'd use the back of his hand across her face, or shove her into a door frame. I tried to intervene, but back then I was scrawny and weak, and could do nothing but watch helplessly. She'd beg and plead with him to stop, but that would just encourage him if anything. She started taking painkillers and sleeping pills, more and more each day to cope with his behaviour, until she was pretty much high every minute of the day. She stopped bothering to clean and cook, and most days wouldn't even come out of her bedroom. One evening, I caught him choking her against a wall. I still remember how big her eyes bulged before I launched myself at him, clawing and scratching at his hands. The next day when we all came back from school, she was gone.

"Where's Mum?"

"She left us." Big Mike threw a beer bottle at me and I flinched as it narrowly missed my head.

And that was when he started on me instead. After that, there was no way I was ever calling him 'Dad' again. He didn't deserve it.

"If he loses his job, he's going to go mental," Ollie frowned, dragging me from my painful memories. "We could take him, you know."

"Take him? What do you mean?" I raised my eyebrows at him.

"You and me. We could take him in a fight. We could beat him together." He clenched his fists and took a fighting stance. I don't even think he realised he was doing it.

"And what good would that do? Say we did beat him, then what? He'd be so pissed that the next time he saw me, when you weren't with me, he'd kill me. He'd literally pulverise me to death." I could see the rage behind Ollie's eyes.

"You need help, mate. I don't know how we make it stop, but we *must* make it stop."

"Listen. It's not that long until I turn eighteen and then I will go to the police, make them give us our own council house, and leave the fucker to rot by himself. I can't risk them taking Georgie and Ryan away from me. Just another year to go, Ollie." Well, closer to eighteen months. But still.

"If you last another year," Ollie mumbled, his anger fading and defeat written all over his face. He knew I was cornered and had no other options. He slumped down in the chair next to me. He was a good friend to me, a *really* good friend, but I had a plan and I had managed by myself for this long. I could make it to eighteen.

After several minutes of silence, each of us no doubt contemplating our next moves in life, someone else started knocking at the door.

"Why is everyone insisting on getting in my damn

business this morning…?" I scraped back the chair, pausing until my head stopped spinning. I yanked the door open.

"What?" I answered, shocked to see Isabel standing there holding a plastic bag. She had her hair scraped back, wearing grey jeans and the bright pink *Buttercups* polo top. With barely any makeup on and her face flushed from the walk over here, she looked gorgeous. Beautiful even.

"I just wanted to check on you. I felt really guilty about not calling for a paramedic and getting someone to check on you properly," she said quietly, giving me a soft smile.

"Well, I'm fine. Thanks."

"Do you need anything? I could…"

"Look. Why are you here?"

"What…what do you mean? I just said," she stammered, looking confused.

"No. Why are you *really* here? Why are you interfering? We don't need your help." I gritted my teeth, jaw going stiff. I needed this girl to get lost. As lovely a sight as she was right now, I couldn't afford to let anyone mess up my plan. I had a feeling she'd cause me trouble if I let her.

"I just…Georgie…"

"Why the interest in my brother all of a sudden? He told me you gave him your number. What the fuck's that all about? He's only nine, you know. It's perverted." I forced my anger to the surface, doing what I usually do when I want to start a fight.

"What?! NO. It's not like that…I just…" I slammed

the door in her face. She'd get the message now, for sure. I stared at the inside of the door, calming myself down and trying to ignore the aching pain in my ribs. I shook my head, returning to the kitchen.

"Was that Isabel Johnson? From school?" Ollie asked, incredulous.

"Don't even ask, mate…"

"No, no. You have to tell me why the fuck she's at your front door at 8.30 a.m. on a Saturday." I started to recount the events of the night before, whilst Ollie began pulling bread out of the cupboard to make us all some toast. However, after a couple of minutes, we were interrupted by Georgie bounding down the stairs. He sailed right past us in his batman pyjamas, opening the front door.

"Where are you…" He grabbed something off the front doorstep, coming back inside with a smile on his face. It looked like the plastic bag Isabel had been carrying.

"No need to make breakfast Ollie," he smiled, slinging the bag on the table in front of us. Ryan came into the kitchen then too, going over to the kettle to make tea. Once Ollie, Ryan and I had steaming cups in front of us, Ryan poured some of the leftover water from the kettle into another mug. He grabbed a bottle of antiseptic from our first aid kit and added some of it into the mug. He then pulled out our stash of cotton wool pads, placing all of it in front of me.

"The back of your head looks bloody awful," he muttered. He dunked a pad into the water, using his other hand to carefully part my hair.

"Shit!" I sucked in a breath. It hurt like a bitch.

"I need to clean this great big cut you've got. Izzy said we can't let it get infected and to check it isn't too deep." I huffed and crossed my arms, sitting back in my chair. I could tell Ryan was being as gentle as possible, but God the pain was almost unbearable. A couple of times I felt my vision grow hazy again.

As the bloody cotton wool pads started building up on the table, Georgie began pulling all sorts of baked goods out of the bag. Pain au chocolats, croissants, cinnamon buns, muffins...there was enough to feed about ten people. Georgie looked over and saw me frowning at the food.

"Izzy text me. She said she had left breakfast on the front doorstep for us. She had to go to work so couldn't come in." He reached over and grabbed a cinnamon bun, shoving it into his mouth. "See, told you she was our friend," he said around the mouthful of food. Ollie was trying desperately not to laugh. I was extremely irritated that not only had Izzy bought a ton of food that I would never have been able to afford, but that she hadn't even ratted me out to my brother that I'd actually slammed the door in her face.

"You know, if you want her to keep her mouth shut you should probably make an effort to be nicer to her. Keep her on your side," Ollie snickered around a croissant.

"Yeah, especially as she keeps buying us food," Ryan added.

"Tell me the rest of what happened," Ollie requested. I refused to speak, sulking because I had a feeling that

Ollie's approach would have indeed been more successful. It hadn't even occurred to me to try and be nice to her. I was such a dick.

Ryan and Georgie eagerly obliged, taking turns to add in little anecdotes. When they started explaining how Isabel had cleaned up my puke, I was mortified.

"What?!" Ollie and I shrieked at the same time.

"Well, you didn't think *we* cleaned it up, did ya?" Ryan laughed.

"What puke? I don't remember throwing up?"

"Georgie said she practically carried you up the stairs 'cos you could barely walk, and when you got to the top, you threw up everywhere. Someone definitely threw up 'cos I had to step over it when I got home." He looked to Georgie for confirmation and he nodded. I dropped my head into my hands. So that was why the carpet looked so clean. She must have scrubbed the whole damn thing! Ollie couldn't contain his laughter any longer.

"Oh mate! She's the first person that's shown you the tiniest bit of kindness in years and you slammed the door in her face! You are a complete prick."

Fuck. My. Life.

Chapter 7

Isabel

Screw you, Joshua Bugg. You self-centred, rude, ungrateful little shit.

When he slammed the door in my face on Saturday morning, I had been pretty upset. OK, fuming was more like it. I'd gotten up early so I could go check on him before work and stopped at a bakery to get everyone breakfast. I had not expected the hostility that had greeted me. I mean, he'd basically accused me of being a paedophile! What the fuck was his problem? I was just trying to be nice. OK, so we hadn't spoken much before and I didn't know him at all, but was it really that weird for me to offer some help? I'd held back angry tears the entire walk back to *Buttercups*.

I'd been distracted the whole time at work, running the events of Friday night and the following morning through my head. By the time Monday rolled round, I still hadn't simmered down. I made up my mind that I would stay out of Josh's way. He clearly didn't want any help and if he was going to be such a dick all the time, then I didn't want to waste my time anyway. He could sort his own problems out. Fucking ingrate.

"Hey Izzy, how are you feeling?" Sophie asked as soon as I breezed through the common room doors before classes. I paused, confused by her question, until I remembered the excuse I gave for missing the cinema last Friday.

"Er, yeah much better thanks. Think I was just over-tired or something," I strained a smile. "How was the film?"

"Well, it was a shit ton better than *I* thought it would be," Ed smirked as Jack nodded his agreement with a grin. The five of us spent pretty much all our spare time at school together now.

"That's only because the leading actress got her tits out," Jess rolled her eyes. We were all sitting in a circle in what had become our regular spot. I raised my eyebrows at Sophie and Jess.

"We thought we'd invite everyone in the end," Jess said, answering my unspoken question. I felt a twinge of jealousy and then guilt. I was jealous that all my friends had gone without me but then again, I had said no. And even if I'd known that Jack and Ed were going, I still wouldn't have gone. I noticed that Sophie and Jack were stealing glances at each other every now and then. I met Sophie's eyes after they did it again and quirked my eyebrow, smiling. She flushed completely red. Yep, there was definitely something going on there.

"Hey, er, Isabel…" I flicked my gaze over my shoulder, seeing Josh standing there looking very sheepish. Nope. I. Was. Not. Interested.

"Jeez, what happened to his face?" Sophie leaned over and whispered in my ear. I shrugged.

"So other than the nudity, was the film actually any good?" I asked Jess, purposely angling myself further away from Josh. Jess looked at me, behind my head, then back to me again.

"Er…yeah it was…"

"Isabel. I really need to talk to you," Josh interrupted, louder this time, moving so that he was standing by my arm. I gritted my teeth. Why was it that people at this school thought they could blow hot and cold and walk all over me?

"I am not interested in anything you have to say, Josh." I kept my face completely neutral, demonstrating just how little I cared. He didn't say anything for a second or two, so I turned back to my friends.

"Listen, I am really sorry about how I acted on Saturday morning. Can we please talk for a moment, in private?" He was avoiding looking at anyone but me and I could see the desperation in his eyes. I held his gaze for a few moments before I felt my resolve crumbling. I sighed. I stood up and grabbed my stuff, following him outside. He led me to an empty bench behind the common room, choosing to sit on the same side as me with his legs straddled. I sat facing out over the table, deliberately not looking at him. He looked around to make sure no one was within earshot, but it was overcast and the breeze was cool, so no one else was outside. Josh ran his fingers through his hair, scratching the back of his head.

"I acted like a complete wanker. I shouldn't have slammed the door in your face. I'm sorry." I could feel his eyes boring into the side of my head as I continued to ignore him, unsure how to respond.

"And I wanted to thank you for everything you did on Friday night. Walking my brother home, buying pizza, cleaning that shitty carpet…" I flicked my gaze at him. He was looking down at his fidgeting hands, his hair flopped over part of his face. He looked so vulnerable and up close, his face didn't look any better than the last time I'd seen him. In fact, it looked worse. The bruises on his cheek had turned deep purple and blue, making it look like he was wearing some kind of weird face paint. He reminded me of Harvey-Two-Face, one half of his face spoiled with the other half of his face pristine. He lifted his chin and smiled at me. Oh wow, what a smile. I don't think I've ever seen Josh smile before.

"And I know I don't deserve it, but I need to ask a favour…" My eyebrows shot up in disbelief.

"Is that so?" I asked, arms folded.

"Please don't say anything to anyone. About what happened at my house Friday night. Or about Georgie leaving school on his own - we'll be right in the shit if his teacher finds out." He looked uncomfortable and a little embarrassed.

"I haven't said anything and I won't. It's none of my business or anyone else's." I turned to face him but kept my arms crossed, trying to at least come off that I was still annoyed, even though inside I had most definitely melted.

"Thanks." There was that smile again.

"You know, sometimes people are nice because they want to be. Doesn't mean they have an ulterior motive or anything. And certainly doesn't make them a paedo…" Yeah, I was still smarting from that comment. Josh had the decency to wince.

"I should never have said that. I was in a bad way still and I'm not used to people being nice without expecting something in return." He looked down again, avoiding my eyes. I started to feel like a bit of a bitch. I was giving him a hard time when he and his family were obviously struggling through something. Maybe I shouldn't have been so hard on him. I should give him the benefit of the doubt.

"It's OK. How about we draw a line under it?" I smiled at him.

"That would be great, thanks." The bell rang, signalling it was time to get to classes. "OK, well er, see you around Isabel," Josh said whilst standing to leave.

"Hey, Josh?" He looked back at me.

"My friends call me Izzy." After a moment of hesitation, he nodded. Right before we parted ways, I could swear the corner of his lips twitched again.

"Well, you have some explaining to do, my friend," Sophie hissed as I entered biology. I climbed onto the stall next to her and rolled my eyes.

"What do you mean?"

"Since when are you and Josh Bugg buddies?!"

"We're not. Well, we might be. I don't actually know…" Sophie's brow furrowed, looking very sceptical.

"Well, you must be if you're hanging out at the weekend." I wasn't sure if she sounded a little miffed that I hadn't told her about it.

"We weren't. I just…bumped into him on the way to work and he was a bit of an arse." It wasn't technically a lie.

"Ah OK, that makes sense. Knew you'd tell me if you'd started dating someone."

"We are definitely *not* dating," I scoffed. This morning was the longest conversation we'd ever had, and it had only lasted around ten minutes.

"I've barely spoken to him to be honest. But I have…a feeling…that he is going through some kind of rough patch. Seems like he could do with a friend." I shrugged. Even without Josh's plea this morning, I wasn't planning on sharing details of Josh's life with anyone. I knew what it was like when people started gossiping about you, whether the gossip was true or not was irrelevant.

Sophie squinted sideways at me, taking out her textbook as our teacher Mr Radley began talking about different organelles of eukaryotic cells.

"So, you don't have anything other than 'friendly' feeling towards him, even if your new *friend* happens to be insanely hot?"

"Definitely not."

"Uh huh." She didn't look convinced, but I laughed her off. Sure, Josh was hot, but there was no way that I'd fall for a hothead like that. No chance.

~

By the time Friday rolled around, the week had been uneventful and perfectly normal. I hadn't spoken to Josh or his brothers again. I had accepted the fact that we probably wouldn't speak again and that everything would blow over and go back to normal. Whatever it was he was dealing with, it appeared to have resolved itself. It didn't stop me keeping an eye out for his brothers after school each day though. If I saw them, Georgie would often wave and smile, but nothing else. It also didn't stop me from visually seeking Josh out wherever I went. I found myself regularly searching corridors or the common room between classes, just to check on him. I tried to stop, but it was like I needed to know he was OK. I felt a surge of relief every day he showed up without any extra bruises.

Although there weren't any new injuries, I couldn't help but notice that he didn't actually seem OK at all. He was quiet and brooding, often avoiding eye contact with anyone. He rarely spoke unless it was with his friend Ollie, and he often sat on his own in the common room. He'd nap or sit quietly, staring off into space. He looked as if he had the weight of the world on his shoulders.

"Earth to Izzy! Hello?" Sophie waved in front of my face. We were waiting by the canteen for the others to join us for lunch. I had no idea what she'd been talking to me about.

"Sorry. I zoned out there for a sec..." I felt my cheeks

redden a little, embarrassed that I'd been lost in thoughts about Josh.

"Hey, do you guys have a free period after lunch today?" Jack asked as he, Ed and Jess approached us. Sophie and I nodded.

"So do we. Fancy going into town to grab lunch instead then? I'd kill for a Nando's," Jack grinned. That boy was obsessed with the popular chicken restaurant.

"Yeah, I don't see why not," Sophie smiled, looking up at him through her lashes. I definitely needed to prod her some more about what was going on there. So far she had stayed very close-lipped, only saying that she'd gotten to know him a little better when they all went to the cinema.

"Wahey! Extended lunch break it is," Ed exclaimed, punching his fists into the air.

"You are such a loser," Jess rolled her eyes, laughing. As we all moved to leave, I saw Josh nearby. He was heading in the opposite direction by himself, his hood pulled up and his hands in his pockets. I couldn't recall seeing Ollie today, so I wondered if he would be by himself for lunch. My friends were a few steps in front of me but I hung back, something pulling me towards Josh.

"Gimme one sec," I called. The four of them turned around and watched as I jogged to catch up with him. I could feel my blood pressure rising a little. It was silly but I felt nervous. We still weren't really friends.

"Hey, Josh!" He didn't reply, continuing on.

"Josh!" I called, louder this time. He startled, turning towards me in surprise.

"Er, hey," I smiled at him.

"Hey," he said, head tilted a little in confusion. "Everything OK?"

"Erm, yeah. A bunch of us are going into town for lunch as we have a free period right after. I was just er, wondering, if you would like to come with us?"

"You're asking me. To go out with you. For lunch?" I swear, his eyebrows were going to crawl right off the top of his forehead if he raised them any higher. Although we'd come to some kind of truce, he had still been a dick the last time I had tried to be nice to him. I started to wonder whether this was actually a good idea. He looked over to where my friends were huddled waiting and back to me again.

"And they're OK with me coming too?" he asked sceptically.

"Yes," I nodded reassuringly, sure that it would be fine, even though I hadn't actually checked with them. There were a couple of awkward seconds of silence and I shuffled my feet, turning to go.

"Fuck it," I heard him mutter as he began to follow, eyes colliding with mine as he gave me a small smile. This boy's whole face transformed when he smiled. He pulled his hood back, pushing his hair out of his face. Even with the faded bruising giving his cheek a greenish glow, he still looked gorgeous.

We walked over to re-join my friends and I grinned at them, trying to appear far more confident than I felt.

"Josh is coming with us too." No one said anything, darting looks back and forth between them. Sophie quirked her eyebrows and Jess looked completely bewildered.

"Well, alrighty then. To the realm of chicken!" Ed said, breaking the silence. He pointed forward whilst doing some kind of weird lunge. He was a strange boy, but I was glad for the distraction. Everyone began moving towards the campus exit, Josh hanging back slightly. I slowed my pace, making sure I fell into step with him. I'd invited him to lunch so I wanted to make him feel included, not like some outsider hanging around whilst we all chatted.

"What classes do you have this afternoon?" I asked him, desperately trying to avoid walking the ten minutes to Nando's in silence.

"Art."

"Oh, you must be in Jess's class then. She has that too."

"Yeah, I've seen her in there." He stared straight ahead, avoiding my eyes.

"What other classes did you pick?"

"P.E. and business studies."

"That's quite an eclectic mix, why did you pick those?" He looked across at me, seeming surprised.

"What?" He was staring at me.

"Er, nothing. I um, like working out and sports so I picked P.E., and Ollie was doing business, so I thought I'd tag along."

"And art?" He sighed, looking ahead again.

"It's the one thing I'm good at. Sketching helps me relax, tune everything out. Escape." He almost whispered the last word. As he stared off into the distance, I noticed again the sadness in his eyes. I surprised myself when I realised how much it bothered me. I don't know why, but I cared. He cleared his throat, shaking himself from his thoughts.

"Where we going for lunch anyway?" We had reached the top of the high street, moving through the hustle of daytime foot traffic. With cobblestone streets, little boutique shops and many cafes and restaurants, Gilleford High street was a popular destination at lunch time.

"Nando's." I nodded towards the sign further up ahead.

"What's that?" He asked, brow furrowed.

"It's a restaurant, sells lots of chicken. South African style cuisine, I believe. You've never been?" I couldn't believe he'd never even heard of it.

"No." His steps had slowed, the space between us and my friends in front growing.

"Everything OK?" I asked as we stopped outside the entrance.

"Er, yeah. I'll be right behind you." He stood still, waiting for me to go in. I shrugged, stepping inside. After a few steps, I glanced back at him over my shoulder. He had turned away from the door and was reaching into his back pocket, pulling his wallet out. I could see him rifling through it, looking flustered. *Ah shit.*

Chapter 8

Joshua

Why the fuck did I agree to go on this little jaunt? When Izzy had strolled over to me, all smiles and big green eyes, I had been completely taken aback that she'd asked me to go to lunch with her friends. No one had ever asked me to go out to lunch with them. No one. Usually Ollie and I hung out and neither one of us would eat that much. We were both conscious of conserving food and money. But Ollie's words from Saturday were ringing in my ears. If I wanted Izzy to keep her mouth shut and butt out, I needed to be *nice* to her.

It had been hard enough sucking up to her on Monday and my pride had taken a major hit. I'd tried to look as disarming as possible, bringing out my puppy dog eyes and even a smile or two. It made me cringe just thinking about it. I usually wouldn't hesitate to turn her lunch offer down, but I'd noticed her looking at me a few times over the week. What if she was having second thoughts? What if she decided to tell her parents or the police about what she'd seen?

I had about four quid in change in my wallet. That would be enough for a sandwich and a can of something from one of the bakeries in town. My mouth watered at the idea of actually having lunch for a change. I mulled it over, trying to weigh up whether the effort of acting like a nice guy would be worth it. Fuck it. I was going to go. I could play nice a little longer if it meant my life stayed private.

I was surprised she didn't stay with her friends when we began walking into town. I'd assumed they'd walk together and I'd planned to hang back, not wanting to bother with making small talk. When Izzy fell into step beside me, I was immediately suspicious. Did she want to get me on my own to talk about last weekend again? But no, she only asked about my classes. I tried to convince myself that telling her about why I chose art was all part of the nice guy act. I ignored the fact that it had caught me off guard how easy it was to talk to her.

But now I was seriously regretting agreeing to come along. Why hadn't I checked where we were going before? There was no way I could afford a meal in a restaurant. I could withdraw some extra cash, but it was likely that I'd need it to top up on food at some point this month. No, I wasn't going to risk Georgie or Ryan going hungry just so I could eat a fancy lunch. I could probably have tap water and a plate of chips or some kind of side. I'd just tell everyone I had eaten a big breakfast or something. Feeling better about my plan and still looking forward to eating chips, I squared my shoulders and held my chin up, pushing through the door and spying Izzy at a nearby table.

"OK, we've ordered. your turn." Jess, the girl in my art class, returned to the table with the rest of their friends in tow. Izzy stood, motioning me towards the tills. I ordered, the waitress frowning when I only had to pay £2.60. What a result! I ignored her, happy to actually be getting some change, and grabbed the glass of tap water she held out to me. Izzy stepped up for her turn and I hesitated. I didn't fancy going to sit with her friends without her. I didn't know any of them. Then again, I didn't really know Izzy either. *Grow a pair, Josh.*

I went back to the table, sitting down across from where I'd seen Izzy sitting. The two guys were at the other end of the table, laughing and joking about something. Jess was sitting in the middle opposite me and another girl, whose name I didn't know, was immediately next to me. They were both quiet, watching me. I raised my eyebrows at Jess as she stared, her eyes roaming over the bruises on my face.

"So...Josh...do you know everyone here?" She asked and I slowly shook my head.

"I'm Sophie." The girl next to me smiled. She looked like she spent most of her time outside, she was so tanned. Both she and Jess were tiny, at least a foot shorter than me.

"That's Jack and Ed," Jess introduced the guys and they paused, offering a chin lift each and then going back to their conversation. Izzy then came back to the table and the girls seemed to visibly relax.

"What did you order?" Jess turned to her.

"Chicken burger and chips," Izzy responded, her eyes darting to me and quickly away again. The girls started talking about their plans for the weekend, some kind of sleepover by the sounds of it, and I looked around the restaurant. It was packed. This place must have some pretty good food and by the smells coming from the kitchen, I was betting that I was going to have some major food envy. As if on cue, my stomach started gurgling, but the restaurant was so noisy that I don't think anyone heard. I couldn't remember the last time I was in a restaurant, but this place was pretty cool. There were bright pieces of random artwork on the walls and lots of plants dotted about. It had a nice, relaxed feel about the place.

"Roulette wings?" A different waitress appeared, balancing a tray of food high in her hand. She was short and curvy, her tight black t-shirt not leaving much to the imagination. I had no idea what roulette wings were, but they looked awesome as she set them down on the table in front of Ed. She slid the food down in front of everyone and I noticed Jess giving me the side-eye when only chips were put in front of me. Thankfully, no one queried it.

"We er, made an extra chicken burger by mistake. Did you want it?" The waitress winked at me, pulling her shoulders back and thrusting her chest out. I sure as hell wasn't going to turn down free food so I reached for the burger, smiling at her.

"Thanks, darlin'." She nodded happily and trotted off, putting a little extra sway into her hips. This nice guy stuff had its advantages.

"Ah mate, what a result! I've been here loads and I've never been given free food. She definitely wanted to get in your pants," the guy called Ed shouted down the table, so loud that I saw a few people nearby smother laughter behind their hands. I laughed, shrugging my shoulders and taking a huge bite of burger. Oh my fucking God, it was amazing. The chicken was juicy and rich and whatever relish they had going on in that bun was heavenly. I ate so slowly, savouring every bite, so that by the time I moved onto my chips, everyone else had nearly finished.

I suddenly had a pang of guilt. Ryan and Georgie would love one of these burgers. My heart was telling me to get the extra cash out and get them one each, but my head was telling me to be sensible and save the money. It was so frustrating, but I knew what the right thing to do was, even though it made me feel like shit.

"Here's your takeaway order too," the flirty waitress reappeared, handing a bag over to Izzy.

"Don't tell me you're still hungry, Iz. I am stuffed!" Jack stretched back and patted his stomach.

"Well, you did have a full plate of wings, chips, garlic bread *and* corn on the cob, so that's no surprise." Jess rolled her eyes at him.

"He's gotta keep his energy up, needs his stamina," Ed smirked, nudging him in the ribs. Jack frowned at him, glancing at Sophie and I saw her drop her head. There was some sort of drama there that I had no

ANGELA MACK

inclination at all to find out about. I had a feeling that my version of drama and Izzy's friends' versions were very different.

It was soon time to head back and as before, I found myself walking alongside Izzy.

"So, what did you think of your first trip to Nando's?"

"The food was fucking incredible. Tasted even better 'cos it was free." I was struck with how much the whole experience hadn't sucked. OK, so I hadn't exactly gone out of my way to have a conversation with any of them, but it was nice to have some company at lunch for a change. And the food was awesome.

"Thank you. For asking me to come. It was nice." Why did it feel so awkward to say thank you? Maybe because I still hardly knew this girl and she was going out of her way to be nice to me, which let's face it, I completely didn't deserve. I wasn't used to people doing that. And the only reason I'd even agreed to come was to try and make her like me enough to keep my secrets. I was a douche bag.

"No problem. We should do it again sometime." I raised my eyebrows at her. "Er, if you want to. I mean," she shrugged.

"Why?" She frowned at me.

"What do you mean?"

"Why would you want to spend lunch with me again? I wasn't exactly amazing company. I barely spoke the entire time." She didn't answer straight away and I wondered if she was going to at all.

"I...we're supposed to be friends, right? Friends get

to know each other…" She looked away, her cheeks colouring faintly pink.

"I don't think you'd like me very much. If you got to know me." Now it was her turn to look surprised.

"We won't know until we find out." Not likely. If I spent much more time around her, she'd figure out that I really was a dick and definitely go blabbing.

~

After eating some actual decent food at lunch, I was feeling pretty pumped about going to a double session of art before the end of the day. Jess had walked with me to class, nattering away the whole time. I was relieved that she took her usual spot at the front, whilst I shuffled to the back. That girl was exhausting and I'd only spent five minutes with her.

Mrs DeLaney, a scatty, eccentric woman, set us our project for the year. She reminded me of Professor Trelawney from the Harry Potter films (yes, I'd watched them all. And yes, I can unashamedly admit I love them just as much as Georgie).

"Inspiration!" She clapped her hands twice, her long skirt swishing around her legs as she swayed a little. Her short, greyish-brown hair was sticking up in all directions and she had ridiculously large hoop earrings in.

"That's the theme for this year. It can be something that inspires you or something you want to inspire other people." Urgh, great. I didn't have a whole lot of experience with that.

"Before you start thinking about your final piece, I want you to research a range of different artists. They can be any style and any medium. But I want you to fill your sketchbooks with little testers. Try out some of your ideas following another artist's style. Show me your journey..." she proceeded to hand out some example sketchbooks from previous years. Wow, some of these people were seriously talented.

"And get out of your comfort zone. Don't fill your sketchbooks up with all sketches or all watercolour. Experiment with oil paint or charcoal or collage..." Well, I guess my idea of spending the year sketching had gone out the window. I had no idea what my final 'piece' would be. I spent the rest of the session flicking through books and biographies of different artists that Mrs DeLaney provided, noting down which ones I could try tester pieces out for during our next class. By the time the final bell rang, I was a little disappointed. I had been enjoying looking at other people's methods for escaping reality.

On the days I wasn't working, Ryan and I would meet over the road outside Georgie's school. With all the hours I worked, I felt like I didn't get to see either of them much, so I made the most of spending as much of my spare time with them as possible. After the incident at the weekend, Big Mike hadn't come home for three days. It was pretty normal for him to be absent a lot, as he worked long shifts at all sorts of hours. However, three days was the longest he'd not come home for in a while. I tried not to get my hopes up that this time, he wouldn't come back at all.

On a typical day, it was rare for him to be home much before 10 p.m. Even if he'd worked an early morning shift, he'd stop by the betting office, or the pub, or both, and not come home for hours. Not that I cared. If anything, it made me feel more comfortable about working so late while the boys were home alone. Rarely would I come home and find Big Mike had gotten home before me, and even if he had, Ryan and Georgie had plenty of practice staying out of his way and locking themselves in our room.

"Hey. How was art?" Izzy jogged to catch up with me as I crossed the road. My God, this girl didn't give up. Surely she was sick of me by now?

"Fine. Where are your sidekicks? I didn't think you went anywhere without them." *Shit.* That didn't sound very nice at all, my true colours starting to show. Thankfully, she seemed to think I was joking and laughed.

"Who, Jess and Sophie? Sophie went straight home after lunch, said she wasn't feeling well, and Jess is staying late to work on her fashion project for textiles."

"On a Friday night? She doesn't seem the sort to stay late on a Friday."

"You'd be surprised. She wants to be a big designer one day and once she's in 'the zone,' she tends to stay late to work on a project."

"I wish I knew what I wanted to do and had that much conviction about being able to do it." Why the hell did I just say that? She didn't need to know that. Besides, with my background, my best bet would be for Martin to take me on full-time at the shop and that would be it.

What a career.

"Me too. I honestly have no idea what I'm going to do after sixth form. I'd like to go to university, but I haven't decided on what course to study." It was a little unnerving at how quickly I found myself opening up to her. Within moments, she had me telling her a little bit more about myself and I could almost see the gears turning in her head, trying to fit the pieces of me together like a giant game of Tetris. I had to keep reminding myself that I was only talking to her so she wouldn't reveal my pathetic life to the rest of the world.

"Izzy!" Georgie saw us approach and came running over from where he was standing with Ryan, a big grin on his face.

"Hey buddy, how you doing?" She appeared genuinely happy to see him and ruffled his hair. I still didn't understand how or why she had formed some sort of bond with Georgie, but I was grateful for someone putting a smile on his face nonetheless.

"Guess what?" she asked him as Ryan caught up, nodding hello to both of us as we all began walking together towards *Martins*. Unlike Georgie, Ryan didn't seem quite as trusting of Izzy. It was more like he'd just make the most of anything good that came from her hanging around.

"We went out for lunch today and Josh brought you some extra food back." She thrust the takeaway bag from Nando's at Georgie. "Oh, there's my bus. I better go." She ran off, completely avoiding my eyes.

"Thanks so much, Joshy," Georgie's face lit up, rummaging around the bag and peeking through the wrapping, trying to see what food it contained. Ryan leaned over, licking his lips in anticipation. I was stunned. What the fuck had just happened? How did she know that I had wanted to bring the boys some food back? My ego was definitely taking a kicking with this girl. She kept buying us food and helping me and trying to be friendly. I didn't understand why.

After shaking off my bewilderment, I started ushering the boys home. Georgie swung the takeaway bag back and forth by his side, a noticeable spring in his step. I spied a slip of paper at the top and snatched it out, smoothing it in my hands. It was the receipt from the order. The waitress must have stuffed it in there, and it was broken down into two sections. One for takeaway and one for eat-in. Under takeaway, there were two chicken burgers and chips, a portion of Roulette wings (hell yeah!) and three lots of corn on the cob. There was probably enough for me to have dinner with them too. I was about to crumple it up when I noticed what was under the eat-in section; chicken burger and chips and an extra chicken burger by itself. I frowned. No way. Izzy hadn't actually purchased the extra burger for me and told the waitress to lie? No. She wouldn't have. Would she?

As soon as we got home, we heated the food up and demolished the lot of it. We had all learned pretty quickly what 'roulette wings' were; you had no clue how spicy each one would be. Georgie ran around the kitchen, eyes streaming and repeatedly gulping down mugs of water at one point. It was hilarious.

"Fuck me, that was awesome," Ryan beamed, sauce

from the wings smeared around his lips. Georgie nodded his agreement with a big toothy grin. He had bits of chicken stuck in his teeth and some kind of mayonnaise streaked across his cheek. They looked like kids for a change, carefree and with full bellies. I was conflicted; part of me was happy to see the boys smiling, but the other part was irritated that it was because of Izzy and not me. I could feed my brothers just fine without her. I'd managed this long without any help.

I thudded upstairs to our room, pulling out my phone and crashing onto my bed. *I do feed them, you know.* I hadn't used Izzy's number before today, but right now the overwhelming urge to message her was too fierce to ignore.

Who is this?

Josh.

I know you do.

So why do you keep buying them food? She didn't answer straight away. I could almost feel her hesitation through the phone. *It makes me feel good to do something nice.* Well shit, how was I going to respond to that?

You paid for my burger today too, didn't you? The one the waitress said they'd made by mistake.

What makes you think that?

Your receipt was left in the bag.

Ah. No point me denying it then.

Why would you do that? I could have bought myself a burger if I wanted one.

I saw you outside Nandos looking in your wallet. You looked stressed so I thought maybe you didn't have enough on you. Oh for fuck sake, she was annoyingly perceptive.

Plus your stomach was rumbling the entire walk there, so you can't tell me you weren't hungry ;) Great. Just great. She's seen where and how we live, so the rational part of me knew it was obvious that we don't have a lot of money. But it irked me to know she pitied me.

I didn't mean to offend you. I was just happy that you agreed to come and I didn't want you feeling awkward or uncomfortable. I kept rereading the text. I had made her happy? I didn't understand this girl at all.

At that moment, my brothers came bundling into the room, both jumping on my bed and I smiled as we settled in for another movie night. I pushed all thoughts of Izzy right to the back of my mind.

Chapter 9

Isabel

"Izzy, you've had a death grip on your phone for the past twenty minutes. Who are you messaging?" Jess threw a cushion at me and it smacked me right in the face.

"Hey!"

"Well, come on. Who's distracting you from the Twilight movie marathon we have going on right now?" Jess gestured to the TV, currently showing the first film. It was up to the part where Bella and Edward won the golden onion. I really did love these films. Usually the three of us were chattier when we stayed over Sophie's, but she'd been rather quiet, so Jess had stuck the films on instead.

"I think I've upset Josh…" I wasn't sure how much I should confide in them, but Josh hadn't replied to my last message for almost half an hour and I was fretting a little.

"How do you have Josh's number? How does he have yours?!" Jess squealed, hitting pause on the film and turning towards me on Sophie's bed. The three of us were sprawled across the huge king size mattress, Sophie and Jess at the end nearest the TV and me propped up by the pillows. I had been alternating between staring at the screen and staring at my phone, willing a new message to appear.

"I can't remember exactly. We swapped a few days ago," I shrugged, trying to appear nonchalant. Jess frowned, clearly not believing me.

"Why do you think you've upset him?" Sophie asked, hugging a pillow to her chest and pulling her knees up. She definitely didn't seem herself tonight. Maybe if I shared a little bit, she'd feel encouraged to do the same.

"You know today at lunch, when the waitress brought him over that free burger?"

"Of course. How could we forget the waitress that practically shoved her tits in his face?" Jess rolled her eyes and I frowned. She had been annoyingly flirty, alright.

"Well, it wasn't actually free. I had paid for it but asked the girl at the till if she wouldn't mind lying about it."

"Why the hell would you do that?" Jess tilted her head, confused.

"I don't think Josh had realised we were going to a restaurant. I got the impression he didn't have much money on him and then when I heard him only order chips and tap water, I was pretty sure he was a bit strapped for cash. I felt bad for asking him to come and not telling him where we were going first," I sighed.

"I must admit, I was shocked you invited him in the first place," Jess said.

"I think it was nice. He only ever sits with that other guy and I don't think he was in today." Sophie didn't have a bad bone in her body and she always knew how to make me feel better about something.

"Yeah well, I guess he found out somehow that I paid for it and he was texting me earlier. But when I tried explaining, he stopped replying."

"OK, so you bruised his male ego a little. So what? I'm not even sure he's that nice a person, Iz."

"What makes you say that?" I turned to Jess, interested to hear what she had to say.

"Well, you've seen the bruises he's covered in. He's always starting fights. I heard he broke some kid's nose because he accidentally knocked a sandwich out of his hand. I was so nervous walking to art with him earlier that I kept blathering on like an idiot!"

"That can't be true. Mr Tapps would have expelled him for that." No way would the Head of Gilleford School have allowed him back to sixth form if he'd broken someone's nose.

"It must have been outside of school or something…"

"I don't think I have ever seen Josh start a proper fight at school," Sophie interjected and she was right. A bit of shoving and yelling, but never an actual fight.

"He's obviously careful about it at school. But I know

for a fact that he and that Ollie kid beat up some students from the private school on the other side of town last summer." Jess crossed her arms, disapproving.

"Look, I know he doesn't scream Mr. Nice Guy but maybe he's a bit misunderstood. You know, like how I was last year," I said pointedly. I knew Josh didn't have a squeaky-clean history, but I was getting a little irritated by Jess' judgemental glare.

"Just be careful, Izzy, yeah? We don't want you getting hurt," Sophie smiled at me.

"It's not like I fancy him or anything. I'm only trying to be nice." Jess snorted at me.

"Yeah, yeah. You keep telling yourself that." She rolled her eyes and I ignored her, shaking my head.

"Don't tell anyone about the extra burger at Nando's please? Last thing I need is Jack or Ed finding out and making some inappropriate joke to him. I was trying to be discreet," I begged and they both nodded.

"So, what's up with you, Soph? You've been a little quiet. I wasn't sure tonight was still going ahead after you left early today." I turned to her, changing the subject but hoping she'd open up. It was unlike her to be so stand-offish, like she had the past week or so. She rested her chin on the top of her knees and I wasn't sure she was going to answer.

"I kissed Jack…" she whispered.

"What?!"

"Oh my God, when?!" Jess and I both gaped at each other, shocked that neither of us had heard about this sooner.

"Earlier this week. His family own the next farm over, but I hadn't really spoken to him much before this year. We hit it off when we all went to the cinema. He was easy to talk to." She smiled, staring at her toes. "He started hanging around the farm, helping me out with the horses and chatting." She shrugged, going quiet.

"Okaaay...go on..." Jess encouraged and Sophie huffed, her shoulders sinking even lower than they already were.

"Well, on Wednesday when he came by, we kind of ended up...kissing. It got pretty heated..." Sophie started turning red and Jess wolf-whistled.

"Sophie! You've been holding out on us." She smiled for the first time tonight but then immediately looked sad again.

"Yeah, well, it clearly didn't mean anything to him," she mumbled.

"Why do you think that?"

"Yesterday I saw him walking down the road with some other girl. He had his arm slung around her shoulders. And she was gorgeous, Iz. Tall, stick thin with huge boobs and long blonde hair. The complete opposite of me."

"Oh, shut up, Soph. You are seriously hot and if he can't see that, he's a moron," Jess said and I nodded in agreement.

"Maybe she was just a friend?" I offered.

"I was naively hoping for the same thing too but after Ed's comment today about stamina..." she rolled her eyes, her mouth straightening into a thin line.

"Have you asked Jack about it?" She shook her head.

"Nah, been ignoring his texts. I was starting to like him, but I am not going to be messed about."

"Good on you! You're right. If he's going to dick about with some other girl, then he's not good enough for you anyway." Jess threw her arm out, pulling Sophie closer to her and squeezing her tight.

"Yeah. You deserve better than that," I echoed.

"Thanks girlies," she smiled.

"Right, come on. You know the last film is my favourite and we're never going to get to it if we keep pausing it." Jess grinned at us both and I felt better now that we had all cleared the air.

"I am not staying up all night again. I have work tomorrow," I laughed, throwing the pillow from earlier back in her face.

"We'll turn the volume down low and you can doze off."

"Fine." I shook my head at her, laughing. I knew full well I wasn't going to get much sleep and I would be a walking-zombie tomorrow.

~

"You seem a lot happier lately, dear," Mary beamed at me, watching me work as I arranged one of the largest bouquets I'd done yet. Mary had lots of laughter lines around her eyes, which were magnified by her round, thick-rimmed glasses.

"I have made some really great friends this year," I grinned. She came closer, inspecting my arrangement as I wrapped it in cellophane and tied it off with a yellow ribbon bow. I caught a whiff of her lavender perfume as she leaned over, her long dark plait falling forward on one side as she examined the flowers.

"Beautiful! You do favour the yellow flowers, don't you?" She laughed.

"It's my favourite colour and the guy said I could pick whatever I wanted." I turned from the back room, heading to the front of the shop and presenting the customer with his order.

"Cheers, love. This should get me out of the doghouse." He gave me a sheepish grin as he passed over a fifty-pound note, gently taking the bouquet and heading out the door. Mary came up behind me, resting her delicate fingers on my shoulders.

"Why don't you grab some lunch, dear? I have some new bridal magazines for us to flick through." I looked over my shoulder at her and nodded. We often spent our lunch breaks getting ideas for wedding flowers, Mary's main passion, and seeing what the latest trends were. Usually I brought lunch with me but after staying up late at Sophie's, I had woken up with exactly seven minutes to get ready before I had to run for the bus.

"Would you like anything?" I turned back to her before leaving the shop.

"No thank you, dear."

As I stepped outside into the crisp, fresh air, I saw Josh sitting on a nearby bench. He had his back to me, with his arms stretched out along the top of the bench and his face tipped up, the sunshine warming his face. It was almost October and although the breeze was turning bitterly cool, we were definitely getting more sunny days than usual for this time of year. I ran into *Martins*, grabbed a large cheese salad baguette and two cans of coke, then headed over to where Josh was sitting. He had his eyes closed so didn't see me approach. His *Martins* black polo top was stretched across his chest and upper arms, like most of the t-shirts he wore, and he was again in his signature black jeans and trainers. The way the sunlight fell on his face meant you could barely see the discolouration and bruising anymore. I felt my pulse quicken a little as I realised just how attractive he looked.

"Hey." I fell back on the bench next to him. He peeked one eye open.

"Hey." I opened the baguette and took a bite out the end.

"There is no way you're going to eat all that." He raised his eyebrow at me and I shrugged.

"When you gotta go back in?" I asked.

"'Bout ten minutes." We sat in silence for a little while, but it didn't feel uncomfortable.

"Your bruises have almost gone." *Way to go and make it uncomfortable, Izzy.* He frowned, not responding and grabbed a cereal bar out of his pocket.

"Tell me that's not all you're eating for lunch?" It was my turn to raise my eyebrows at him.

"Sorry, Mum," he mumbled around a mouthful.

"I'm sure your mum would agree with me that a cereal bar is not a sufficient lunch." Why was I using such a patronising voice all of a sudden? Urgh.

"Ha! Doubt that," he huffed and I tilted my head, not sure whether to voice the question on my tongue. "I haven't seen her for over a year. She doesn't care about me or what I am or am not eating for lunch." I grimaced. I should have just been content sitting in silence. I vaguely remembered Ryan saying something about their mum not being around, but I didn't realise he meant *at all*. I thought he had meant just for that night. I picked up the extra can of coke and held it out to him.

"Peace offering?"

"For what?" He asked cautiously.

"For annoying you yesterday."

"You didn't annoy me. Why would you have annoyed me?" He looked puzzled.

"I thought you might have been mad about me paying for your burger?" He shrugged.

"You don't need to keep buying me food, I eat when I'm hungry. But it was an awesome burger." There was a hint of a smile playing on his lips.

"I bet Georgie loved it." I was probably playing with fire, bringing up that I had also bought his brothers food again, but he didn't seem to mind. In fact, his face brightened instantly.

"You should have seen him when he took a bite out of one of those roulette wings," he chuckled.

"Oh no. He didn't get a super spicy one, did he?" He nodded and we both laughed.

"OK, well I better get back." I wrapped the remaining half of my baguette back in its packet, set it on the bench and jumped up. "See you Monday." I walked off before he had a chance to notice I'd left half my lunch next to him. I paused at the Buttercups doorway, turning to watch him. After a few seconds he went to stand and saw the baguette. He shook his head, his lips twitching. He went to walk away but after half a step, changed his mind, grabbed the discarded food and walked back into *Martins*.

Chapter 10

Joshua

"Come on guys, hurry up or you're going to be late," I called to Ryan and Georgie as I descended the stairs. If we didn't leave in the next ten minutes then they would both be late for school and Georgie's teacher, Mrs Abernathy, was already causing issues. She'd rang last week and left me a voicemail, asking if we could meet to discuss Georgie. She said she was concerned about how withdrawn he was at school and how he didn't have any friends. She also said he was behind in most subjects compared to other kids his age. Of course, she thought she was leaving a voicemail on Big Mike's phone, not mine.

When we first moved to this shitty neighbourhood and things with Big Mike started getting rough, the teachers at both our schools began to notice the difference in all three of us. Georgie especially had been a very happy, confident little boy and his sudden U-turn in behaviour was cause for concern. Although Ryan had always had a streak of rebelliousness in him, he grew even mouthier and more disruptive in school. The teachers would call Big Mike and most of the time I don't think he answered, but occasionally I'd over-hear him telling one of them to fuck off. He'd then be in a foul mood and prone to a violent outburst. I'd cringe, holding my breath at school the next day, waiting for a teacher to say something to me. They were bound to make a comment about either his inappropriate phone manner, or the bruises on my arms I tried to keep hidden under my school shirt. One day my form tutor kept me behind in the morning and asked 'if there was anything going on at home' I wanted to tell him about. I knew then that we had to start keeping up appearances better.

I decided to steal Big Mike's phone. It was risky but necessary. I could pretend to be our dad and try to placate the teachers' concerns. Big Mike had gone mental when he thought he'd lost his phone, turning our house upside down and even ripping a few doors off the kitchen cupboards in his rage. Eventually he calmed down, bought himself a new phone the next day and forgot all about it. Meanwhile, I kept his phone on silent in the den under the floorboard with all our other contraband. I checked it every night, listening to voicemails and either calling back the next day or using the computers at school to email replies instead (from a fake account in his name, of course). I preferred email but sometimes only a phone call would do the trick. So far, I'd avoided going in for a face to face, obviously that wasn't going to work, by saying that 'I' worked long shifts. I'd call Mrs Abernathy at some point today and try to put her mind at ease.

It bothered me though, that Georgie didn't have any friends. He used to always get invited to birthday parties and now that I thought about it, I couldn't remember the last time he mentioned anyone at school he hung around with or when he didn't spend all weekend with either me or Ryan. Actually, Ryan didn't hang around with anyone else either. They either spent all their time together at home alone, with me watching movies, or we'd all go to the playground down the road with Ollie. That was about it. They both seemed their normal selves around me though, so it was hard for me to understand that they were so different at school. I was going to have to talk to them both about it at some point.

I breezed into the kitchen, intending on making the boys some toast to go, when I froze. Big Mike was sitting at the table reading the newspaper and eating some toast himself. As if it was the most ordinary thing in the world for him to be sitting there. He was *never* up this early. I heard Ryan and Georgie barrel down the stairs behind me until they both crashed into my back, unaware that I was glued to the spot. They peered out from behind me and I could hear Georgie's sharp intake of breath. Big Mike didn't react, as if we didn't exist. Several moments of silence passed and then I felt Ryan start to inch forward. I glared at him, but he purposely stayed facing forward, ignoring me. I went to grab his arm but he shook me off. I watched as he squared his shoulders back and waltzed over to the table, heading for the loaf of bread next to Big Mike. What was left of it anyway. We had almost a full loaf yesterday and judging by the mountain of toast next to Big Mike's paper and the slack in the packaging, we'd be lucky to have four slices left in there. Greedy shit.

As Ryan's outstretched hand reached for the bread, Big Mike snapped his head up and grabbed his wrist. I took a step forward and Big Mike turned his glare to me, daring me to come forward. I could feel the anger starting to seep to the surface, my jaw tense and my fingers twitching.

"This is my food. Not yours. You don't earn the money round here that puts food on this table. You're not worthy enough to eat my food." Big Mike spoke so low it was almost a growl and his eyes locked with Ryan's in a fierce leer. That was his favourite insult to us all; *we weren't worthy of this, we weren't worthy of that, we were worthless pieces of shit*, blah, blah, blah.

"Don't kid yourself, old man. Josh puts food on this table, not you." A second ago, I thought Ryan was trembling with fear but by the look on his face, it was actually rage he was visibly shaking with. I was momentarily taken aback. I had taught Ryan and Georgie to never back-chat, to avoid confrontation with Big Mike at all costs, and whenever he was home, hide out in their room. I would deal with Big Mike and take the brunt of his mood swings, so that they didn't have to. What Ryan was doing right now, was incredibly dangerous. And stupid.

Big Mike swung his gaze to me, narrowing his eyes as I took two more steps forward. Ryan was within my reach and Georgie had backed up further away, staying behind me.

"I pay the rent around here. I keep the roof over your heads. Whatever is under this roof is mine." The rent was the only damn thing he did pay. And the amount of hours he worked, I knew he must have enough to cover the other bills too. But he never did. If I didn't pay them, he'd let the electricity get shut off and the water dry up. He didn't give a shit about us.

His eyes were wild, his pupils so big that if you asked me what colour eyes he had right now, I would have to say black. He flung Ryan's wrist away with such force that he spun, colliding with me. I wrapped my arms around him to keep him from falling to the floor and when he went to lunge at Big Mike, I squeezed tighter.

"What the fuck, Josh...let me go!" I was holding him off his feet now and his legs were flailing. Big Mike had gone back to eating his toast and ignoring us. I turned around to Georgie.

"Out. Now." I nodded to the front door and he scurried out.

"So you're just going to let him eat all our food and talk to us like shit..." I dragged Ryan out the house as he yelled at me, his thrashes becoming more and more forceful. I lengthened my strides, marching down the street with him still locked in a bear-hug. Once he stopped flailing, I set him back down on the ground. As soon as his feet touched the floor, he spun around and faced me, his chin tipped up and his breathing laboured.

"You are lucky he didn't clock you one round the face, you stupid shit. What the fuck were you thinking?" I was furious with him. Why the fuck did he think antagonising him was a good idea?

"Lucky? LUCKY?!" he was practically spitting at me. "Why didn't you do something? That was *your* food that *you* paid for and you *let* him get away with it!"

"Do you think I wanted to do that? Don't you think that I wanted to snatch the bread off the table, swipe his plate to the floor and punch him in his smug fucking face? Of course I fucking did! But have you missed what has been happening the past couple years, Ryan? I CAN'T FUCKING WIN! I cannot beat that miserable, fat shit. Don't you remember me trying?" My chest was heaving with the effort of not punching something and expelling all the pent-up frustration sitting in my stomach, weighing me down.

"Have these bruises faded so fast that you've forgotten the last beating I took?!" I pointed to my face as Ryan's eyes filled with angry tears.

"I HATE YOU! We could have beaten him. Just then. The two of us. We need to stand together and show him he *can't* win against us." His tears were flowing now, his fists balled and shaking. I laughed and shook my head.

"You are twelve years old, Ryan. You are less than half my size and definitely less than half my weight. Honestly, what advantage do you think you'd have given me back there?" He looked like I'd slapped him in the face.

"I can fight…" he muttered, looking down at his shoes.

"Can you? Can you really?" He avoided my eyes, not answering. "No. I didn't think so. You know the plan, Ryan. It's not that long 'til I turn eighteen. And then I am going to get us all out of that shithole and away from that prick." He still wasn't looking at me. I sighed, walking over to him and crouching down so that I was peering into his eyes.

"Ryan, look at me buddy." I used my thumb and forefinger to turn his face until we made eye contact. "I'm sorry. I am so sorry that this is how our life has ended up. I'm sorry that I am not strong enough yet. I'll keep training and maybe we won't have to wait until I'm eighteen and I'll be able to beat him instead. But until then mate, you need to lay low. I would...I couldn't..." I took a deep shuddering breath, trying to keep it together. I looked around and saw Georgie, reaching out to him until he stepped into my embrace too.

"I could not *stand* my life without you two in it. Do you hear me? I *need* you to stay smart, stay strong and most importantly, stay alive." I looked at my two brothers, forced to grow up so young. "I can't do this without you." I whispered the last sentence, leaning my forehead forward so that it touched both of theirs. A stray tear escaped from under my eyelid and I roughly palmed it away. They both nodded at me, but Ryan wouldn't meet my gaze any longer.

"OK. So, we are going to pick our battles, bide our time, and soon we will all be free." I smiled at them both, trying to reassure them when we all knew it was a promise I wasn't sure I could keep. We walked the rest of the way to school in silence, although Georgie did take my hand and let me hold it all the way to the entrance of his school. Usually Ryan and I walked him up to the front gates and then crossed the road together to enter Gilleford Secondary. However, as I turned towards St James', Ryan turned in the other direction and walked off without saying goodbye to either of us.

"He just needs a little space right now, buddy," I said to Georgie as I bobbed down, giving him a firmer hug than usual.

"I know. He's angry with himself that he can't help you more. He wishes he was bigger. Stronger." He tried to smile at me but it looked more like a grimace.

"I need you to do me a favour today please, mate." He looked up at me shyly as I tried to change the subject. "I need you to try and make some friends today. Say hello to some of the other kids or sit with them at lunch or something. Your teacher is starting to leave me messages again." He sighed, his little shoulders sagging.

"Fine." I was surprised he didn't fight me on it more but then again, we'd had a long morning already. I gave him another quick hug and said goodbye, watching as he walked towards his classroom. His shoulders were stooped, his gait slow and his head down. It was heartbreaking to witness and I almost ran over to him and scooped him up. I desperately wanted to take him far away, where we could escape all the chaos. It wasn't the right time yet, though.

As I headed towards school, I was struggling to keep a lid on my emotions. I could picture myself punching Big Mike in the face, over and over until his face was a bloody mess. *He* was the one that wasn't worthy. He didn't deserve to breathe the same air as us. But then my inner vision would switch to Big Mike hitting Ryan over and over, whilst I just stood there and watched. It was like a nightmare reel on repeat, alternating between blinding, furious hatred and paralysing fear.

"Woah, sorry mate," a guy apologised after crashing into my shoulder, making me stumble. I had entered the common room, spying Ollie at the bench we'd grown accustomed to meeting at, when this prick rammed into me. I whirled round, watching the guy laughing with his mates as he walked away from me.

"Think that's funny, do ya?" I snarled at him. The guy looked over his shoulder, frowning at me. "Don't walk away from me, you prick." He had been about to continue towards the doors but paused, turning around to face me.

"What's your problem, Josh? I said sorry. You weren't exactly watching where you were going." He shrugged at me, turning away. I saw red, seething fury starting to leak into my veins. I sprang forward, grabbing the guy's bag on his back, yanking him backwards and launching him behind me. His bag took most of the impact, but I saw his head snap back and rebound forward with the force of it. I threw my own backpack onto the floor next to him, jumping on top of him and sitting my full weight on his chest. His eyes grew wide as I pulled my fist back. I was about to connect with his cheekbone when someone came charging into me, knocking me off him. I sprawled on the floor, hastily sitting up, ready to jump into action and pounce on whoever had decided to join the fray. My rage instantly halted, replaced by confusion when the only person in the immediate vicinity was Izzy. I looked up at her from the floor.

"What the fuck are you playing at, Josh?!" I don't think I've ever seen a girl angry before but boy, was Izzy pissed. I was rigid, my adrenaline still pumping but with nowhere appropriate to go. The other guy scrambled up and made a run for it with his mates.

"*You* were the one that came in here like a raging bull. If anything, *you* collided with Tom, not the other way around." Well, at least I knew his name now. "Does it make you feel good?" I was puzzled by her question, unsure how to answer. She crept closer to me, towering over my prone form still on the floor.

"Does it make you feel good to pick on someone weaker than you? To start fights for no reason? Do you feel like a man now?" She was shouting at me, right in my face. She turned to leave, but something made her hesitate. She faced me again, this time crouching right down so her eyes were level with mine.

"I am so disappointed in you," she whispered, eyes shining. The bell rang and with that, she left. She didn't look back once. Everyone else started filing out until the common room was almost empty. I hadn't moved an inch.

"Well fuck me, I wasn't expecting that." I looked over my shoulder and saw Ollie standing behind me, staring at the door after Izzy. "You know she just saved your arse, right?" I frowned at him. "If you had hit that kid, you'd have been expelled. And maybe even worse as you looked like a murderous, raving lunatic, if I'm honest." I knew it had to be bad if not even my best mate was backing me up. Fuck.

Chapter 11

Isabel

Shit, shit, shit. Why did I do that? Why did I do that? I was back to pacing in the girl's bathroom again, trying to keep it together.

"Izzy! What the hell was that?" Sophie and Jess came ploughing through the doorway, Jess' face mirroring the shock that was reverberating through my bones.

"I don't know…" I don't know how it happened. It was all a blur.

"You literally shoved him off of someone." I don't know whether it was awe or surprise on Sophie's face.

"I…it reminded me of all the times Ellie said something to me and everyone sat back and watched, not intervening, even though deep down they knew it was wrong." I don't know how I'd gotten up the courage to push Josh away from Tom. There was something about the scared look in Tom's eyes that triggered me. I didn't think. I just acted.

"OK, but Josh is like, huge. You could have gotten hurt." Sophie came forward, touching my arm and peering into my face with concern.

"I told you he wasn't a nice guy…" Jess folded her arms and shook her head.

"Maybe you're right. But I don't think that's true," I disagreed, even though defending Josh was the last thing I wanted to do right now.

"After what you just saw in there? How can you say that?" Jess gestured wildly at the door behind her.

"That's not the real Josh. It's like he's putting on a mask or something." I shrugged, not sure how to explain it.

"I didn't think you knew him that well…" Jess raised an eyebrow.

"I don't. I don't know how to explain it, but I…I have this feeling…" Jess laughed at me and rolled her eyes.

"More like you're blinded by his muscles…" Her comment irritated me, this was nothing to do with how Josh looked, but I wasn't going to start an argument with her. And she was right, I didn't know Josh that well to be coming up with any kind of conclusions. Plus, I was furious with him for acting like a complete dick back there.

"Come on. We've missed the first fifteen minutes of class already, so why don't we head to the library and study for a little while instead?" Sophie tugged me gently towards the door and I nodded. There was no way I'd be able to pay attention in history anyway. As we left the bathroom and began walking down the corridor towards the library, Ollie came through one of the side entrances. He paused when he saw me, waiting whilst we moved closer towards him.

"Hey Izzy. Have you got a sec?" I'd never spoken to Ollie Boon before. The general consensus was that he was a funny guy, but with one hell of a mean streak. Whenever someone was telling a tale about Josh getting into a fight, Ollie's name was never far from their lips either. Jess and Sophie both looked to me, soundlessly asking if I wanted them to stay.

"I'll meet you guys in the library in a few minutes." They brushed past Ollie, Jess giving him a side-eyed scowl as she passed.

"I er, just wanted to say thank you," Ollie said, whilst nervously rubbing his face.

"Thank you?" I repeated, lacing my voice with distrust.

"Yeah. If Josh had hit that kid, then he would have been expelled. So, thank you for stopping him."

"I didn't do it for Josh. I did it for Tom." I crossed my arms. Preventing Josh from getting kicked out of sixth form hadn't exactly crossed my mind. Ollie nodded and turned to go.

"Don't give up on him," Ollie twisted back towards me. "He hasn't, erm, got the easiest life. At home."

"What do you mean?" I eyed him curiously as he stared back at me, searching my eyes as if he was trying to silently communicate something to me.

"He has a lot on his shoulders. And I know he doesn't make it easy, but stick with him, yeah? He could use another friend." Ollie walked away before I could ask any further questions and I felt my anger towards Josh waning. Just as I'd start to think I should stay out of his way, something would make me change my mind. This was starting to become a habit.

~

"Hey! If it's not our very own Tyson Fury!" I didn't know who Ed was talking about, but given the fact that he was prancing around on the balls of his feet and swinging his fists, I'm guessing he was making a joke about the incident this morning. I rolled my eyes at him as we all gathered in the common room for lunch.

"So, I have great news!" Jack announced, sitting forward. "I have officially passed my driving test!" He started waving his plastic photo card around. Ed high-fived him and Sophie beamed at him, a large grin stretched across her face. I didn't know what, but something had clearly changed between the two of them since last weekend.

"And I have been invited to a house party Saturday night. It's a guy from footie and he's turning eighteen. He lives over in Brittlesford, which usually we would have to pay a fortune on a cab for, but I am graciously offering to be your designated driver. So, you all up for it?" Ed high-fived him again and they both swung their gazes to the three of us.

"Are you sure we are invited too?" I asked. The last thing I wanted to do was gate-crash some random guy's eighteenth birthday.

"Yup. I told Jeremy that I wanted to bring a few friends and he said the more, the merrier." I couldn't remember the last party I'd been to and I could feel the first inkling of excitement tingling.

"Oh, and his dad is some kind of policeman. Although he'll have the house to himself, he has made it very clear no drugs of any kind. Alcohol is fine, but nothing else." We all frowned at him.

"And er, why would you feel the need to tell us that? You know none of us do that shit!" Jess chastised him.

"Oh, no I know. Just in case you wanted to tell your parents or something, might make 'em feel better," he shrugged. Good point, actually. My parents had been pretty slack about me seeing my friends, grateful I was going out again I suppose, but I hadn't really tested that by going anywhere other than Jess's or Sophie's houses.

"Count me in," I smiled as Sophie and Jess nodded their agreement too.

"We'll come over to yours to get ready, Iz, right Soph?" Jess' smile was a tad too bright and she was looking very pointedly at Sophie, who looked ever so slightly confused.

"Okkaaay…"

"Great!" Jess had a glint in her eye that made me nervous.

Chapter 12

Joshua

I stared at Big Mike's phone in my hand, planning out in my head what I was going to say to Mrs Abernathy. I was going to play the 'Mum walked out on us and he's still trying to adjust' card. It happened over a year ago, but it couldn't hurt to remind her, try and drum up some sympathy.

I was about to dial when the phone started ringing and 'Gilleford Secondary' started flashing on the screen. *Shit.* Someone must have grassed me up for the incident this morning. Although nothing much happened, thanks to Izzy, I was on very thin ice with Mr Tapps. He promised me that even though he'd allow me back to sixth form, if I so much as even swore at another student, I'd be out. I was so surprised he'd caved in the first place that I had hastily agreed. My grades were average, maybe even a little less so, and I had no ambition or clear career trajectory. I had a feeling that the number of students wanting to stay on for sixth form were lower than expected, and so that was the real reason why he'd agreed to it.

"Hello?" I answered, making my voice a little lower but trying not to overdo it.

"Mr Bugg?"

"Yes?"

"This is Mr Tapps, Head Teacher of Gilleford Secondary School. I'm afraid we have had a bit of a situation with your son this morning." This was going to be a pain in the arse to deal with.

"I'm sure Joshua didn't…"

"Oh, my apologies, Mr Bugg. I meant your other son, Ryan." What. The. Fuck? "Mr Bugg? Are you still there?"

"Sorry, yes. What happened?"

"I'd prefer to talk about this face to face, if you are able to come by the school?"

"There is no way my, er, boss is going to let me leave after I have only been here a few hours. I have another six hours to go on my shift…" I was scrambling for excuses. I was so not prepared for this conversation.

"I see…" I could hear the disapproval in his voice.

"I'm on my break now though, so why don't we talk it through on the phone and then I will send Josh down to your office afterwards?" *Please, please,* I prayed.

"That is a little unorthodox, but I know how hard you work, Mr Bugg, so yes, let's come to some kind of arrangement."

After a fifteen-minute conversation to which I spent the entire time wishing the ground would swallow me whole, I learned that Ryan had been in a fight. He had attacked another student and had given him a black eye.

"You understand from our previous discussions, Mr Bugg, that Ryan is not exactly a model student. He is rather disruptive and his blatant disrespect for authority has caused us no end of issues. However, this is his first offence of violence. I also understand that Ryan was provoked by the other student, an inappropriate comment of some sort. As such, I have explained to the other student's parents about your, er, situation, and we have agreed that a one-week suspension is appropriate." A fucking whole week at home? By himself? Fuck.

"I do hope you agree that this is rather lenient of me but understand that should something of this magnitude happen again, Ryan will be expelled."

"Yes, Mr Tapps. Thank you very much for your generosity." Urgh. Kissing up to this jackass left an incredibly sour taste on my tongue.

"If you could arrange Josh coming to collect Ryan from my office and escorting him off the premises as soon as possible, please, that would be most appreciated." Is it possible to sense someone's smugness coming through a phone?

"I will call him straight away. Thanks again for your understanding." I hung up before he could change his mind. This was 100% my fault. I could just predict how the conversation with Ryan was going to go; *You said I didn't have any experience fighting, so I got some…*

I started heading to Mr Tapps' office when I saw Ollie rounding the corner.

"Hey mate. I need a really big favour. Like, a huge one." Ollie grinned at me.

"Don't tell me the great Joshua Bugg is actually asking his mate for help?" He smacked his cheeks with the palm of his hands, pulling his face into an over-the-top shocked expression.

"Yeah, yeah, I know. Listen, Ryan has been suspended for a week."

"What the fuck for?" he reeled back in alarm.

"Punched some kid in the face. Gave him a black eye." Ollie gave a long, low whistle.

"Surprised Tappsy didn't expel him."

"Yeah, you and me both. Anyway, Big Mike was at home this morning and er, things didn't exactly go well…" I could see Ollie's eyes cloud over instantly, his whole body tensing as it always did whenever I mentioned Big Mike. "…I don't want to send Ryan home in case Big Mike's still there. You know how unpredictable he can be, but Ryan has to leave school property straight away. Can I take him to yours for the day instead?" I didn't have a clue what I was going to do for the rest of the week, but that was a problem for tomorrow.

"Of course, mate. No problemo. Mum's working at the shop most of the day, so won't even be in. I'll shoot her a text now to let her know though. We keep a spare key in the little frog statue on the doorstep. Lift it up, it has a false bottom."

"You're a life-saver, mate, thanks."

"What you going to do about the rest of the week though?"

"I honestly don't know."

"OK, I have a great idea." Ollie looked too pleased with himself for me to like wherever this was going. "Mum's working most of the week and she loves you and your brothers anyway, so it won't be an issue. Send him over to mine every morning."

"OK. And what's the catch?" Ollie clutched his chest, feigning some kind of heart attack.

"I am appalled, dear friend, that you would think I would want something in return."

"Yeah, yeah, get on with it," I laughed at him.

"OK so you know Mum's new fella, Detective Pole-shoved-up-his-arse-so-high-I-can-see-it-when-he-speaks?" I couldn't help but chuckle. Tracy had been seeing a local policeman the past few months and Ollie was none too impressed with him. I nodded for him to continue.

"Well, turns out it's getting pretty serious. Mum says I need to make more of an effort." He rolled his eyes. "He has a kid of his own and he's got some kind of house party Saturday night. I promised Mum I would go and now, my man, you are going to accompany me." I groaned. I hated parties. Just a load of people I didn't talk to getting drunk, or high, or both, and making fools of themselves.

"Why would you promise her that?" Ollie hated parties as much as I did. Especially because the last one we went to, we got chucked out of for, yes you guessed it, starting a fight. Although in my defence, Ollie was the one caught with his tongue down the throat of some guy's girlfriend.

"As much as I don't like the guy, this is the first time I've seen her happy in a long time." Ollie looked serious for a moment, staring at something far off behind me. "Plus, it's going to be filled with drunk girls, my favourite," he quickly switched back to his usual light-hearted self. I sighed.

"Fine. I don't have a choice anyway, do I?"

"Nope."

"Thought as much. Right, I better get going before Tappsy gets the arse-ache with me for taking my time." I held my hand out to Ollie before I left and he grasped it tight, whilst I slapped him on the back. "Thanks though, mate. Seriously. I didn't like the idea of Ryan at home all on his own all week."

"Don't mention it." God, I was lucky to have him in my life right now.

~

"But why do I have to stay at Ollie's all week? Why can't I stay at home and watch films all day or something?" Ryan was getting on my last nerve. He had indeed spun me a bullshit line about trying to get some fighting experience, and when some kid had shouted an obscenity at him about our mum, he had fully taken advantage of the situation. I already felt guilty as hell without him rubbing my nose in it.

"Because I do not want you at home all day by yourself all week. We have no idea what shifts Big

Mike's working or when he'll be home, and I'll be worried sick the whole time."

"But you leave us at home on our own when you're working." I ground my teeth.

"And you know I hate doing that. But I have no other choice. This, I have a choice with. Actually, if you want, you can start going to Ollie's every day after school too until I get back from work?" I was bluffing and we both knew it. There was no way I'd put that kind of burden on Ollie or Tracy; they didn't have a pot to piss in either. But that didn't stop Ryan from glaring at me as we neared Ollie's house. Not only did I escort him out of school, but I was going to walk him all the way to Ollie's myself. With how temperamental he was being lately, there was no way I trusted him to go there alone.

"Look. You can take a bunch of DVDs over to Ollie's and watch them there. And you can catch up on your homework while you're at it." He rolled his eyes at me and we both knew there was no chance of him doing that.

"If you don't go over to Ollie's, then I am going to have to stay home with you all week too. Then Tappsy is going to expel me for skipping so many classes and then…"

"OK, OK, OK. I'll go over to bloody Ollie's house." He balled his hands into fists as he trudged along next to me. We reached Ollie's and I retrieved the key from the stupid, little frog statue and let us in. His house was two streets over from ours and almost a mirror image. Same layout, same number of rooms. Only difference was, Tracy actually gave a shit about her son and the conditions he lived in. She kept it clean and tidy with a few homey touches, and although to most people it still looked like a shithole, to me, it looked heavenly. I was actually a little jealous that Ryan would be spending his time here; a much better alternative to school or home. He dumped his bag on the floor in the living room and slouched into the sofa, switching on the TV. I grabbed the remote from him, switching the TV off again and taking a seat next to him.

"Make sure you clean up after yourself, don't leave a mess for Tracy to clean up when she gets back. Try not to eat any of their food, you've got your own," I gestured to the bag of food we'd bought from *Martins* on the way past. I also wanted to stop by and personally thank Tracy for helping us out before I dropped Ryan off. Ryan didn't respond.

"Hey." I shifted closer to him, nudging his leg with my thigh. He reluctantly looked over to me.

"You know I love you, right?" He looked momentarily stunned by my admission. With the exception of this morning's little display, I did not show my emotions much (unless it was rage or anger, of course). But I felt like both Georgie and Ryan were slowly slipping away from me. I was doing everything I knew how to, yet they were both malnourished, withdrawn or disruptive, and failing in school. I was failing as a parent miserably.

"I just want to keep you safe. It's my job to keep you safe and I promise, soon we'll be looking back on this part of our life and laughing. We'll have it so good that this will be a distant memory." I smiled at him as I ruffled his hair. Surprisingly, he shuffled closer to me and wrapped his arms around my waist, snuggling into me. I squeezed him.

"I better get back so I make it in time for my other classes. But text me if you need anything at all, OK? And you'll meet Georgie like normal and walk him home after school still, yeah?" He nodded at me and I stood to leave.

"I'll be home around half nine as usual. See you soon." As I walked out the room, Ryan called out to me.

"I love you too, brother."

Chapter 13

Isabel

"Hi Sammy!" I heard Jess call as she and Sophie breezed through the front door. I rolled my eyes at the name my mum insisted my friends call her; Samantha was her actual name.

"Hi Jess, Sophie. You girls looking forward to tonight?" Mum smiled as she embraced them. It was a little awkward as they were each carrying bags of clothes to change into and Jess also had a humongous, rectangular box squeezed under her arm. Mum managed to more or less wrap her arms around them both.

"I can't wait. I haven't had an excuse like this to get dressed up for in ages!" Jess squealed.

"Hey!" I called down the stairs to them both. I had not long gotten out of the shower and had slung on some tracksuit bottoms and a vest for the time being.

"I hope you're not planning on wearing *that* tonight?" Sophie laughed up at me.

"Well it's this or my Buttercups uniform," I joked.

"Actually, you have no say in what you're wearing tonight. Sophie and I are going to decide," Jess grinned whilst my mum tried to smother a giggle. I narrowed my eyes at them, starting to guess at why they had insisted on getting ready over mine. Jess never approved of my outfits, regardless of the occasion. My clothes were either too boring or not flattering enough. They both came charging up the stairs, dragging all their bags with them. They bundled into my room, slinging their stuff on my bed.

"What's with the box?" I gestured to the package in Jess' hands. Sophie and Jess looked at each other, smirking.

"We bought you something for tonight," Sophie smiled. Oh shit, I definitely wasn't going to like this.

"Guys, you know I love you, but I can't wear the same kinds of things as you. What are dresses for you two are tops for me. And I cannot pull off the same things that you skinny bitches can," I ribbed playfully. Jess rolled her eyes and thrust the box at me.

"Just open it. Then you can bitch about whether you like them or not." I took a deep breath, lifting the lid a little and peeking inside, praying that it wasn't some kind of body-con dress that Jess seemed to be favouring lately. I lifted the lid off completely, admiring the pair of boots that sat inside.

"They're in your favourite colour, they're flat, and

your mum gave us your size, so we know they'll fit," Sophie grinned, bouncing a little on the edge of my bed. Typical of my mum to be in on something like this too. They were gorgeous though. Black suede with a slight point at the toes and lace-up ribbon criss-crossing at the back of them. I pulled one out and realised they were over the knee, thigh-high boots. They were very stylish, but certainly not something I would ever have picked for myself.

"Do you like them?" Jess asked, seeming a little nervous. She took fashion very seriously and prided herself on picking things out that people usually wouldn't go for, but still looked fabulous. I hoped she was right this time too.

"They are beautiful. Although I've never worn anything like them before," I laughed.

"They'll look gorgeous on your long legs." Jess held one of them up against my leg.

"They must have cost a fortune. You didn't have to do this, guys." I would *not* cry over a pair of boots, but boy did I appreciate these two girls. They both bounced over to me and squeezed me in a group hug.

"Now, what are you going to wear with them?" Jess strolled over to my wardrobe and started rifling through the clothes inside. "I'm looking for something sexy, but something you'll be comfortable wearing…"

"Good luck with that," I huffed. I did not own a single item of sexy clothing.

"Ah ha! Bingo!" Jess pulled out a plain black, long-sleeved dress.

"I'm pretty sure I wore that to my great nan's funeral

last year…" I scoffed.

"Trust me. With those boots and the make-up and hair I'm about to do for you, you will look like you're going anywhere *but* a funeral." That gleam in her eyes was back again.

Almost two hours later, we were finally ready to leave.

"Oh, my! Charlie, get in here!" Mum shouted to my dad. "Doesn't she look gorgeous?" My dad choked on the cup of coffee he had been sipping as he looked at my outfit.

"Why is it that you are pretty much covered up, but I still want to ask you to go upstairs and change?" he laughed.

"You will do no such thing!" Mum smacked him on the shoulder. "You look amazing honey." She kissed me on the cheek and I was horrified to see her eyes watering.

"Mum! Don't embarrass me!"

"Sorry, love. I'm just so happy you became friends with these two girls." She came over and enveloped us all into a group hug. "And Jess, you are so talented! That's a great outfit for my Izzy. Classy but still sexy."

"Urgh, Mum. You can't say sexy. It's weird." She rolled her eyes at me.

"You really do look lovely," Dad said, kissing me on the cheek too.

"And this Jack, he's a good driver, yes?" Mum asked for the twentieth time since I told her I was getting a lift.

"The instructor wouldn't have passed him otherwise, Mum."

"I know how boys can be once they get behind a wheel, Isabel. They suddenly think they're Dominic Toretto…"

"Who?" Sophie and Jess chorused. I sniggered.

"Never mind. Look, here's forty quid for a cab. I am trusting you, Isabel, to say something and get out the car if you feel unsafe. So if you don't want a lift home, you take a cab." She gave me a stern look as she handed me the cash.

"I'll be fine, Mum. I promise."

"And you can call me anytime if you need something. And make sure you text me when you are on your way home, so I don't worry, please." I rolled my eyes as I gave her a squeeze goodbye.

"Yes, Mum." We heard a horn sound outside and I peered out the front door, happy to see Jack pulled up out front in his silver Renault Clio. It was an old model that had definitely seen better days, but it was a car nonetheless.

"Be safe…" Mum called after me as we hurried to the car. Jack gave her a little wave as we climbed in.

"You all look seriously hot!" Ed twisted round in his seat in the front, waggling his eyebrows at us as we laughed. I'd seen the way they had both watched us all as we approached the car. They were definitely looks of admiration and for once, I was pretty sure I was on the receiving end too. My dress had a high neckline and was made from a stretchy fabric, so that it hugged every curve. Jess had pulled the dress up a little, so that the clingy fabric was somewhat creased around my waist. This pulled the previously respectable hemline up about two inches. However, with the thigh-high boots, Dad was right in that I had hardly any skin on show. Maybe a couple inches or so of leg and that was about it. But I felt confident and with the heavy makeup and loosely curled hair that Jess had carefully crafted, I didn't even recognize myself.

After about twenty-five minutes of Jack's overly cautious driving (Mum needn't have worried about him emulating the Fast and Furious), we pulled up outside a large, detached house a couple of villages over from mine. It was surrounded by farmland and had a long, winding driveway that was already bumper to bumper with parked cars. We managed to squeeze on the end and could still hear music thumping from this far back.

It was the opposite to our new build home and looked old enough to perhaps be Edwardian. There were large bay windows on the ground floor and the first-floor windows had intricate brickwork above them, highlighting the pointed arch of each one. As we neared the house, it looked like there might be a second floor too. There were some further windows at the side of the building that looked like some kind of loft extension.

Jack rang the doorbell but there was no answer. With the music so loud, I wasn't surprised that no one could hear us. Jack tried the handle and the door swung inwards, allowing us entry. We stepped over the threshold into a long entryway, tiled in terracotta and cream coloured diamond-shaped tiles. You could tell that the place had been renovated recently. It still had some period features, such as the tiled flooring, but with a modern twist. The walls were a crisp white and a large staircase off to the side was also painted white with a light grey carpet. A cluster of pendant lights encased in a geometric wire frame dangled from the ceiling, their light dimmed low. It was very atmospheric.

"Hey, Jack! You came!" A very tall guy rounded the corner and pulled Jack into a typical guy, back-slapping greeting.

"Guys, this is Jeremy. Jeremy, these are my friends I was telling you about," Jack introduced us.

"Nice to meet you all. There's a ton of booze in the kitchen, so please help yourself. There's also some pizza and various other snacks 'round the place…" We all followed Jeremy as he began guiding us through the house. The downstairs was open-plan with a huge kitchen-diner-living room as the main focal point. There was an iPod and speaker system blaring the music and the diner-living room part had been turned into a dance floor, the furniture pushed haphazardly to the edges. There were about fifty people crammed in, jumping and twisting to the music. The large, white kitchen had an island in the middle and lots of people perched atop bar stools, choosing to stay close to the booze.

"The garage is out of bounds. Feel free to venture up to the bedrooms, but clean up whatever mess you make." Did he just wink at me? "If you need some fresh air, the backdoor to the garden is open, but we have horses in the next field over so try not to make any loud noises or they'll spook." He was shouting now, trying to ensure we could hear him as he busied himself pouring drinks in the kitchen. "And if I catch anyone doing drugs, you'll be chucked out. My old man's the

Superintendent for Suffolk and he will majorly kick my arse if he so much as gets a suspicion that any of that is going on tonight. What do you drink?" Jeremy looked pointedly at me. And yes, it was definitely me, because I looked behind me to see if anyone else was there and there wasn't.

"Er, Malibu and Coke?" He laughed at me whilst nodding his head to the music, grabbing a bottle of coke from the fridge. The cupboard next to it was stocked with every kind of liquor imaginable and Jeremy poured me a *very* generous shot of white rum. He finished it off with some ice and a straw and handed it to me.

"What's your name?" He leaned on the kitchen island, angling his body towards me, his gaze trailing me up and down. I could see Jack and Ed start to wander off in my periphery, whilst Jess and Sophie nudged each other and tried not to smirk at me.

"Izzy," I smiled. Not only was this guy at least four inches taller than me, but he was extremely good-looking in a typical Prince Charming kind of way. He had muddy blonde hair that was longer on top, combed upwards to form an untidy quiff. It was the type of hairstyle that looked as if he'd just rolled out of bed, but judging by the rest of his impeccably presented exterior, he had probably spent a considerable amount of time getting it just right. He was in light blue, tight jeans and a dark blue *Ralph Lauren* polo top that made his blue eyes sparkle. There was no denying that Jeremy was a very attractive man.

"Come on Izzy! I love this song!" Jess grabbed my

elbow and dragged me towards the dance area. I wiggled my fingers goodbye at Jeremy and he lifted his drink in farewell.

"Dear Lord, that boy is insanely hot!" Jess shouted in my ear as I laughed at her.

"Someone definitely took a shine to you," Sophie nudged me in the ribs with her elbow. Tinie Tempah's *Drinking from the Bottle* was blasting through the room and Jess tugged us right into the centre. They both started rhythmically moving, swaying their hips and gyrating to the bass. I took a big gulp of my drink and tried to loosen up, pushing my self-consciousness away. I was not particularly coordinated and didn't have a lot of experience dancing in such close proximity to complete strangers. After a couple more gulps, I started to relax and could feel the beat pulsating through me. A few songs in, Jeremy pushed through the throng of people to stand next to me. To my surprise, he took my now-empty glass from my hand, replaced it with a new one, and tilted himself towards me, starting to dance. Was he trying to dance? With *me*? Jess and Sophie both nodded encouragingly at me, grinning like idiots. I felt incredibly insecure and unsure, but I carried on dancing, trying to enjoy the fact that an incredibly handsome guy was actually paying me some attention.

Chapter 14

Joshua

"Holy shit, mate. This place is ridiculous!" Ollie and I stopped dead in our tracks, staring at the colossal house in front of us.

"No fucking way is this Detective Dickwad's house!" He looked at me open-mouthed and I shrugged.

"This is definitely the address, so must be."

"Shit. Now I feel like a complete prick," Ollie sighed.

"Why?"

"I've been giving him such a hard time about spending so much time over our house every weekend. I mean, he's been glued to my mum's hip the past few weeks…"

"You sure it's her hip he's glued to?" I sniggered, interrupting him.

"Fuck off. Anyway, last week I accused him of

sponging off of us. Eating our food, watching our TV...and all this time, he lived in this place! He didn't say anything to me once. He must be pretty high up in the police. And no way Mum would feel comfortable coming over to a place like this. She'd feel well too self-conscious and out of place. She'd definitely do a runner. And he must know that, which is why he's been hanging around our shithole instead of living it up in this palace!" Ollie looked genuinely bereaved at this development. "Why couldn't he live in a council house like every other fucker that's ever shown any interest in Mum?"

"Because they were all fucking morons and maybe Detective Pussy-Whipped is better than her usual type?"

"Do NOT start fucking calling him that. That's my mother you're talking about!" Ollie slammed into my shoulder, almost knocking me over as I burst into hysterics. He stomped away from me, heading straight for the front door. I had to jog a little to catch-up with him. He pushed his way through without knocking and the chavvy dance music was infinitely louder now we were inside.

"Do you even know what this guy looks like?" I asked. "You've not met him before, right?"

"Mum showed me a picture. He's some hotshot captain of a local football team or summin.'" Ollie took the lead, going through the nearest doorway. In search of some alcohol, no doubt. Holy shit, my house could fit into the downstairs of this place about three times over. High ceilings, sparsely furnished and pristine, it looked like a fucking show home. Not exactly homely but stunning nonetheless. Ollie began rifling through the fridge, smiling when he found two beers. He then started searching through the cupboards, grabbing two shot glasses and a bottle of vodka. He poured the shots, passing me one along with the beer. I raised my eyebrows at him.

"We need more than just beer to get through tonight, my friend," Ollie announced as he downed his shot. I followed suit, feeling the comforting burn as the liquid slipped down my throat.

"We do not look like we belong here," I pointed out, referring to the fact that almost everyone else was in designer labels. I was in my black jeans, white t-shirt and black trainers. Again. Nothing special.

"That's because we *don't* belong here, mate. But it's free booze, free pizza and it'll make Mum happy that I came."

"You should make sure you say hello to the birthday boy, then. So he corroborates that you actually turned up," I advised. He turned to look out over the crowd of people dancing in the centre of the room, scanning faces.

"I er, think I found him." He nodded in a vague direction.

"Where? Which one is he?" I had already built up a very clear picture of a preppy, pretty-boy footballer and was curious to see if reality measured up.

"The tall guy in the middle. The one your girl is grinding up against." Ollie took a sip of his beer, avoiding my eyes. I frowned in confusion, scrutinizing the mob of people. There was a slight shift of bodies and there she was; Isabel Johnson.

"She's not my girl," I responded flatly. But right now, I was kind of wishing she was. Fuck, she looked good. Really fucking good. She was in a tight black dress that was slowly riding up her thighs as she danced. And I hadn't quite seen a pair of boots before like the ones she was wearing. They rose all the way above the knee, highlighting the bare skin between them and the hem of her dress. Her long hair was delicately curled and trailing down her back. At that moment, she rang her fingers through her hair, pulling it back off her face. Her eyes were dark and smoky. Mesmerising. I couldn't seem to pull my gaze from her.

Some kind of 50 Cent song was playing and she was dancing with a tall, blonde guy. It wasn't exactly grinding, they were facing each other for Christ's sake, but the mutual interest between the two of them was clear. An absurd bolt of jealousy ran through me. I was blown away by how desperately I wanted to kick this guy's arse and swap places with him.

~

After exploring the place for a while, Ollie and I drifted back to the kitchen, propping ourselves up on the bar stools around the kitchen island (which was bigger than my bed, for fuck sake). I shot a text off to Ryan, asking if everything was OK. He had promised to text me before they went to sleep to let me know everything was alright, and also to let me know if Big Mike got home before I did. It was getting close to 10.30

p.m. and I still hadn't heard from him. It was making me nervous. I was trying not to overreact, but my imagination started running wild. Willing myself to stay calm, I set an alarm on my phone for 11 p.m. and if I hadn't heard from him by then, I promised myself I'd leave and go home.

Ollie mumbled something to me around a mouthful of food. I couldn't hear him over the music, but judging by the satisfied expression on his face, he was thinking the same as me; the pizza was awesome. There were boxes strewn all over the counter and although it was starting to go a little cold now, Ollie and I knew how to make the most of a free meal. We were halfway through demolishing our third pizza when the birthday boy himself strutted over. There was no sign of Izzy as he helped himself to more beer.

"Hey Jeremy," Ollie shouted over the music, lifting his chin. The guy turned and looked a little baffled. "I'm Ollie. Boon. Your dad's dating my mum…"

"Nice to meet you, mate!" He shook Ollie's hand and threw a cursory glance in my direction before turning back to him. "I've barely seen him the past month. Reckon he must like your mum a lot." Ollie grunted in response as a group of people approached Jeremy, snatching away his attention. I rolled my eyes at Ollie and he shrugged.

"We can probably leave now. I've said hello, drank a loada beer and stuffed my face. No reason to listen to this shit any longer," Ollie pointed to the ceiling, referring to the bassy music. I nodded, keen to get home and check on my brothers.

"Josh! What are you doing here?" Jess frowned at me. "Never mind. Doesn't matter. Have you seen Izzy?"

"No. Why?" She seemed a little frantic. Sophie approached from a different direction, looking equally flustered.

"I can't find her!" She shouted to Jess. They both looked around, their agitation clear.

"What's wrong?" I asked again.

"Ellie is here," Jess said, not looking at me and still scanning the room.

"Who the fuck is Ellie?" Did they expect me to know what they were talking about?

"She used to go to our school. Her and her mates bullied Izzy for about two years, pretty nasty stuff," Sophie filled me in.

"We need to find Izzy and give her a heads up before she has a meltdown." Jess turned to leave, grabbing Sophie's hand and pulling her in a different direction.

"I'm going to go help them look." Ollie jumped down to follow them and I almost fell off my chair in surprise. I raised my eyebrows at him.

"She is fucking hot!" He mouthed to me whilst doing some kind of weird thrusting behind Jess' back. I laughed, rolling my eyes. Trust Ollie to make the most out of any opportunity. I looked around and saw the backdoor propped open. If I had been dancing all night, I'd probably want some fresh air. I stood up and pushed my way through the crowd. As I stepped outside, the cool night air was pleasantly refreshing from the sweaty humidity inside. There were some outdoor lights illuminating the immediate area, which was good as it was pitch black outside now. It seemed like there were as many people out here as there were inside. There was a large decking area in front of me with an L-shaped sofa and armchairs. People were crammed all over them, sprawled out across each other and perching on the arms or the backrests. I was about to turn around and go back inside when I heard a group of girls laughing. There was something about the way they laughed that made me head closer to them instead.

They were on the periphery of the crowds outside and as I pushed closer, I could see a group of four or five girls huddled together. They were all facing in one direction and when I followed their eye line, I could see Izzy stood on her own a few feet in front of them. Her head was bowed, shoulders rounded and her fingers were twisting around each other nervously.

"There is no way you came here with Jack Conners. He's way too cool to be hanging around with a nobody like you." A short blonde at the front of the group sneered at her, flicking her hair over her shoulder as her friends snickered. Izzy remained silent.

"You know, it doesn't matter how slutty you dress or how much makeup you cake on, no one wants you. Jonny didn't want you, he still doesn't want you, and no one else even bothers to look at you." The girl, presumably Ellie, took a step closer. Izzy was still planted in position, her eyes averted. This wasn't the feisty girl that had pushed me off Tom earlier on in the week. Where was *she*?

"And I mean, what the fuck are you wearing anyway? You think that dressing up as a whore in those terrible boots will make guys look at you? Oh honey, you are naive." Her friends were laughing as if she had said the funniest thing in the world, but my anger was slowly starting to brew. I had no idea who this girl was, but she wasn't anything special. Izzy was ten times more attractive than she was, and why she thought she could get away with talking to her like that was beyond me. It felt like my blood was boiling and all I wanted to do was prove to Izzy how wrong Ellie was. Without thinking through my next move, my feet started moving towards Izzy.

Chapter 15

Isabel

"Hey babe, I've been looking for you." My head snapped up as I watched Josh approach. How long had he been standing there? How much had he heard? And why the hell was he calling me *babe*? He stopped right in front of me with his back turned to Ellie. I searched his eyes, trying to figure out what the hell he was doing. We hadn't spoken since the incident with Tom and I was still a little pissed at him. But right now, he was the lifeline I needed to escape Ellie's torment. I prayed that he'd help me.

"Have I told you how beautiful you look tonight?" I heard Ellie huff out a laugh behind him and I glanced over at her. Josh reached out, cupping my face and tilting my chin up a little to look at him instead. I felt my breathing hitch, confused by the look of desire dancing on his face. He smiled at me and it reached all the way to his eyes. He lowered his face slowly, maintaining eye contact the entire time. It was as if he was giving me a chance to back away, but I was rooted to the spot. My heart pounded and I found myself desperately hoping this was going the way I thought it was. His lips gingerly touched mine. He pulled back again, waiting to see how I'd react. I continued to seek some sort of explanation in his eyes, wanting to understand. But the overwhelming urge to feel his lips again won out. I leaned forward, feeling a searing heat spread through me as I kissed him. He applied more pressure, his fingers reaching up and knotting my hair until he gripped the back of my head. I lifted my hand, stroking the stubble along his jaw as I pulled him closer. He made a kind of guttural noise deep in his throat, which vibrated through me as he parted my lips with his. I could feel his tongue slip into my mouth, moving gently, cautiously. There was this fire burning in my chest and though I didn't quite understand why this was happening, it wasn't enough. I wanted more.

I lifted my other hand, pushing my fingers up through the back of his hair. Our bodies were touching pretty much the whole length, my chest pressed into his and my thighs pushing into his legs. I wasn't sure, but I thought I could feel something of his pressing into me too.

He pulled back, coming up for air. I looked around and Ellie and her friends had disappeared, nowhere to be seen. Josh frowned a little, staring intently at me as if I had the answer to something. His phone started ringing with a loud piercing squeal and he fingered it out of his pocket, cursing as the screen lit up. He looked up from the screen, to me, and back again.

"We're even now. You saved Tom, I saved you..." he slowly walked backwards away from me before turning, hurrying back into the house. I stared after him, feeling like I was drowning and couldn't suck enough oxygen into my lungs no matter how hard I tried. I had never felt anything quite like that. Sure, I'd been kissed before, but not for a long time. No boy had so much as even glanced at me since Ellie decided I wasn't worthy, but Josh had gone against all the rules. He'd turned his back to her and kissed me so passionately, my heart was still thumping. It felt like it might break right through my ribs and escape my chest altogether.

But it didn't mean anything to him. He was a bloody good actor, I'd give him that. I was sure that had been real passion, real *feelings* I'd seen reflected in his eyes, but I was wrong. It was his way of apologising for what he'd done to Tom. His way of making it up to me. *We're even now. You saved Tom, I saved you...*

His words rang in my ears, the disappointment spearing my chest making me feel a little nauseous. Go*dam*mit, I hated Joshua Bugg right now. I clenched my fists, my fingers digging into my palms so hard that I was surprised my nails didn't draw blood. How *dare* he? He couldn't kiss me like that and then walk away. He couldn't toy with my emotions like that. One minute we were close to being friends, then he'd do something to infuriate me, and then he went and did this! He kissed me! I mean, I'd cleaned up his sick for Christ's sake and he couldn't even *respect* me enough to be real with me? Nope, I wasn't accepting that.

I charged towards the door to the house, relieved that my legs were working. I'd been frozen to the spot for so long I was afraid I'd somehow become paralysed. Pushing through the throng of people, my eyes slid left and right, right and left, searching for Josh. My annoyance intensified with every second I couldn't locate him. At some point my brain registered that Sophie and Jack were in the corner kissing, but I ignored them, too focused on finding Josh and letting him have a piece of my mind. I stormed through the kitchen and living room, breaking through into the hallway and growling in frustration when I couldn't find him. I was about to give up when I glimpsed something out front. The front door was ajar and I could see Ollie jogging away from the house. I darted through the door, smiling in victory when I could see Josh just ahead of him. I broke into a run, chasing him down.

"The bus doesn't come for another thirty minutes, mate," Ollie called to Josh, out of breath as he tried to keep up with him. Josh was almost sprinting and I was struggling to gain on them, just catching the sounds of their conversation.

"Then I'll run all the damn way home. I need to make sure they are OK!" Josh shouted over his shoulder, not slowing down.

"Josh! Wait! WAIT!" I hollered as loud as I could, panting like a dog. Ollie slowed, staring at me in confusion. I bent over, gripping my knees as I tried to gasp lungfuls of air. I was so bloody unfit. I was relieved to see Josh pause, turning to jog over to me. Relieved that is, until the anger took over, the memories of what happened earlier lighting a fire in me. He hesitated a metre or so in front of me, unwilling to come closer.

"You. Don't. Get. To. Leave. After. That." I was still panting, struggling to get my words out.

"I don't have time for this, Izzy. I'm sorry, OK? I'm sorry I kissed you and took off, but I *have* to go..." he half turned away from me again, edging down the driveway.

"Did it mean anything to you? Or was it all for show?" I glared at him, grateful that my breathing had finally evened out. I felt my heart jump as I realised I sounded as if I cared if it meant something to him or not. A mixture of embarrassment and shock rippled through me. He let out a frustrated growl.

"I don't have *time* for this!" He repeated, running his fingers through his hair. "It doesn't matter when I can't fucking think straight!" His chest was heaving and sweat was dripping down his brow. He had a wild look in his eyes. My anger started to fade when I realised it was fear.

"What's wrong, Josh?" I asked in a softer tone. He looked so panicked and fearful. Something else was bothering him.

"I just...I need to go home...I need to make sure Ryan and Georgie are OK..." with that, he turned away from me completely, moving further away.

"I told you, the bus doesn't come until half past. No point rushing to the bus stop, mate. And you can't possibly run all the way home..." Ollie sounded apologetic but Josh howled. That's the only way I can describe it. He literally tipped his head to the sky and *howled.* It sounded like he was in physical pain and I could see the anxiety shuddering through him as he stopped, stamping his foot with his back to us. It would have been comical if he hadn't looked so serious.

"Hello? Yeah, I er, need a cab as soon as possible please…" I pressed my phone into my ear, watching as Josh whirled round to face me. I reeled off the address as Josh stared at me, hanging up only after the taxi company promised that the driver would be here in five minutes. I started searching through the little black clutch bag that was slung over my shoulder, pulling the money out my mum had given to me earlier.

"The driver'll be here in five," I said, thrusting the money towards him. Josh looked torn. He didn't move to take the money, but I could see an internal battle raging through him.

"Take the money and go check on your brothers, Josh." I shoved the money in his hands, having to pry his fingers open in order for him to hold it. He looked over at Ollie but he only shrugged at him in response.

"Why…? I'm not… I'm a shitty human being…Why do you keep coming to my rescue?" He looked flustered and was almost vibrating on the spot. He pulled out his phone, grinding his teeth after he looked at the screen.

"Why haven't you text me back?" He mumbled to himself before I could respond, shoving his phone in his back pocket. I saw headlights pause at the end of the driveway, the car not able to actually turn down it due to all the other cars parked up.

"That's our ride, come on…" Ollie started moving towards the car but stopped when Josh didn't move. He was still standing there, watching me. Ollie looked at me over Josh's shoulder and I gave him a slight nod. He jumped forward, grabbing the sleeve of Josh's shirt and tugged him towards the cab. Reluctantly, Josh turned away. As soon as our eye contact broke, he started to pick up pace until he was back to a flat out run. I watched as he and Ollie dove into the back seat, door slamming behind them, the sound echoing into the night.

"Because I think you might be worth rescuing…" I whispered to thin air.

Chapter 16

Joshua

Why were we going so fucking *slow*? I swear the cab driver was doing this on purpose, not breaking the speed limit even a little.

"What was that back there? We saw you and Izzy kissing..."

"Not now, Ollie. Not fucking now. I can't concentrate. I need to get to my brothers." I rocked forward, willing the car to go faster. I had a terrible feeling in the pit of my stomach, fear clawing at my throat and making it hard to breathe.

"I'm sure everything's fine, mate..." I silenced Ollie with a thunderous look, my jaw starting to hurt from grinding my teeth so hard. He knew what Big Mike was capable of. There was a very good chance that everything was *not* fine. I pushed all thoughts of Izzy far from my mind, focusing only on getting to Ryan and Georgie.

"Can't you go any faster?" I snapped, finally losing my patience with the driver. He rolled his eyes at me in the rear-view mirror and it took all my self-control not to scream at him. Especially when I was sure he lifted his foot from the accelerator. I watched the houses and streets crawl past, praying that they would soon become familiar. After what seemed like hours, I finally began recognizing our surroundings. My hand gripped the door handle, knuckles turning white, ready to leap out of the car as soon as it pulled up outside my house.

"That'll be..." I threw the money at the driver without waiting to hear how much it was. I lunged from the car, scrambling to get my footing and racing to the door. I heard another door slam behind me and quick footsteps following.

"Ollie, I..."

"Don't even bother, Josh. I'm coming with you." As Ollie ran beside me, I could see the determination in his eyes and that there was no point arguing with him. I fumbled my keys in the door, my hands shaking as the adrenaline coursed through me. I pushed inside, taking the stairs two at a time. I tried to throw our bedroom door open but it wouldn't budge.

"Ryan! Georgie! It's Josh. Let me in!" I hammered the door, pounding with my fists. Why weren't they answering? I raised my foot to kick the door in when I heard the click of a deadbolt retracting. And another one. And another one.

"Hey," Georgie yawned, rubbing the sleep from his

eyes. I collapsed to my knees in front of him, gripping his shoulders and looking him over in detail. No cuts, no bruises. No blood.

"Are you OK? I've been worried sick. I haven't heard from you or Ryan all evening." I searched his eyes, imploring him to be OK.

"Ryan's got some kind of stomach bug." Georgie swung the door open and stepped back, letting Ollie and I enter the dark room. It was then that I noticed the faint tangy smell of vomit. I could make out Ryan curled up into a ball with his back to me, sleeping in his bottom bunk. His face looked a little sweaty and a large plastic bowl was next to him on the floor.

"He told me not to tell you, didn't want you rushing back. We wanted you to have some fun for a change," Georgie whispered. He began clambering up the ladder to his bed, tiredness making the ascent slow and clumsy. I was still panting and my legs shaking, unspent energy and concern pulsing through me. Ollie clapped me on the shoulder, sighing in relief.

"See? Told you they were fine," he smiled triumphantly before collapsing on my bed.

"Where's Big Mike?" I asked Georgie as he pulled the covers up to his chin.

"He...went back out." He hesitated and I could feel suspicion creeping up on me. But then he yawned and stretched, making me feel bad for keeping him awake. Georgie was a terrible liar anyway so I'm sure I'd be able to tell if something else was going on.

"Has he thrown up much?" I nodded towards Ryan.

"Just a couple times," Georgie yawned again, turning

over.

"Night bro," I murmured whilst pulling my t-shirt over my head. Ollie had already stripped and wiggled under my quilt, grinning at me. I rolled my eyes, nudging Ryan over in his bed a little. He muttered something in protest, but I stroked his hair, trying to soothe him.

"It's just me, Ry. Just Josh. Go back to sleep ..." He scooched over some more, letting me in next to him. I hadn't slept next to either of my brothers for a long time. Sometimes they climbed into bed with each other on a really bad day when they needed comfort, but very rarely did I join them. After the panic and fear that had been threatening to consume me for the past hour or so, I was only too happy to lay next to Ryan and listen to his steady breathing. Besides, I sure as hell wasn't climbing into bed next to Ollie. Especially as I could hear him snoring from across the room already.

My phone went off, indicating I had a text. I carefully rolled over, using my hand to rifle around in the dark. I managed to locate my jeans pocket, tugging the phone out and gently laying back down so as not to wake Ryan again. I flicked my phone to silent and dimmed the screen before looking at the message. It was from Izzy.

Everything OK? Georgie and Ryan OK?

Yeah, all good.

Sure?

Turns out I was overreacting for nothing. Ryan's got some kind of stomach bug, that's all.

Glad they are OK. Hope Ryan feels better soon.

Thanks. And thank you for the cab money too. I'd have

gone crazy waiting for the bus.

No worries. Just glad everyone's OK.

I'll pay you back, promise. I was going to struggle with that one as I didn't even know how much she'd given me. What kind of arsehole just chucks someone else's money away without even bothering to check the amount? Me, that's who. *Don't be ridiculous, Josh. My mum gave me the money to use for a cab anyway.*

Shit, how did you get home then? I'm so sorry. I didn't realise you needed the money to get back.

Relax. I didn't. Mum gave it to me in case Jack turned out to be a Dominic Toretto fan. But he most definitely was NOT. So I got a lift back with him, no big deal. I felt a twinge of jealousy at the idea of her going home with someone else. Was something going on between her and Jack?

Ryan loves those films. Fast and Furious is his favourite.

That's the 4th one right? Where Brian tries to prove himself to Dom? That's my fave too :) We spent the next hour or so texting, talking about nothing really. Films mainly. Turns out Izzy is a movie buff too. I could feel my eyes starting to get sore, but I didn't want to go to sleep. She was so easy to talk to. *I better go to sleep now. I can barely keep my eyes open.* I sighed in disappointment as she echoed my own thoughts. *Yeah me too.*

Before I do, I should really say thank you to you too.

Thank you? For what?

Saving me from Ellie. I know that kiss didn't mean anything to you but you saved me. And it was amazing. So thank you.

Ah yes, that kiss. I closed my eyes, letting my head squash back into the pillow. If I concentrated hard enough, I could still feel the pressure of her lips on mine. I could feel her nails raking through my hair. Her gentle fingertips tracing my jawline. That kiss *was* amazing. And it wasn't meant to mean anything either. I don't even know why I did it, I only wanted that bitch Ellie to stop saying those nasty things to her. I wanted to prove to Izzy that it wasn't true, she was beautiful and sexy and Ellie was chatting complete bullshit. But fuck, I wasn't expecting the intense burn of desire that swept through me when we kissed. She had started off so timid and unsure but had soon taken control, pushing against me and deepening the kiss. I hadn't expected that at all.

But getting involved with Izzy was a bad idea. A terrible idea. She was already interfering, and I could just tell that she was the kind of person who would want to know everything about you. If she found out about Big Mike, she'd want to help. She'd definitely go blabbing to someone and I couldn't have her do that. No, I had to steer clear of Izzy. The idea of not kissing her again was disappointing, but I knew what I had to do to protect my brothers. I knew I had to stay away from her. Yet as I felt sleep tug me into oblivion, a smile danced on my lips as I replayed that kiss in my mind.

Chapter 17

Isabel

"We saw you, Izzy, so don't even try to deny it!" I could hear the accusatory tone in Jess' voice through the phone. It was Sunday night and I was stretched across my bed, listening to my friend grill me about what had happened last night. I had been very close-lipped during the ride home. Thankfully, Ed had been boasting about some girl he'd gotten off with, so I could ignore the sideways glances from Jess and Sophie until I escaped the car and through my front door. However, Jess had tried calling me three times already and I'd finally caved and answered her this evening. How I was regretting that decision now.

"Soph and I were worried shitless that Ellie would bump into you before we got a chance to tell you she was at the party. We were running 'round like headless chickens and there you were, sucking the face off of Joshua Bugg! And what was he even doing at that party anyway? Hardly his crowd." I tried to smother a giggle as her description conjured up a replay of that kiss. I could feel the blush creeping up my neck and was grateful she couldn't see me.

"Ellie *did* find me. She was spouting her usual crap at me in front of a huge crowd of girls and as per usual, I froze up. Why do I do that, Jess? I've just started standing up for myself and acting more confident, but as soon as I am back in front of her again, I revert back into that pathetic little girl that doesn't have a backbone." I sighed into the phone. It was so frustrating.

"It's conditioning," she replied.

"Conditioning?"

"You have spent years being afraid of her. Every time you see her, your body shuts down because that's what you always used to do. It's been *conditioned* to act a certain way. You know, like Pavlov's dog…" I pulled the phone away from my ear and stared at it incredulously.

"Who are you and what have you done with my friend Jess?"

"What? I can be intelligent sometimes too, you know," she laughed at me.

"Hey, I know that. I was only joking." I felt bad for teasing her. I knew Jess was a little insecure around Sophie and I sometimes. She felt like she was the 'dumb one' of the group, even though that was completely inaccurate.

"If I am being totally honest, we read about it in my

textiles class the other week. About how some people will react a certain way to colours or graphics because of past experiences. You know, like how Sophie will buy absolutely anything with animals on, even if it isn't particularly flattering, because she grew up on a farm." I laughed at her and rolled my eyes. If anyone overheard that they might think Jess was being catty, but she wasn't. That was just Jess; blunt and to the point.

"That reminds me, I saw Jack and Soph kissing before we left too. I thought she was mad at him? Because he was getting off with that blonde she told us about?"

"Apparently, when Soph saw Jack and the girl the other week, he was taking her home to explain that their casual 'friends with benefits' thing they had going on had to stop because he'd met someone he really liked. Not sure I believe that bullshit, what guy turns down no-strings-attached sex? But Soph seemed happy enough."

"So, what was Ed's comment about the other day at Nando's?" I asked.

"Again, apparently Jack hadn't said anything to Ed at all about spending more time with Sophie, so he had no idea Jack was ending it with the blonde." I could hear the scepticism in her voice.

"Anyway, enough with that. Stop changing the subject. How did you end up kissing Josh?"

"Well, like I said, Ellie was being a bitch as per usual and I stood there and did nothing. Next thing I know, Josh is strolling over to me and kissing me! It was so unexpected."

"So, he just walked right up to you and kissed you? In front of Ellie?" I could hear the disbelief in her voice.

"Yep. But it didn't mean anything. He was only being nice…"

"Being nice?! What the hell does that mean?"

"Er, afterwards he said that we were even now, because I'd saved Tom and he'd saved me. He was basically saying that he'd only kissed me because he knew I needed saving from Ellie." I let out a surprised huff in disappointment and prayed that Jess didn't catch it.

"Ah. And you were hoping it meant something? You wanted it to mean something?" No such luck, she'd heard me alright.

"I…he confuses me, Jess. I was sure that he was enjoying that kiss as much as me, but then he said that. And we were texting for ages last night. Not about anything important, but I felt comfortable talking to him. Then I had to open my big mouth and bring up the kiss and he didn't text me back. He clearly just wants to forget all about it."

"OK, one, let me tell you that he most definitely enjoyed kissing you. What moron wouldn't? And two, what exactly did you say to him about the kiss?" I could feel the heat colouring my cheeks again. It was so embarrassing.

"Oh Jess, you don't want to know. I made a complete tit of myself."

"Come on, you're not getting off that easy. Tell me what you said."

"No."

"Yes."

"NO."

"*Yes.*" I groaned.

"OK, let me put you on speaker and I'll read it out to you." I scrolled through my phone, locating the text and groaning again but even louder when I read it in my head.

"Tell me!"

"OK, so I said: *Thank you for saving me from Ellie. I know that kiss didn't mean anything to you but you saved me. And it was amazing. So thank you.*"

"You said *thank you*?! Oh jeez, Izzy…"

"I know, I know! You don't have to make me feel like even more of an idiot. Who bloody well says thank you after someone kisses them? And why did I tell him it was amazing? I am such an idiot."

"And he didn't reply after that?"

"Nope."

"And you'd been texting for ages before that?"

"Yep."

"Shit."

"Exactly."

"OK. Well you know what? *He's* the idiot if that kiss didn't mean anything. He should be damn grateful that you kissed him back instead of slapping him. You're going to strut into school on Monday, looking as fine as ever, and ignore him. You hear me? You're going to *ignore* him. Trust me, he'll soon be chasing after you, begging for more."

"Haha, yeah right. But thanks for trying to cheer me up, Jess," I laughed at her. "And I am going to have to ignore him anyway. I'll die of embarrassment if I so much as even look at him again." Jess started giggling down the phone.

"It's not funny!" Her giggles turned into full on laughter.

"I'm...imagining him...kissing you...then you curtsying...saying thank you..." She could barely get her words out now she was laughing so hard.

"Shut UP! It wasn't like that, you tit." But I was giggling now too, the mental image of me in a tutu bowing at Josh causing me to burst into fits of my own laughter.

"OK, I'm hanging up now, bitch..." I could still hear her peals of laughter as I hung up. A few seconds later, my phone pinged. *I love you really ;)* I shook my head smiling, pulling a pillow tight over my head. If I could please suffocate now so I didn't have to go into school tomorrow, please, that would be great.

~

So far, I had successfully managed to avoid Josh all day. I had purposely arrived at school bang on 9 a.m. so I could go straight to class and I studied through lunch and my free periods, avoiding the common room like the plague.

"So, you've not spoken to him? At all?" Jess asked. Jess, Sophie and I were walking to the bus stop and were almost there. A few more minutes and I'd be sitting on the bus without a care in the world, not having to worry about bumping into Josh.

"Nope," I grinned. "Have you spoken to Jack at all today, Soph?" I wiggled my eyebrows at her, changing the subject. She immediately blushed.

"Don't even ask, Iz. They were all over each other at lunch. You were lucky you were in the library. I'm going to join you tomorrow if they keep it up." Jess rolled her eyes playfully as Soph bumped her shoulder.

"We were not!"

"You bloody were!"

"Are you and Jack together now? Like officially?" I questioned, feeling very happy for my friend. Before she could answer me, we were interrupted.

"Izzy! Iz!" I turned around and saw Josh waving, trotting towards me. "Hey."

"Hey," I replied, praying that my face wasn't turning bright red.

"I didn't see you at lunch today." He looked down at me, dragging his fingers through his hair and pulling it to the side, out of his eyes. My heart skipped a little as we made eye contact.

"I was, er, studying," I muttered, looking at my shoes.

"Why hello ladies. A pleasure to see you as always." Ollie strolled past Josh and I, throwing his arms around Jess and Sophie's shoulders whilst winking at me. Sophie giggled but Jess huffed, knocking his arm off and turning away.

"Don't pretend you can't feel it, Jessie girl," Ollie called after her as she dragged Sophie away.

"Feel what?" she responded, confusion drawing her eyebrows close together.

"This." He pointed his finger between the two of them. "There is some chemistry here, baby." Jess laughed at him, flipping him the bird over her shoulder as she walked away.

"Ouch!" Ollie clutched his chest over his heart, staggering backwards before chasing after Jess.

"He's an idiot," Josh laughed, shaking his head.

"I think he's funny," I laughed along with him and he cocked an eyebrow at me, narrowing his eyes. I was definitely blushing now, the intensity of his gaze making me uncomfortable.

"Anyway, I wanted to give you something to say thank you for last night. You must have thought I was a right psycho, stressing out over my brother when all he had was a stomach ache." Now it was Josh's turn to look uncomfortable as he tugged his backpack off his back, rummaging through the contents.

"I don't know if you've seen it or not but figured it might be your kinda film." Josh tugged a DVD out of his bag, handing it over to me. I turned it over, analysing the front cover. *Rush. The merciless 1970s rivalry between Formula One rivals James Hunt and Niki Lauda.*

"How did you know?" I asked, completely shocked.

"Know what?" he frowned at me.

"My family and I *love* Formula One. My dad was telling me about this film a while ago, but I couldn't find it on Netflix. I have been wanting to see this for ages." I could feel my cheeks pushing up into my eyebrows, I was beaming at him so hard. Josh scratched the back of his head, breaking eye contact.

"I'm glad you like it," he choked out. "And don't

worry, I will still pay you the money for the cab back, promise." We started walking and I felt more comfortable now we were side by side and I didn't have to look directly at him.

"Josh. I told you not to worry about that. Honestly. It's fine."

"But I feel like a complete shithead. You're always paying for stuff."

"It's the twenty-first century and it's my choice. So get over it," I smiled over at him as he snorted.

"Well, I better get going or DeeDee will have my balls if I'm late again." Josh tilted his head towards *Martins* as we rounded the corner.

"DeeDee?" I queried, laughing.

"Don't even ask…" He gave me a little wave, heading off into the direction of the shop. My bus pulled up and I could see Sophie gesturing at me to hurry up from the doors. I climbed up the first step when I heard my name being called. I turned and saw Josh watching me.

"Come find me when you've watched it. Let me know what you think," he nodded at the DVD I was still clutching in my hand. I smiled in agreement as I climbed onto the bus, spying Josh still watching me from the corner of my eye.

"Told ya it would work. *Treat 'em mean, keep 'em keen* works every time," Jess leaned over from behind me and whispered in my ear. I laughed at her, shaking my head. I couldn't help but smile the whole way home.

Chapter 18

Joshua

I couldn't stay away from her. I'd promised myself that night after the party that I'd steer clear, and as much as my head was screaming it at me, my heart had other ideas. I had no clue why I'd picked up that DVD the following morning. All I knew was that I wanted to show my appreciation and do something to make her smile. I hadn't expected it to escalate from there though.

She'd watched *Rush* that night, tracking me down between classes the next day to tell me how much she loved it. As she regaled her favourite parts, I couldn't help but study her facial expressions. The way her eyes creased when she smiled, or how she tipped her chin up when she laughed, or how she cocked her head when she was trying to figure something out. I was fascinated by her.

Later in the week, she brought me a DVD to watch too (*Death Race,* an epic Jason Statham film) and we fell into an easy habit, taking it in turns each week to bring the other a movie to watch. We didn't always agree. She did not appreciate *Anchor Man* (note to self, Izzy hates 'pointless comedies.' Her words, not mine) and I thought *Pitch Perfect* was a total piece of crap (though Georgie loved it), but we gradually started spending more time together. For the first time in my life, I was ignoring my instincts and better judgement and doing what felt good instead. What felt *right.* And being friends with Izzy definitely felt right. Problem was, every time I looked at her, all I kept thinking of was that kiss and how much I wanted to do it again. But that really was a terrible idea. Being friends with Izzy was risky enough. I couldn't let it develop into anything else.

"Oi, Josh! Josh!" Ryan waved his hand in front of my face and rolled his eyes.

"Sorry man, must have spaced out a little there." The three of us were sitting around the kitchen table, picking at our dinner of tuna pasta. Ryan had been talking for the past couple of minutes, but I hadn't heard a single word.

"I'm not sure I like tuna anymore..." Georgie muttered.

"But it's better than Pot Noodle, right?" I asked.

"I guess..." My wages had taken a hammering, what with the time off I'd had thanks to Big Mike's last beating. I ended up missing sixteen hours in total this month, which might not sound like a lot, but given how far our money had to stretch, it had a big impact on us.

I was sick of tuna pasta too, but it was cheap to make and more filling than a Pot Noodle. And it meant Ryan and Georgie got a little more protein in their diet.

I looked across at Ryan and was pleased to see him finish the whole bowl. He had served his week suspension without fuss, staying over Ollie's all week and promising me not to get into any more fights. So far, he'd kept that promise.

The sound of keys rattling in the front door caused me to tense, bracing myself. Big Mike stumbled in, eyes wide, pupils dilated and reeking of booze. He had a whiskey bottle in his hand and was slurping it straight from the bottle. I'd never seen him with whiskey before, he preferred beer, and it struck me that Ollie was right. He was getting worse.

"Where's mine?" he slurred, slamming the door shut behind him.

"Where's your what?" I asked, keeping my back to him. I was suddenly very fascinated with spearing the pasta on my fork and bringing it to my mouth.

"Dinner, fuckface. Where's my dinner?" I shrugged, still not facing him.

"Look at you, you worthless fucks. The three of you playing at happy families. Well, I am the head of this family and I should fucking well have dinner on the table when I get home from work!" His fists clenched by his side, his breathing laboured. I stood up, grabbing mine and Ryan's bowl and putting them in the sink. Georgie had only eaten about half and judging by the tremors quivering through his body, he wasn't about to finish it anytime soon. I scraped the leftovers into a discoloured lunch box, leaving it in the fridge for tomorrow. Neither Ryan nor Georgie had moved a muscle.

"Come on, let's go up to bed," I gestured to the pair of them, motioning them towards the stairs.

"Don't fucking ignore me, boy!" Actually, ignoring him was a safer bet. Sometimes not giving him a reaction led to him giving up and leaving me alone. It was like he was doing it on purpose to torment me and it wasn't any fun if I didn't fight back. Sometimes his mood was so bad that nothing I did mattered. Nothing would calm him down or diffuse the situation.

I filed in behind Georgie and Ryan as they left the kitchen, being careful to keep between them and Big Mike at all times. As I lifted a foot towards the bottom step of our rickety staircase, I felt a hand grab my hair and yank backwards. I could feel some of the roots being torn from my scalp as I stumbled, clutching my head in my hands as I swivelled to face him. He was smirking at me, provoking me. I scowled at him, pouring every ounce of hatred through my eyes as if I could kill him by sheer willpower. I had never hated another human being so much in my life.

"Josh...?" Georgie called from behind me, voice quiet, unsure.

"Upstairs. Now. Lock the door." I heard two sets of frantic footsteps climb the stairs and I traced their sounds, all the way to our room, until I heard the three deadbolts slide. They sounded like gunshots in the tense quiet of our kitchen.

"Those shitty little locks won't stop me and you

know it." He laughed maniacally and I started to wonder if it was only alcohol that was behind his behaviour. Maybe something stronger? Drugs? He looked like a crazed lunatic, his eyes starting to bug out of their sockets.

"Leave. Them. Alone." I growled, adopting a fighting stance.

"They're safe. For tonight at least. I prefer someone who can put up a fight," he grinned. The kitchen light bulb gleamed off of his yellow, chipped teeth, making them appear even more sallow than usual.

"Fuck off. You are never touching them! Not whilst I am here!" My body was convulsing so hard that I didn't know how I was still standing. The rage was all-consuming, and it took everything I could not to unleash on him. He laughed so hard this time that he had to lean over, hands resting on his knees, whilst he coughed uncontrollably for a solid minute. Good, maybe the fucker had pneumonia, or a lung infection, or something.

"You're fucking clueless as well as worthless. A fucking moron. No wonder your mother left you here to rot. You're not worth the fucking hassle!" I would *not* react. I would not give him the satisfaction. My fight or flight response was confused. I so badly wanted to kick the shit out of him, but my body instantly trembled at the notion, knowing full well that would mean some kind of pain coming my way too. I felt sick with shame; I was pathetic, standing there, doing nothing. Staring up at the fat mammoth in front of me. I also didn't want to turn my back to him, knowing that was too risky.

Especially as he seemed to be boiling for a fight tonight.

After another minute, he forced my hand, growing impatient for me to make a move. He launched the whiskey bottle at my face and I ducked just in time. Ducking bought him a second of advantage, catching me off guard as he barrelled towards me, arms wrapping around my waist. He lifted me high off the ground, slamming my back against the kitchen wall. This was becoming a favourite move of his. He knew I stood a chance if I had my feet on the ground, when I could throw my weight behind every punch, every kick. He kept me pinned to the wall, my feet dangling a few inches above the ground as he brought his hands up, tightening his grip around my neck.

"This'll teach you to not have my fucking dinner ready, you bastard!" He squeezed tighter and tighter, causing my vision to blur around the edges. Hours of watching self-defence YouTube videos the past few years weren't for nothing though. I pressed my hands together in a prayer position, lifting them sharply between his arms and slamming my wrists and elbows outwards. His hands left my neck immediately, arms flying wide with the force. He lifted his fists to block a punch and so, despite not quite having enough oxygen in my lungs still, I kicked out at his balls as hard as I could. I yelled in triumph as my foot connected with its target and he crumpled to the floor, rolling around in agony. I don't know whether it was the alcohol, drugs or something else that was causing him to react so slowly, but I was fucking grateful for it. If I knew what was good for me, I'd run up the stairs and leave the fight there. But I was too damn angry and resentful. I lifted my foot and stamped on his goddamn face. His nose erupted and blood sprayed everywhere. I'd never been so fucking happy to see someone's bodily fluids expelled from their body. I was definitely going to pay for that later, but whilst he lay passed out on the floor, the blood pooling around his face, I could feel nothing but ecstasy.

I'd won! I'd actually motherfucking won! I was the last one standing. I knew it was a fluke. If he'd been sober, I wouldn't have stood a chance, but I had a slight skip in my step as I made my way up to Ryan and Georgie.

"Open up, it's me." I rapped on the door three times and was immediately rewarded with the door unlocking. Ryan was standing in the doorway, a sharp kitchen knife lowered by his side. We kept two in our room; one under my bed and one under Ryan's. We'd never had to even brandish one at Big Mike so far. Usually our fights ended with me being unconscious whilst the boys barricaded themselves in our room. Once Big Mike proved himself superior, it was like all the fight left him instantly. A balloon deflating. He didn't bother with Ryan or Georgie. And on the one or two occasions in the past when, like tonight, I was victorious, he would sleep it off and act as if nothing had happened the next day. Although he seemed to be twice as vindictive the next time we fought, and I have never won two times in a row. Never. But you couldn't be too sure how he'd react and so we kept the knives here for emergencies. I thanked God every day that we hadn't had to use them. Yet.

Ryan wrapped his arms around me briefly, smiling proudly up at me. Georgie was in Ryan's bunk, quilt pulled up to his chin, trembling. I took the knife off of Ryan, re-locked the bedroom door and sat cross-legged on the floor in front of it, facing the doorway. There was a chance Big Mike wouldn't be unconscious for long and would come looking for me. I wanted to be prepared.

Ryan switched off the light before climbing into bed with Georgie. I could hear him whispering reassurances to him as I turned the knife over in my hands. I shouldn't have broken Big Mike's nose. He was going to be so pissed in the morning. The adrenaline was wearing off and in its place was pure, unadulterated fear. I was glad that my brothers couldn't see the tears filling my eyes and the shivers racking my body. Fuck, I was weak. The shame built in my throat, the taste of vomit palpable. I should go downstairs and finish him off, plunge the knife into his chest. I don't know how long I sat there, visualising ending his life. Occasionally there would be a creak or a random sound, causing me to jolt. Was that him? Had he regained consciousness? Did he want revenge? I felt the sweat rolling down the side of my face and soaking my t-shirt. I had to protect Georgie and Ryan at all costs. I *had* to.

I sat that way all night, crying softly at how disturbingly pitiful I was. I should sacrifice my freedom and kill the bastard, leaving Ryan and Georgie to live their lives free of pain. Free of suffering. But my limbs were frozen, unmoving. I couldn't do it. I just couldn't do it. Pathetic.

Chapter 19

Isabel

"Happy birthday to you, happy birthday to you. Happy birthday dear Isabel, happy birthday to you!" My mum was so cheesy. I was turning seventeen and she was still singing happy birthday to me, making me blow out the candles on the chocolate cake she was holding. Mum, Dad and I had spent the day at the zoo together. I know, I know, not your typical seventeen-year-old birthday party, but I enjoyed spending time with both of them and we hadn't done it much lately. To be honest, I was feeling guilty about the distance I'd put between us all over the past couple of years. We had been close, especially Mum and I, but I'd isolated myself once Ellie's bullying had started. I'd chosen to retreat into books rather than go out shopping with Mum, fearful that we'd bump into someone from school and they'd start shouting obscenities at me in front of her. I'd stay locked in my bedroom all day, watching movies and trying to escape into another reality. Now though, I was keen to get our relationship back on track and a day at the zoo, followed by a family dinner cooked by Dad, was exactly what I needed. Dad was a fantastic cook and he'd made my favourite; salmon en croute, dauphinoise potatoes and green beans.

"Here you go sweetie," Mum beamed at me as she passed a card to me.

"But you already gave me my cards and presents this morning," I commented as I peered at the card curiously. They'd given me a bunch of new clothes, a lovely pair of earrings and a one-hundred-pound Amazon voucher. They had already spoiled me rotten, as they did every birthday.

"Well this is your main present," Dad smiled, reaching out to hook his arm around the back of Mum's shoulders. The pair of them sat across from me at the dining table, smiling so widely that I felt my own face morph into a grin.

I gently tore the envelope, sliding the card out. It was a plain card with a vintage microphone stand on the front; the kind of card you could get in the 'other' section of a card shop without a message inside. As I opened it, two tickets fell out.

Nickelback Greatest Hits Tour, Saturday 3rd November
O2 Arena, London

"No way! That's in two weeks' time!" I beamed at

them and Mum laughed.

"I'm sorry we could only get you two and not three, but considering how many jokes people make about that band, their UK tour sold out bloody quick!"

"And I'm sure Jess or Sophie will understand that you could only take one of them," Dad smiled encouragingly. Actually, both of them *hated* my taste in music. Sure, I liked the modern pop hits too, but the likes of Nickelback, Paramore and Blink 182 had stuck with me since going through my grunge phase. I didn't think either Sophie or Jess would want to go with me, although I knew one of them would reluctantly agree if I begged them enough.

"Actually, I might ask someone else…" I started to voice my idea out loud before properly thinking it through.

"Oh really? Who?" Mum asked. To my embarrassment, I could feel myself blushing and turned away.

"Ah. It's a boy, right?" Mum smiled knowingly as Dad frowned.

"I didn't know you were seeing someone?" he questioned, eyebrows drawing together and his tone a little more serious than usual.

"I'm not! We're er, just friends. But he might enjoy the music more than either Jess or Sophie," I muttered, my cheeks definitely flaming an even deeper red than before.

"Well, I think it's a lovely idea. We'd love to meet your *friend*, wouldn't we Charlie?" She patted Dad's chest, leaning towards him whilst trying to smother a laugh.

"Hmmmm," he replied, not convinced at all.

"Well we'll see, he might not want to go," I shrugged.

"Oh, I am sure he will, honey," she winked at me.

~

Why was I sweating so bloody much? It was frickin' October, the frigid wind was lifting my hair and throwing it all over my face, and yet I was yanking my jacket off and throwing it over my arm. My palms were *damp* for Christ's sake. Thank God I had a thin knitted, loose jumper over my t-shirt 'cos no doubt my sweat patches were out of control right now.

To make matters worse, I'd missed my bus and had to wait for the next one, so now I was doing a weird walk-shuffle-run to try and get to school as close to 9 a.m. as possible. All because I'd been up most of the night, tossing and turning and fretting. Every time I had thought about today, I'd been hit with a wave of nausea. It was a bad idea. He wouldn't want to go. What if he said no? Why did I even care? I should ask Jess. She'd go.

By the time I saw the school gates in the distance, I was out of breath and my face was on fire.

"Izzy! Hey Izzy!" *No, no, no.* Please, no. I jolted to a stop, glancing over my shoulder. Oh, for fuck sake.

"Hey. You're running late today as well it seems," Josh smiled as he slowed his jog to walk beside me. I garbled something unintelligible and glared a hole into my shoes, praying he wouldn't notice my shiny complexion.

"Hey, you OK?" Josh tugged on my shoulder, turning me to face him and grinding us to a halt by the school's entrance.

"It was my birthday at the weekend!" I blurted out. What the hell did I say that for?

"Oh." He dropped his hand from my shoulder and took a step back. "I didn't know." There were a few seconds of awkward silence and if by some miracle my face hadn't resembled a beetroot before, it definitely did now.

"Are you mad?" He looked off behind me, not meeting my eyes.

"Mad?" I repeated, confused.

"'Cos I didn't get you anything for your birthday?" Again, he wouldn't meet my eyes.

"NO! No. God no…"

"You just seemed off, so I thought…" Great. How was I going to dig myself out of this hole?

"No. Sorry. I'm not mad." *Pull yourself together, Isabel.* I took a deep breath.

"It was my birthday and my mum and dad got me tickets. To a concert."

"Okaaaay." Josh cocked his eyebrow and tilted his head.

"I don't know if you've heard of them or even like them, or would want to go with me anyway…" Josh was staring at me like I was crazy, confused by my babbling. Was I really going to do this?

"Do you want to go?" I gushed. He didn't respond straight away.

"Go? Go where?"

"To the concert. With me. Saturday the 2nd of November. Nickelback." Jeez, I was *such* a bumbling idiot.

"You want me to go to a concert with you?" He sounded incredulous, as if it was the most ridiculous thing he'd ever heard, and my heart sank.

"Forget I said anything..." I muttered, turning away and slowly putting one foot in front of the other.

"No, wait! I..." I flicked my eyes up at him as he ran his fingers through his hair. "I don't really listen to music." Well, that was the lamest excuse I'd ever heard of. I huffed, picking up my pace.

"No, Izzy! Wait!" Josh hurled himself in front of me and I almost crashed straight into his chest. "I want to. Yes. Yes, I want to go."

"Really? You really want to go with me?" I tried to stop my heart from doing a little dance, cautious that he'd change his mind. "But I thought you said you didn't listen to music." I crossed my arms.

"I don't. I probably won't have ever heard of whoever is playing. But I'd like to go with you anyway."

"Are you sure? You weren't just trying to find a lame excuse to not go with me?" Josh looked like I'd slapped him and I instantly felt bad for doubting him.

"No. I had genuinely meant it." He ground out, jaw tight. "I don't get to listen to music because we don't have a car, so no radio. We don't have a working TV, just one hooked up to a DVD player, so no music channels. I don't have a smartphone..." he angrily grabbed a tiny black, ancient phone model out of his pocket and waved it in my face. "...so no Spotify or iTunes or shit like that. So, when I said I didn't listen to music, I was basically saying that my family's so piss poor that I had no *way* of *listening* to *music*!' He shouted the last word at me, brushing past me.

"Josh, wait! Don't go!" Now I was chasing after him and I felt like the world's biggest bitch.

"I'm sorry. I'm so sorry. I've just been really nervous about asking you and I barely slept, then I missed my bus and I'm grumpy when I'm tired and I didn't think you'd say yes," I rushed at him, praying he'd forgive me.

"You were nervous? Why?" He frowned at me.

"Well er, we haven't hung out outside of school and I didn't know if rock music would be your thing…"

"Hang on. *Rock* music? Who did you say we were going to see?"

"Nickelback. They're a rock band. Well, more like pop-rock."

"So, we're going to see a band? Like, a gig? Not some chavvy boy band or rapper or something?"

"Are you trying to say you think I'm chavvy and are surprised by my taste in music?" I teased, raising my eyebrows.

"Well…yeah I suppose so," he laughed, and I playfully slapped him on the arm.

"I went through a grunge phase and the music has kinda stuck with me."

"Well, now I'm actually pretty excited to be going." And he did look genuinely happy. As we headed to class, my brain was going into overdrive. *Oh my God, I can't believe Josh Bugg agreed to go on a date with me.*

Chapter 20

Joshua

Shit, Izzy was going to be so pissed at me. Or worse, she'd cry. I really, *really* wanted to go with her on Saturday. I was still in shock she'd asked me in the first place. I was even more surprised that she still wanted me to go after I blew up on her about the whole 'I'm too poor to listen to music' thing. Urgh. It made me cringe just thinking about it. I must have sounded like a right prat.

But now I couldn't go. After the initial excitement wore off and I started asking for more details, the more I realised that there was no way I could go. First, Big Mike had disappeared for over a week now, ever since I'd broken his nose. He hadn't come home once. As much as I'd like to think I'd scared him off for good, I knew he was only biding his time, waiting to get his own back. And the concert was in London and didn't start 'til 7 p.m. According to Izzy, the doors would open at 6.30 p.m., but some kind of support act goes on first. The main band wouldn't come on 'til around 8.30 p.m. That means we aren't going to be home 'til about midnight and there is no way I can leave Ryan and Georgie on their own for half the day. Second, I'd have to change my shift around at work and finish early; something we couldn't afford to do. And thirdly, and most importantly, how the hell was I going to afford to go in the first place? The train ticket, the food and drink...it was all going to mount up. I'd spend a whole week's worth of wages in one night. Izzy has been yammering on about it almost every day and now I was going to have to let her down. Shit.

As I walked down the corridor alongside the library, I peeked in through the window and saw Izzy sitting at a nearby table. She was sitting with Jack, just Jack, and I immediately felt a pang of jealousy. I knew from Izzy that he and Sophie had some kind of thing going on, but that didn't make me feel any better. God, she was pretty. No, so much more than pretty. She was gorgeous. She had her head tilted to the side as she poured over some kind of textbook, pen perched between her lips as she read. She had a notebook, highlighters and post-it notes spread out all around her, taking up over half the table. Her long hair was pulled around to one side, curving around her neck and flowing down her shoulder. Jack leaned closer to her and she laughed at something he said. Jealousy reared its ugly head again and my feet picked up their pace of their own accord. As soon as I was a metre or so away from her, intense nausea kicked in and I slowed right down. I did *not* want to do this. I didn't want to let her down.

"Izzy? Can we talk a moment?" I whispered, gesturing at a nearby table. I knew she had a free period today and would be studying in the library. I thought that if I told her in here, she wouldn't be able to react too extreme and make a scene, she'd have to stay quiet. It was pathetic and cowardly, yes, but I couldn't stand the idea of making her cry. She nodded at me and stood, following me over to a table near the back.

"What's up?" she smiled.

"Erm...it's about Saturday..." Immediately her face fell and I could see the disappointment shining through already. Fuck, this was going to be hard.

"I didn't realise but my, er, dad is working the night shift. I can't leave Georgie and Ryan on their own for hours whilst I'm at the concert with you." I had practiced the lie I don't know how many times, but it still left a sour taste as soon as the words left my mouth.

"Oh." She started picking her nails and dropped her head, watching her fingers fidget.

"I'm sorry, I really do want to go, I even changed my shift at work and everything..." Another lie. But I wanted her to know that I did genuinely want to go. She was quiet and as the minutes ticked past, I contemplated getting up and leaving, not sure if she wanted to be around me right now.

"What if your brothers stayed over mine?" She looked up at me hopefully and I reared back in surprise.

"Huh? What do you mean?"

"Bring 'em over with you on Saturday. Mum and Dad won't mind. They can have dinner over ours and stay the night in the spare room. You'd have to stay on the sofa bed in Mum's office most likely, but you could all totally stay the night…" she was talking in an excited whisper, smiling at me reassuringly.

"I'm not sure…"

"Honestly, it's no problem! Then you can still come!" She was beaming at me now.

"To be honest, Iz, I'm not sure how I'm going to afford the train and…"

"Oh, don't worry about that. Mum and Dad gave me some money for the day too, as part of my birthday gift, so they're paying. They thought I'd be taking Sophie or Jess and they still gave me the money, so it's honestly nothing to do with you or anything."

"And you're sure your parents don't mind that you're taking me or that my brothers are going to stay over?" I could feel myself caving. Resistance was futile.

"Yup. I'm sure. I'll text you later tonight to confirm, but I know it won't be a problem."

"Well, er, great! Guess I can come after all…"

~

"So, tell me again why we are all dressed up and going over your girlfriend's house for a sleepover?" Ryan scowled at me as we got off the bus, tugging at his collar. It was only a polo top for Christ's sake, but you'd think he was wearing a shirt and tie the way he was complaining.

"For the tenth time, she's not my girlfriend. And you know you can't stay at home on your own all night. What if Big Mike comes back? He is going to be in such a shitty mood, and I can't risk you being there on your own."

"Right. And why are we in our best clothes?" 'Best' wasn't exactly the right word for dark jeans, polo tops and trainers but they were the nicest things we had. I'd bought Ryan and Georgie's tops especially for today, only wincing a little when I handed over the cash in the charity shop.

"We need to make a good impression. It's a bit of a risk staying over there and we need to make sure we don't look like…"

"We're living in a shit hole with an abusive, dickhead of a father," he interrupted me.

"Exactly."

"If it's so risky, why are we going? Why couldn't we stay over Ollie's instead?"

"I told you. Ollie's mum is dating a detective and he is over there all the time. We definitely can't risk him asking too many questions."

"Well, you shouldn't have bloody agreed to go tonight in the first place then." Before I could bite out my retort, Georgie jumped in.

"Ryan, shut up, will you? Josh hardly ever goes out and you know it. He always stays home with us. Leave him alone. He deserves a night out with Izzy. I'm looking forward to seeing her," he beamed.

"Thanks buddy," I smiled as I ruffled his hair. I looked over at Ryan and stuck my tongue out at him.

Completely childish, yes, but it made him laugh. Well, he rolled his eyes at the same time, but still.

"Woah…" Ryan looked up at the house in front of us. "Is this it?" It wasn't anywhere near as big as the mansion that Jeremy and his detective dad lived in, but it was still pretty damn nice. The street was so pretty that it wouldn't look out of place on the front of a postcard. The houses looked new and neat, with trimmed hedges and pretty flower beds out front.

"Is that a playground?" Georgie asked, pointing down the road. It certainly didn't look anything like the crappy, run-down one near us. I nodded, took a deep breath, and rang the doorbell.

Izzy had assured me that her parents didn't have an issue with my brothers coming over. But it was fucking weird and I knew it. Who brings their little brothers with them on a first date? Wait, this *was* a date, right? I mean, it was dinner and a gig. That counted as a date, yeah? Or did it not count if she asked me and not the other way around? I didn't have a chance to think about it any further as the front door opened.

"Hi. You must be Josh, Georgie and Ryan." The lady smiling widely at us was definitely Izzy's mum. You could tell they were related a mile off. They had the same colour hair (I'd finally settled on calling it mahogany), same green eyes and same welcoming smile. Izzy had a few more freckles sprinkled over her nose and Izzy's mum's hair was short, just above the shoulder, but they looked very similar otherwise.

"Hi. Nice to meet you." Ryan sniggered at me as I held my hand out by way of greeting. He was loving how awkward I felt.

"I'm Sammy. Come in, come in." She stepped back and pulled the door open for us. OK, so although the house wasn't as big as Jeremy's, it was definitely as stylish. If not more so. The walls were painted in a soft grey, with hardwood flooring that had tinges of grey and beige throughout. We followed Sammy down the hallway and into an open plan lounge-diner.

"Oh my God!" Georgie ran over to the huge TV mounted on the wall. It must have been at least a sixty-inch screen. There was a long, narrow TV stand underneath that was stuffed to the brim with DVDs.

"My husband and Izzy are really into their movies," Sammy laughed as she watched Georgie crouch down and run his fingers along the DVD cases. "You can watch whatever you want tonight whilst Josh and Izzy are at the concert." Georgie almost fell backwards as his mouth gaped open, and even Ryan headed over, both of them rummaging through and selecting their favourites. I stood uncomfortably in the middle of the room, not sure what to do.

"Izzy will be down in a few minutes, she's just finishing getting ready. Would you all like a drink? We've got pineapple juice, diet coke, hot chocolate...whatever you like." Sammy walked through an archway at the back of the room into a sleek, dark grey kitchen. The cupboards were so shiny I could literally see my face reflected in them.

"Pineapple juice, please."

"Hot chocolate!"

"Diet coke, please." Sammy laughed as all three of us

reeled off completely different drinks. My brothers' eyes snapped to mine, widening. We had lived off of water or very weak squash for so many years now that I could practically see them salivating from here. And I was embarrassed to admit that I was too. Even when Big Mike's business had been going well, he and Mum had never paid attention to the drinks (or food) we liked. Mum always bought squash, wine and beer when she went shopping and rarely anything else. Maybe some tea bags too, if we were lucky.

Sammy started filling up the kettle and I reached for the glasses she had retrieved from one of the higher cupboards.

"Let me help you," I smiled tightly at her. I was so out of my comfort zone right now.

"Thank you, Josh." They had a huge double fridge at the end of the kitchen, also in matching dark grey, with one of those water and ice dispensers built into the front of it. I filled my glass with a little ice and then opened the door to grab the juice and coke. Holy shit. This thing was jam-packed with food. Fresh fruit and vegetables were spilling out of the bottom drawer, the other shelves packed with fresh pasta, yoghurts, a whole chicken, lamb cutlets, a salmon side, bottles of milk, cheese, ham, and on and on.

"Everything OK, Josh?" Sammy called over her shoulder, concern flitting across her features briefly.

"Er, yeah, sorry." I'd been staring at the inside of the fridge, motionless, like a complete idiot. I finished making our drinks and handed Ryan his juice, whilst Sammy handed Georgie a hot chocolate, complete with whipped cream and marshmallows on top. She winked at him as Georgie giggled at her.

"So, what do you boys fancy for dinner tonight?" A man came through the backdoor, wiping his hands on a cloth as he strolled straight over to Sammy to give her a kiss on the cheek. He was in loose, black trousers that had a ton of pockets, a tight black t-shirt and work boots. He was taller than me by an inch or two and looked like he worked out a lot. He'd probably be able to give Big Mike a run for his money. Maybe.

"Charlie. Izzy's dad," he held his hand out and gripped mine tight.

"Hi. Josh. Izzy's, er, friend." He laughed at my hesitation.

"Good answer," he teased. "So, any preferences for food tonight?" Charlie walked over to Georgie and Ryan, shaking both their hands too and waiting for an answer.

"Er, no. We aren't fussy eaters," Ryan replied quietly.

"Chicken enchiladas OK then?"

"What's an en, an enchillyda?" Georgie asked.

"An enchilada is a tortilla filled with chicken, peppers and mushrooms and then baked in the oven, smothered in cheese and spicy tomato sauce. Well, that's how I make them anyway."

"That sounds awesome!" Georgie squealed.

"Great. Enchiladas it is then. I'm going to go get cleaned up and then I'll make a start." I watched Charlie leave the room and turned back to Sammy, who I noticed was watching me as she sipped her tea.

"What does, er, Charlie do?" I asked, fumbling

through an attempt at trying to make conversation.

"He has his own construction business. He does restoration and renovation work mainly. Old cottages, listed buildings, stuff like that." Sammy smiled kindly and there was something about her that instantly made me feel at ease. I could feel myself relax a little.

"Hey! Sorry, it took a bit longer to get ready than I thought," Izzy breezed into the room and gave me a little wave as she headed straight for Georgie. To his utter delight, she swooped down and gave him a big squeeze, arms wrapping around him.

"Hey buddy," she smiled, ruffling his hair.

"Hi Izzy! You have so many movies! I'm going to watch them all tonight," he beamed and Ryan rolled his eyes. Izzy nodded at him in greeting and then started looking through the small tower of DVDs Georgie had piled up next to him. She knew Ryan hadn't quite warmed up to her as much Georgie yet.

"Well, I'm not sure you'll have time for all these, but you should definitely watch...this one...this one...and this one." She pulled three DVDs out and put them on top of the pile.

"Black Panther, The Greatest Showman and Instant Family..." Georgie read the titles and nodded approvingly.

"You ready to go?" Izzy straightened and looked at me. Jeez, she looked incredible. She was squeezed into tight, black skinny jeans, with black converse and a sleeveless black vest with 'Nickelback' across the chest in white font. Her eyes had some darker makeup on than usual and her hair was a little wavy. Not full on curls like at the party last month, just a slight wave.

"You look...amazing..." I took a step towards her but hesitated, conscious that Izzy's mum was watching. Not that I would have done anything anyway. We'd only had that one kiss, which I'd kind of been a bit of a dick about anyway, and we never normally greeted each other with anything other than a 'hello.' But for some reason, I wanted to do more tonight.

"Thanks," she blushed. She grabbed a leather jacket from a nearby cupboard and slung a bag over her shoulder.

"Text me and let me know when you get to the O2 or I'll worry, OK? And don't forget to let me know what time you'll be at the train station afterwards so I can come get you. You are definitely not getting the bus back from there that late." Sammy hugged Izzy goodbye after making her promise to follow her instructions.

"Have a great time. Call us if you need anything," Charlie called after Izzy as she headed towards the front door. I was rooted to the spot, staring at Ryan and Georgie. Was I actually going to leave them in a complete stranger's house? Whilst I trusted Izzy, I didn't know her parents at all. Charlie's size was a good thing if he ever came up against Big Mike, which obviously he wouldn't, but actually he could do some real damage to my brothers if he chose to. I pulled them both into a huddle quickly.

"You have your phones on you?" I whispered and they nodded. "Good. Call me or text me if you have any issues and I'll come straight back, OK?" Georgie looked a little nervous at my questions.

"Josh, we'll be fine. They look harmless." Ryan rolled his eyes and I flicked my gaze over my shoulders, seeing Charlie and Sammy standing together, looking at us quizzically.

"Josh, they'll be fine, I promise. My parents will stuff them full of food and probably drive them crazy, but they will be well looked after. Promise," Izzy interrupted, lacing her fingers through mine before tugging me towards the door. Georgie followed and gave us a quick hug and a wave, before running back over to his DVD tower. Izzy dragged me out of the house, locking the door behind her.

"You sure your parents don't mind them being over?" I asked again, still feeling uncertain about leaving them.

"Positive."

"OK then. Let's go," I exhaled a long breath, unsure what was in store for the rest of the night.

Chapter 21

Isabel

It was lame how happy I was right now. I'd thought that Josh was going to end up cancelling, especially as he tried to back out the other day. It was a bit pathetic how I'd convinced him to bring his brothers over to stay at mine whilst we went out. I mean, desperate much? I wouldn't have blamed Josh if he thought I was a complete lunatic, but he surprised me by agreeing. Yes, I'd had to basically kidnap him to get him to leave the house, but hey, he was here now. Somewhere in the back of my mind, it registered how scared Josh looked to leave his brothers, but I didn't pluck at that train of thought. I was too excited for the concert.

"So, we have about an hour and a half before we need to go in. Where would you like to go to eat?" I asked him as we ambled through the O2 arena; the second largest indoor music venue in the UK. We had chatted easily on the bus and then the train here, but he'd been quiet ever since we entered the arena. He was looking all around him, head swivelling from one side to the other as he took it in.

"Josh?" I prompted after no response.

"Oh, huh? Sorry. This place is incredible!"

"Where do you want to go for food?" I repeated, trying to hide a laugh. He looked like a kid in a toy store, eyes wide with awe.

"I don't mind. Oh, actually, ever since your dad mentioned enchiladas, I'm kinda craving Mexican?" He phrased it as a question, asking for my permission. "But this is your birthday present, so you should pick," he rushed.

"I love Mexican food too. Come on, we'll go to Alejandro's." I grabbed his hand and gently steered him in the right direction. This was the second time I'd held his hand today and I was thrilled again when he didn't pull away. I had done it back at home without even thinking, but this time was more premeditated. We'd developed an easy friendship the past few weeks and I didn't want to ruin that, but I knew deep down that I wanted more. I hadn't admitted it even to myself in the beginning, but ever since we'd kissed at Jeremy's birthday party, my feelings for Josh had grown. The longer we were friends, the more I yearned to get out of the friend zone. And the more risks I took, like asking him out on a date and holding his hand. In all the movies and all the books I'd read, the guy always made the first move. I'd thought at first that Josh wasn't interested in being more than friends. Hell, maybe I was right and he didn't think this was a date at all. I was the one who'd asked him, after all. But after speaking with Jess and Sophie last weekend, they had encouraged me to be brave and make a move myself. So that's what I was planning on doing tonight at some point. *Make my move.*

Alejandro's was crazy busy and I should have booked a table, judging by the queue outside. It seemed to be shrinking pretty quickly though.

"Is there much of a wait for a table of two please?" I asked the waitress at the door.

"Just two? No, I can sit you now. They're all large groups," she gestured at the other people waiting and grabbed some menus, leading us inside. The interior was modern but under-stated, with exposed brick walls, plain black, metal chairs, and minimal furnishings. We followed the waitress to a little table near the back, which was set up so that we'd be sitting next to each other at adjacent sides of the table, rather than the opposite ones. The lights were dim and candles flickered, but the music and chatter surrounding us meant we needed to almost shout to hear each other. It was a great, lively atmosphere.

Josh had been staring at his menu in silence for almost ten minutes and I was starting to feel a little nervous.

"Anything you like? We can go somewhere else if you want?" I leaned in to be sure he heard me and he jumped, almost hitting me with his menu.

"Er, sorry! There's just so much to choose from, I

don't even know where to start!" He smiled at me and I relaxed. OK, indecisiveness I could handle.

"Want me to order for you? They have another restaurant not too far from home and it's my mum's favourite, so I've tried pretty much everything on the menu."

"Er, sure. Why not?" He sat back and put his menu down and right on cue, a waitress appeared.

"Did you want to order some drinks?" She tilted her body so that she was facing more towards Josh, her shoulders pulled back and a sweet smile stretched across her face. Girls could be so predictable sometimes.

"Actually, we're ready to order food too. We'll have a frozen strawberry margarita, a Desperado and some water for the table. And then we'll have nachos to share to start, I'll have the Mexican Sandwich with a side of fried beans and sour cream, and he will have the El Superior Burrito with a side of sweet potato wedges please." I handed my menu to her, praying that she wouldn't ID us when I ordered the alcohol. I was acting far more confident than I felt.

"Sure thing." She looked impressed and after scribbling everything down, scurried away.

"What? You said it was OK for me to order for you, right?" Josh was staring at me and I was starting to feel uncomfortable again.

"That was brilliant! I have no idea what you ordered, but it all sounded amazing."

"I ordered you a beer, was that OK? Well, it has tequila in it too, but it tastes like beer apparently. My dad loves them." As it dawned on me that I had no idea what kind of food or drink Josh actually liked, I was starting to doubt myself. Maybe I shouldn't have ordered for him.

"And the burrito has almost everything in it; pork, chicken, steak, guacamole, salsa…"

"I'm sure I'll love it." He smiled at me again and it hit home how attractive this boy was. No, I should say man. There was nothing boyish about him at all. He was wearing his signature black polo and black jeans again and he looked freshly shaven, with only the slightest bit of stubble around his jaw. He was way out of my league and I wondered why he bothered hanging around with me at all. Maybe he still wanted to be sure I wouldn't tell anyone what I'd seen that time at his house when he'd collapsed? I hadn't said a word to anyone about it, and I hadn't asked Josh or his brothers about it again either. I still had no idea what Josh was into that caused the bruises and cuts that appeared periodically, but I was sure it wasn't drugs now. He always acted completely normal and I'd be able to tell if he was on something, right? I was leaning towards money problems, some kind of loan shark perhaps, but I'd not found the courage to ask him yet. In fact, we'd never spoken about his family or anything serious at all. We only spoke about movies, my family, my studies or my friends.

"I don't know much about you," I blurted, immediately embarrassed. My brain didn't want to function properly around him.

"What do you want to know?" He shuffled around in his seat. "You know where I live, you know I have two brothers, you know where I work...I think you actually know a lot," he joked.

"I suppose…" He didn't look comfortable with this topic, but I didn't know how to back-track. "What do you plan on doing after sixth form?"

"Well, if I even make it that far, I…" my eyebrows shot up. What was *that* supposed to mean?

"…I haven't thought about it much, to be honest," he finished, pointedly looking down at the table and avoiding my eyes.

"I'm thinking of studying biochemistry at university when I finish next year," I said, shifting the conversation back to me. He was going to think I was self-centred and self-absorbed, but I didn't know how to talk to him about himself when he seemed so affected by it.

"So you've made your mind up now? Which university?" He continued to grill me about my future career choices and soon we fell back into our easy banter. I still didn't learn a damn thing about him though.

Chapter 22

Joshua

Well, tonight sure as shit hadn't turned out how I expected it. At all. First, Izzy had turned all dominant and bossy and ordered my food for me. I don't think I'd ever been so turned on in my life, which was ridiculous, but her taking control was definitely something I enjoyed. I was used to being the one in charge and having to look after other people all the time. It was nice that I could let her take charge and relax. Well, like I said, it was more than nice.

And don't even get me started on this concert. I know Izzy had said they were 'pop-rock' but I was not expecting this. The arena was rammed with people, mostly grungers, and although near enough everyone had seats, no one was sitting down. Everyone was on their feet cheering, head-banging or dancing, even the ones way above us up high in the stands. Our seats were brilliant too; the first row of seats that wrapped around the edge of the arena, slightly to the right of the stage.

"What do you think? Do you like them?" Izzy shouted across at me, moving her body in rhythm to the music whilst shouting the lyrics towards the stage. She looked a little sweaty and for the second time tonight, I found myself extremely turned on. She was shaking her head from side to side, her hair whipping across her face as the band played a song called *If Today Was Your Last Day*.

"Actually, yeah! I really like the music," I shouted back, and I meant it too. The songs were relatable and catchy, and more than once I found myself singing along to a chorus or two. The energy in the hall was exhilarating and I had never felt so carefree before. I felt like a regular teenager for a change.

As the hours ticked by and the music flowed, I felt myself letting go more and more. With every fast tempo song, I found myself jumping around right alongside Izzy and laughing with her. And with every softer, gut-wrenching tune, I would get lost in the lyrics and really listen to the words. I was surprised by how much I was enjoying myself.

"OK everyone, this is our last one now…" The lead singer shouted to the crowd and I laughed as a bunch of people booed. "Thank you, London, you've been awesome. This is my all-time favourite one of ours, just for you!" He started to strum a melody on his guitar and the whole place fell silent, immersing themselves in the music. The song was called *Savin' Me.*

I felt my arms break out in goose bumps as the lead guy turned and sang directly *to me*, which I know sounds absurd, but that's what it felt like. It was as if they'd written the song about my life and I shivered as the words coursed through me. By the time they neared the end of the song, I was lost.

The arena erupted into cheers and screams but I couldn't move, I was completely paralysed. I felt embarrassed and stupid at how much the words had spoken to me, but suddenly, for the first time in a long time, I felt hopeful. Maybe I really could come out the other side of this shitty life and make a new one, a better one. One that was free of my shithead father and one where I could afford to keep Ryan and Georgie well-fed and dressed. I felt Izzy's hand wrap around my wrist, squeezing. I looked up at her and she wore a serious expression.

"You are," she leaned in and shouted in my ear over the noise. I pulled back, frowning, not understanding.

"You are worth saving."

~

Izzy was babbling excitedly at me on the train, recounting her favourite parts of the show. The train was over-crowded, so we were standing up near a set of exit doors, squashed right into the corner. Her chest was inches away from mine, with her face tipped up towards me as she spoke a million miles an hour. I don't think I'd managed to say a word since we left, but I was grateful, needing the time to process through my emotions in my head. I had a twist of sadness, hope, lust and maybe something more swirling through my stomach. I was reeling from both the music and what Izzy had said to me. I was confident in saying that Izzy and I were friends, and as much as I promised myself that I would keep her at arm's length, I knew I wouldn't be able to keep that promise. After tonight, I was 100% sure that I did not want to be friends anymore. I craved more.

The train arrived at our stop and we fell off the train, squeezed out by the mob of people behind us. It was pummelling with rain and we ran over to a parked car that Izzy pointed out, her holding her jacket above her head with one arm.

"Hey you two, how was it? Josh, didn't you take a jacket? You're soaked already! Did you have fun?" Sammy prattled off as we climbed in, not giving me a chance to answer.

"It was so awesome, Mum, thanks so much for the tickets!" Izzy continued to fill her mum in on the details of her favourite parts all over again.

"How were Ryan and Georgie? Did they behave themselves?" I interjected as soon as Izzy took a breath. Ryan had text me half-way through the night saying I'd have to drag Georgie away kicking and screaming when we left tomorrow, which I had taken as a good sign, but I was desperate to know for sure.

"They have been an absolute pleasure, Josh. They both helped clear the table after dinner and then we watched three movies back-to-back. Charlie had to carry little Georgie up to bed, he could barely keep his eyes open, bless him." Sammy's eyes flitted to mine in the rear-view mirror and I saw something flash through them, although I couldn't quite put my finger on what it was. They then crinkled a little at the edges, so I knew she was smiling and I relaxed, pleased that things had gone well.

"You are welcome over ours anytime you like. Anytime at all. *All* of you." Again, there was an undertone of something I couldn't quite make out in her voice. We pulled up back at the house around 1 a.m. and all the lights were off. Sammy opened the door quietly, ushering us inside. We followed her up the stairs and she pointed at a closed door.

"Your brothers are in the guest room," she whispered and I nodded. "My office is up those stairs and I have made up the sofa bed for you." She nodded her head at a narrow, spiral staircase ascending to another floor.

"Night sweetie, glad you had a good time." Sammy embraced Izzy, kissing her on the cheek. "It was great to meet you, Josh. I'm glad Izzy has a friend like you." To my complete horror, Sammy hugged me and kissed me on the cheek too. She pulled back, pausing to look me in the eyes and squeeze my shoulders, before turning around and entering a different room. The door closed softly with a click behind her.

"Sorry. She can be quite full-on sometimes. Always wants to be friends with my friends," Izzy chuckled in a whisper. I didn't know how to respond. I felt completely taken aback by Izzy and Sammy and this whole bloody night. I padded silently over to the spiral staircase, unsure how I felt about sleeping in a different room to

Ryan and Georgie.

"Josh, are you OK? You've been quiet since we left. I didn't mean to upset you. With what I said at the end of the concert, I mean." She wouldn't look me in the eyes and I felt terrible for making her feel bad.

"You didn't make me feel bad, Iz. I'm just a little...overwhelmed..." I didn't know how to voice the tumultuous feelings pulsing through me. Izzy nodded, looking a little disappointed, turning away from me.

She opened yet another door and started moving through the doorway.

"Iz...wait. I, er..." Shit. What should I say? I was holding so much back from her, but I wanted her to know that I did care. I *really* cared. I stepped towards her, shrinking the distance between us until we were as close as we were back on the train. I lifted my hand, my thumb grazing her cheek as I lowered my head. I gently pressed my lips to hers and watched as her eyes fluttered closed. Our first kiss had been intense, a bit flustered, and very erotic. This was completely different. I wanted to show that she meant something to me.

My right hand was still caressing her cheek and I let my left hand trail down her arm until I found her fingers. I tangled my fingers through hers, squeezing them as she parted her lips and I let my tongue tenderly explore. I moved slowly, real slow, trying to put into the kiss exactly how grateful I was to her. How much I needed her in my life right now. How much she was brightening my dark world. Without warning, some of the lyrics from Nickelback's last song floated into my mind, causing waves of hope and despair to crash into me at once.

I pulled away, avoiding eye contact as I fled up the staircase, embarrassed by the tear that had escaped and slid down my cheek whilst kissing her.

Chapter 23

Isabel

I knocked gently on the bedroom door, being quiet so as not to wake Josh upstairs. I had spent most of the night replaying our kiss over and over again, but couldn't understand why he had pulled away so suddenly. He was the one that had initiated the kiss, but then he'd abruptly run away, without so much as even a 'goodnight.' He confused me and I was planning on avoiding him all morning until he left. Maybe he'd sleep right through breakfast and then I could escape to Jess or Sophie's before he even woke up.

"Ryan? Georgie? Dad's making breakfast if you'd like to come down…" I called softly, easing the door open a little.

"Mmmm…huh?" someone groaned, and I pushed the door open a little wider.

"Breakfast is…" I trailed off as the door thudded into something. I frowned, squeezing my head through the gap and peering into the room. Josh was laying on the floor next to the double bed where his brothers were sleeping, a quilt wrapped around him. He rubbed the sleep from his eyes and the quilt slipped, revealing his muscular shoulders and chest. I'd seen him shirtless before but there was something about him lying in bed that made me blush. Well, laying on some form of a bed on the floor.

"Why are you on the floor?" I whispered, careful not to wake his brothers.

"Er…" he shook his head, sitting up a little. "I, er…" He clearly didn't want to answer.

"Dad's making breakfast. If you're hungry." I retreated from the room, pulling the door shut silently. So much for avoiding Josh all morning.

I padded downstairs, tiptoeing into the kitchen and helping Mum lay the table.

"They coming down?" Mum asked as she lined the middle of the table with place mats.

"I'd be willing to bet a million pounds that they are coming down. I've never seen kids pack away so much food so quickly! They definitely won't miss this," Dad laughed as he flipped some bacon over in a pan. We'd already delayed breakfast as late as possible; the Bugg boys obviously weren't early risers. Fifteen minutes later and a herd of elephants came crashing down the stairs.

"We didn't miss breakfast, did we?" Georgie called as he skidded into the room breathlessly.

"Nope. I was just about to dish up. Take a seat, boys," Dad gestured to the table with the spatula he had in his hand.

Georgie and Ryan eagerly sat at the table, waiting for the food to come out.

"Morning," Josh greeted warmly as he entered the room. I was pouring pineapple juice into Georgie and Ryan's glasses, my back purposely towards Josh as I concentrated too intently on the task at hand. But a moment later he came into view, taking the juice from me and kissing me on the cheek.

"Morning Sunshine," he smiled as he put the juice back in the fridge for me. *Morning Sunshine?* And a kiss? Well, I wasn't expecting that after last night. I glanced at Mum and Dad by the oven and they were both pretending to be very busy, dutifully not looking in our direction as my face went bright red.

"Do you need a hand bringing anything to the table?" Josh asked them.

"No thanks, honey. You go ahead and sit down. You too, Izzy," Mum nodded at the table. I sat opposite Georgie and Josh slotted next to me.

"Be careful, the plates have been in the oven," Dad announced as he placed them down on the table in front of everyone.

"These are hot too," Mum said as she started piling food up in the middle of the table. They'd gone completely overboard, with a mountain of bacon, sausages, mushrooms, fried tomatoes and scrambled egg. There was even some black pudding and hash browns.

"Bon appetit!" Dad sang as he and Mum sat down. After a few mouthfuls, I noticed that neither Josh nor his brothers were eating. I paused, watching as Ryan and Josh stared at Georgie.

"Everything OK, Georgie?" Mum leaned over to him. She was sitting between Georgie and I at the head of the table.

"There's just..." Georgie's bottom lip quivered and his eyes filled with tears.

"Georgie..." Josh uttered a warning with a slight shake of his head.

"It's OK honey, you can tell us," Mum smiled encouragingly at him. The whole table fell silent.

"There's so much food," he whispered. "You have so much food. I bet you don't ever go hungry." How does anyone respond to that? Josh groaned and dropped his head into his hands, avoiding looking at anyone.

"Well, I hope you're going to help us with this lot. Charlie did a little too much, as always." Mum started ladling food onto Georgie's plate until every inch was filled with food, but I saw the sadness in her eyes. I had to turn away as my eyes went a little blurry too, but when I turned back, Georgie was cramming food into his mouth and was back to his usual smiley self. Ryan was also stuffing his face, but Josh hadn't moved, his head still bowed. I reached under the table and squeezed his hand, winking at him when he looked up. He still didn't move, so I copied Mum and started piling food onto his plate. I nudged it towards him and it seemed to kick-start him into action as he picked up his cutlery.

"Thank you," he whispered, squeezing my knee before tucking into breakfast.

"So, you boys have any plans today?" Dad asked between mouthfuls and I immediately became suspicious as Mum ducked her head, avoiding me.

"Nope. We'll just head on home once we've helped clean up," Josh replied and I saw Georgie's shoulders droop.

"Well, Sammy and I were thinking of taking Izzy to the cinema, as a final birthday treat. Did you want to join us?" Neither of them were looking at me now and I could tell it was because they hadn't asked me if I was OK with this. They needn't have worried though. I was delighted at the idea of spending more time with Josh and his brothers.

"Hell yeah!" Ryan exclaimed but Josh shuffled in his seat, kicking Ryan in the knee judging by Ryan's quiet 'ow' and rubbing of his leg.

"Great! Georgie was telling us all about how he loves the Marvel films and Izzy and I have been desperate to see the new Avengers film *Endgame*. Have you all seen the previous ones?" When Dad finally glanced at me, I smiled at him to show I really was OK with this and he relaxed in his chair. Mum too.

"Oh yeah! We love those. Josh always gets them on DVD as soon as they appear in the charity shop near home," Georgie twittered excitedly, whilst Josh choked on the mouthful of eggs he was chewing. Josh looked as if he was growing more and more uncomfortable as the minutes ticked by, but I wanted to show him that he could be himself around us. He and his brothers could trust us with anything. I'd spend today proving that to them all and once again, I was grateful for having such nurturing, intuitive parents.

~

"Hey honey, did you have a good day today? You didn't mind your dad and I meddling a little did you? We got the impression that the boys didn't get out much, so your dad and I thought it might be nice if they joined us." Mum poked her head around my bedroom door. I was sprawled out on the bed with the biggest grin on my face. I'd had a fantastic day. We hadn't bothered looking up the film times so when we'd arrived at the cinema, we'd had an hour to kill before the next showing with any free seats. We'd ended up going bowling and although Josh offered to pay at every opportunity, you could see he was relieved every time my dad rejected the offer. After a while, he seemed to loosen up and let his guard down. I had taken a ton of photos and selfies, trying to capture the way Georgie crumpled over when he laughed too hard or how Ryan pursed his lips after he said something sarcastic. Mum had also taken some snaps; the pair of us were obsessed with taking photos at every available opportunity.

"I have had such a good weekend, Mum, honestly. Thank you so much." I gave her a squeeze as she sat down beside me.

"Good." She smiled but hesitated, not getting up to leave.

"Everything OK?" I asked.

"Um, yes darling. But I want to talk to you about Josh." I swear, if she was going to give me the awkward sex conversation again, I was going to *die*. "Well, about his brothers. And his situation." OK, not sure where this is going.

"The night you and Josh went to the O2, Ryan asked if he could use our shower after dinner and of course I said yes. He must have left his clothes in the guestroom, as he came out of the bathroom with only a towel around his waist."

"O-kaaayy," I frowned, completely bewildered.

"Well...I noticed some marks..." Mum fidgeted on the spot, taking her time before she continued. "Bruises. And some scars. Along his ribs and back." I felt the air leave my lungs. "And they are all so skinny. You heard what Georgie said at breakfast and whenever we offered them food, they ate as if it would be their last meal. What's going on Izzy? Is everything OK at home for them?" My mum looked at me so earnestly that horrifyingly, I felt myself well up a little.

"Erm, they live over on the Black Cross estate. They don't seem to have much money." It was a pathetic response, but I didn't know what to say. Josh was so proud and secretive and that I knew he wouldn't want me to say too much. Not that I really knew much anyway.

"And what about their parents?" Mum prodded.

"Their er, mum, isn't around anymore and their dad works long shifts at the pharmaceutical factory. That's all I know."

"And is Ryan getting bullied at school or something?

Is someone hurting him?" I frowned, unsure how to answer.

"Josh kind of has a reputation for fighting outside of school." It was a terrible idea to tell Mum this kind of thing, she'd only worry and I didn't want her to think any less of Josh and his family, but I knew she'd never let it go. "And Ryan was suspended a few weeks ago for fighting at school."

"Hmmmm." Mum scrunched her nose as she thought about what I'd said.

"But you saw how protective Josh is of his brothers. I'm sure he's handling it." I hadn't given much thought to Josh's circumstances lately. I was so concerned with trying to befriend him and maybe persuade him into something more than friendship, that I had pushed the niggling questions at the back of my mind aside. I felt shame wash over me. I should have asked him more questions and probed harder about his life, instead of shying away from it.

"The way he first looked at Daddy when he met him made me think that...never mind...it sounds like it's just typical teenage tempers getting the best of them," Mum shrugged. I promised myself that I'd ask Josh about Ryan's bruises and that I'd try harder to find out more about his family life.

Chapter 24

Joshua

That had been one of the best weekends we'd had in a long time. Maybe even ever. I hadn't seen Georgie or Ryan laugh so much or be as relaxed as they were around the Johnsons. And we had all eaten so much that we jokingly complained of stomach aches Sunday night. I felt so full I could have exploded and I hadn't spent a penny all weekend. I'd been so fucking relieved when Charlie wouldn't take any money off me. If he had, we'd literally be in the dark with only dry bread to eat for the rest of the month.

"Hey Sunshine, how's your day so far?" It was strange that Izzy wasn't sitting in the common room at lunch with the rest of her friends, but she'd text me to ask if we could meet in the library instead. I was secretly pleased we got to have some more alone time together.

Ollie and I had gradually fallen into the routine of sitting with Izzy and her mates at lunch, Ollie doing everything possible to impress Jess (who barely batted an eyelid at him) and me pretty much exclusively talking only to Izzy. But it was nice to be included for a change.

"Hey. Yeah good, although I have a ton of coursework to catch up on for biology. Didn't get much done over the weekend," she laughed as we sat at the back table again. She blushed when I called her Sunshine, same as she did the first time I did it, but it just felt natural now. It was as if I'd had a eureka moment and knew that she *had* to be a part of my life, spreading her warm glow through me, like a fire would thaw frozen fingers in winter.

"So, what did you want to talk about?" I leaned a little closer to her, hoping she was going to make the first move and ask about us being more than friends. Or even hinting at something like it. I was sure she was feeling this connection as much as me, but it wouldn't hurt to be 100% positive before I did something like make a fool of myself. Especially when it was a terrible idea anyway.

"Umm...my mum and dad really liked spending time with your brothers..." she started. Right. Not exactly how I thought this would go but OK...

"Ryan, er, used the shower at ours."

"Yeah, I know. He wouldn't stop raving about it afterwards, about how powerful it was. I'm sorry if he used all the hot water?" I offered, wondering if Sammy had complained, or something. Although it was hard to imagine her complaining about anything.

"No, no. He didn't. But after, when he was finished, he came out of the room with only a towel around his waist and um…" Where the fuck was this going? I had a terrible feeling settling in the pit of my stomach.

"Mum said she saw some marks. Some er, bruises. And she was concerned that…"

"Where?!" The rage was clawing its way to the surface again and I could feel control slipping away from me.

"Where? Where, what?" Izzy's brow furrowed in confusion.

"Where. Were. The. Bruises. On. Him?" I gritted my teeth.

"She said there were some over his ribs and some cuts or scars on his back." I stood up, the chair crashing over behind me, the noise echoing through the calm library. The librarian looked over and frowned as some other students at nearby tables turned to look at us.

"Josh! What…"

"I need to go." I turned on my heels and fled the library. If this was a scene in one of Georgie's superhero movies, I'd be turning green and shredding my clothes right about now. Very rarely had I sought Ryan out at school, knowing it was better for him if he didn't have his older brother hanging out with him in front of his friends, but today was different. I wanted answers and I wanted them now.

I stormed over to one of the playgrounds that the younger kids usually frequented and frantically checked my surroundings. There were groups of kids everywhere, but I couldn't see Ryan at all. I was about to swivel and try somewhere else when I saw a group huddled in the very back corner, as far away from the supervising teachers as possible. I was pretty sure I caught a glimpse of Ryan amongst them so I headed over, using every ounce of my self-control to not run over there and throw him over my shoulder.

"RYAN!" I shouted at the group and they parted, turning towards me. Ryan was in the centre, a cigarette hanging from his lips. As soon as he saw me it fell from his mouth, hitting the floor and rolling away. I lurched forward, grabbed him by his collar and hauled him away.

"Josh, stop…" I dragged him as far away as possible until we came around the back of the art building. It wasn't exactly private, but it was as secluded as we were going to get.

"When?" I demanded.

"That was the first time I tried one, I swear!"

"I'm not talking about the cigarette, dick. And don't fucking lie to me about that, you looked well too natural for that to have been the first time, but we'll get back to that later. When. Did. He. Start. Hitting. You?" The colour drained from Ryan's face and I could see a slight tremor shoot through his body.

"I don't know what you mean…"

"DON'T FUCKING LIE TO ME! Sammy saw you get out the shower. She saw the bruises. Izzy just fucking told me. I don't know what has fucked me off more; the fact that Big Mike has been using you as a punching bag and you didn't tell me, or the fact that you thought it was clever to parade around your battle scars in front of

Izzy's mum!"

"I didn't...I wouldn't have..."

"WHEN DID IT FUCKING START?" I was panting and bouncing on my feet in a frenzy of violent, barely controllable fury.

"About a year ago," he muttered. Immediately all the anger drained away and I staggered back, as if he had punched me himself.

"A year ago?" I whispered in disbelief and he nodded.

"Why didn't you...you didn't say anything? I would have..."

"I know you would have. But you fight with him all the time and most of the time you hardly come out of it alive. I can handle it. It's not so bad." Tears filled his eyes and one by one, they trickled down his face. I grabbed him in a fierce hug, burying his head in my chest.

"I'm sorry. I'm so sorry, so sorry Ryan. I should have known. I should have done more." My voice cracked as I desperately tried to keep it together in front of him. An even more horrifying thought occurred to me.

"Has he been hitting Georgie?" I choked the words out and had to smother a wail when he didn't answer straight away. His silence spoke a thousand words.

"When he comes back, and he *will* come back, I'm going to kill him. I will fucking kill him." Ryan was sobbing quietly into me, his tears soaking right through my shirt, and every whimper felt like a knife to the heart.

"I promise, I'm not going to let him touch you again. He won't ever hurt you or Georgie again, I promise." He nodded into my shirt and I pulled him back so I could look at him. I hunched over, getting down to his level.

"I'm sorry I shouted at you. None of this is your fault, OK? It's my fault. I'm a shitty brother. But I'm going to fix this, OK? I'm going to fix it. Go get cleaned up and go back to your friends. I'll meet you after school as usual." He nodded, wiping his face on the back of his hands before turning away and disappearing around the corner of the building. As soon as he disappeared from sight, I collapsed to the floor and lost it. I completely lost it. I was crying so hard I couldn't breathe. I was gasping for air, but I was drowning. Drowning in shame and fear, and more shame.

"Josh! Shhh, Josh. I got you." Out of the blue, Izzy was next to me, sitting on the dirty ground beside me and grabbing my face between her hands, turning me to face her.

"Deep breaths. Calm down. You need to breathe, Josh, breathe. Come on, copy me." She took long, slow breaths in and then released them equally as slow, looking me in the eye the entire time. She repeated it over and over until gradually, I began to mimic her, my breathing slowing to a more manageable rate. But I couldn't stop the tears. I didn't feel the embarrassment that should have come with crying in front of a girl, in front of Izzy. I was too consumed with failure. She pulled my head to her shoulder, cradling me whilst I sobbed my heart out. Little Georgie, my poor little Georgie…

I don't know how long we sat like that for, but eventually I became aware of her fingers running through my hair, making soothing little circles at the base of my head. My tears slowed until they dried up all together and we sat there in silence. A bell rang in the distance but neither of us made a move to leave. It was freezing out here and I could see Izzy shaking a little with the cold, but she didn't say anything. My thread-bare jacket wasn't doing much to keep the November icy wind at bay either, but I deserved the discomfort. Hell, I deserved a fucking lot more than just discomfort. I deserved pain.

"I don't know who Big Mike is, but we will make him stop. I don't care what we have to do, we will make him stop," Izzy declared, a ferocious edge in her voice that briefly made my heart soar in affection. But all the fight had left me. I was broken, completely broken.

"He's our dad…" I confessed softly.

"What?! Big Mike is your dad?" she pulled me away from her shoulder until we were at the same eye level again. I didn't react. I couldn't believe I'd told her. Ollie was the only person other than my brothers that knew what was happening at home. Although apparently, I didn't have a fucking clue what was going on at home either, if he'd been battering them for over a year. A fucking year! New teardrops formed at the thought and they streamed down my face, trickling off of my jaw and splashing onto my chest.

"Oh Josh. You should've told me. We need to tell the police or…"

"NO! No! No, Izzy. They'll take them away from me. I can't lose them. They are all I have!" It was getting tough to breathe again.

"OK, OK, OK. Josh, calm down. No one is taking anyone away."

"No, you don't understand. I'm not eighteen yet. Social Services will come and take Ryan and Georgie and put them in a foster home. And I'm not having them get molested. They need to stay with me. We need to stay together."

"But…"

"He's gone. He's gone, Izzy. He hasn't come back home for almost two weeks now, since I broke his nose."

"You broke his…"

"Yes. And he hasn't come back since. Maybe he never will." My mind flicked back to the night in question and our argument came flooding back to me: *Fuck off. You are never touching them! Not whilst I am here!*

You're fucking clueless as well as worthless. A fucking moron. No wonder your mother left you here to rot. Fuck! He was fucking hinting at it and I didn't even pick up on it.

"We should still tell someone. You don't honesty think he's not going to come home for the next *year*, do you? Come on!"

"Izzy. Please. *Please.* I'm begging you. I know it doesn't sound likely, but what if he really doesn't come back and we tell someone, and the boys get taken away from me and it's all for nothing? Hmm?" I could see the gears turning in her mind as she mulled it over.

"Please. I promise I will tell you if he comes back and if he does, we will go straight to the police station, yeah? OK? Just give me a chance." I was desperate for her to agree. She had to agree. I couldn't risk losing them, I couldn't. She nodded and I almost passed out from relief.

"But you better bloody well tell me Josh, I mean it. No more secrets. I'm dead serious, Josh." She had that look on her face like when she pushed me off Tom; almost murderous.

"Yes, Sunshine. I promise."

Chapter 25

Isabel

For the second time since I had gotten home, I was staring into the bottom of the toilet bowl after retching and vomiting. How could a *parent* want to hurt their own child? Their own flesh and blood? It was unfathomable.

I thought back to the time I had walked Georgie home and Josh had collapsed on me. It had been his father that had done that to him! His father had literally beaten him to a pulp so that he couldn't even stand up.

Everything started clicking into place; the excessive amount of locks on the bedroom door, the broken beer bottles in the other bedroom, the poor living conditions and lack of food. It was all screaming abuse and I had completely missed it. I thought it was a loan shark, for Christ's sake! Josh was my friend and yet if I hadn't followed him out the library, I would never have overheard his conversation and would still be none the wiser. I'd still be avoiding asking him about his life for fear of a difficult conversation. God, I am pathetic. And bloody useless. And I agreed to keep his secret. That was the worst part. It didn't feel right to not talk to Mum at least, she'd know what to do, but I was still haunted by the sheer terror in his eyes at the thought of Ryan and Georgie being taken away. I'd never forgive myself if I was the reason that his family was torn apart. No, for now, I'd keep quiet, but as soon as that monster showed up, I was calling the police myself.

"Love, are you OK?" Mum knocked on the bathroom door.

"Yeah! Just one of those twenty-four-hour hour stomach bugs, I think," I lied.

"I'll go grab you some water." For some reason, this set me off again, tears running uncontrollably down my cheeks. My mum was getting me a glass of water to help me feel better, whereas Josh's dad was AWOL, nowhere to be found, and that was a *good* thing.

My phone started vibrating in my pocket and Josh's name flashed on the screen. I immediately willed myself to calm down. He needed me to be strong for him.

"Hello?" I answered, sounding far calmer than I felt.

"Hey. What you up to?" Josh also sounded normal. I'd begged him to come back to ours again tonight, but he'd refused, saying he needed time alone with his brothers.

"Just, er, chilling in my room. Everything OK?"

"Yeah. No. I mean, yes, but I need a favour."

"Anything. What do you need?" I sat up straighter, ready to pounce into action.

"I can't leave Ryan and Georgie at home on their own anymore. In case he comes back and I'm not there. I'm going to swap my shifts around at work, so I only work weekends and Ollie is going to look after them on Saturdays, but is there, er, any way on Sundays that maybe…"

"Yep. Not a problem. They are welcome over anytime." There was silence at the end of the phone. "Josh? You still there?"

"Yeah, sorry. Thank you. That means a lot, Izzy. I hate to ask but I can't risk…" he sounded a little hoarse.

"Hey. It's absolutely fine, I promise."

"Will your parents mind? Will they start asking questions?"

"No, they won't mind, but yes, they'll ask why. I'll just say…that you didn't know about Ryan's bruises and that he's been getting into fights at school. Erm, you and your Dad work the same shift on Sundays, so you need someone to make sure Ryan doesn't get into trouble?" It would be a miracle if Mum and Dad fell for that, but I needed to tell them something.

"OK. Fingers crossed they believe it," he voiced my thoughts aloud.

"Isn't that a bit much for you now, though? Working all weekend? You won't get a day off."

"I'll actually be doing less hours, and I don't even know how we'll make that work, but I'll be fine."

"Josh, are you sure we shouldn't talk to someone about this? You shouldn't have to work so much to support your family and…"

"Izzy. No. We aren't telling anyone. You promised, remember? I'm trusting you not to tell anyone." Guilt and shame settled in my stomach, raising another round of nausea that I fought to keep at bay.

"OK…" I whispered.

"Thank you. For everything, Izzy. I'm sorry I was such a mess today. It was just a shock. But we have a plan now, and I have you. You're my sunshine in this shitty life right now." My eyes welled up and my throat turned dry, making it difficult to speak.

"I'm always here for you, Josh," I croaked. "And for your brothers too." I hung up, not trusting myself to not break down on the phone with him. He needed me to be the strong one, to be his rock and his shoulder to cry on. Not the other way around.

"Here's your water. Can I come in?" Mum called softly through the door. Shit, how long had she been standing out there? How much had she heard? I replayed our conversation in my head. There wasn't anything too incriminating she'd have heard from only my end of the conversation. I took a deep breath, roughly wiped my face and unlocked the door.

"Oh honey, you look terrible."

"Thanks Mum," I grumbled, taking large gulps of water. She sat cross-legged on the tiled floor opposite me, peering at me in concern.

"Are you sure it's a bug? There's nothing else going on? Sounded like you were having a pretty serious conversation with Josh?" I hated lying to her, but I repeated the story I'd come up with.

"Oh, it was nothing. Well, except Josh's dad's shifts have changed at work and he now has to work Sundays. But Josh already works Sundays and his manager won't let him swap. And Josh asked if we'd mind having Ryan and Georgie over on Sundays. So Ryan doesn't get into any more trouble and Georgie isn't on his own…" I was rambling, my lie building more and more as I struggled to make my excuse sound good enough.

"Of course. No problem. What are they doing on Saturdays? Do they need to come over then too?" It was times like this that I really loved my mum. She was always wanting to help others, no matter the cost. Dad always joked that it was a miracle we had a roof over our heads with the amount of money she donated to charity.

"They're with another friend on Saturdays."

"Well, they are welcome over anytime. They are lovely boys who have clearly been dealt a bit of a rough hand in life. Did you find out what happened to Ryan?" I gulped before answering.

"Yeah, it was just fighting at school, like I told you. That's why Josh doesn't want to leave him on his own at the weekend, in case he gets into trouble." I avoided her eyes like the plague, knowing she'd see right through me. She nodded.

"But you need to promise me that you'll tell me if something else happens, Isabel, OK? If Ryan's getting bullied or fighting too much or, anything, promise me you'll tell me?" I nodded, feeling like a fraud. "Good. We'll help in any way we can. Especially if their own parents aren't around much. Georgie is such a sweetie.

They all are." She smiled at me through her concern.

"I'm worried. About Josh," I blurted out. Mainly to distract myself from the nausea that was back again. "He's working so many hours at the weekend just to pay the bills and…"

"What's his father doing? Why is Josh paying bills? I thought you said his dad worked long shifts?" Mum interrupted, a deep frown splitting her forehead.

"He does. He's hardly ever home! But it's not enough to cover all the bills and food and stuff. So Josh works to make up the difference." All these lies were leaving a terribly sour taste in my mouth.

"Hmmm…" she stared at me as if she could read my mind and I looked away again, not wanting to cave and blurt it all out and betray Josh's trust.

"Leave it with me. I'll see what I can do." I was worried what that meant but I couldn't carry all this on my own. It was exhausting. I needed someone to help me at least a little bit too.

Chapter 26

Joshua

I can quite comfortably say that this week has been the worst of my life. I couldn't think about my meltdown in front of Izzy; the shame and embarrassment were too overwhelming. It was like I was treading water with weights attached to my feet and there were almost too many for me to stay afloat. My chin was above the water and every time my mind started wandering back to that day, the water would slap at my face, threatening to drown me. And if I thought back to the conversation I'd had with my brothers later that night, it was like someone had a death grip around my lungs, squeezing and forcing every inch of air out of me.

We hadn't actually spoken many words. It was more like a cruel, sick, twisted version of show and tell. They showed me their scars and bruises and I forced myself to listen to exactly how they got each one. *Punched. Kicked. Back handed. Whipped.*

One small mercy was that Georgie didn't have many. The downside to that was that it was because Ryan had taken it all. I had to run to the bathroom and throw up repeatedly when he showed me his back. Sammy hadn't even seen the half of it. The belt marks across the backs of his legs were the worst. It reminded me of the scene in The Da Vinci Code where Silas uses self-flagellation and you see the horrendous wounds he inflicts on himself. Except in Ryan's case, he was an unwilling participant.

It turns out that Big Mike was getting home from work a lot earlier than I thought. He'd get back around 6 p.m., take out his frustrations on my little brothers, then go back out to get drunk or high, or whatever the hell else he was doing. I'd get home from work after 9 p.m. and be none-the-wiser, relieved that he hadn't yet returned from work. What a fucking idiot.

Well, it sure as shit wasn't happening again. I've switched my shifts at work so that I only work weekends, meaning I can be damn sure nothing happens to either of them after school. Ollie said that his mum had finally started going over to Detective Dipshit's house (his words, not mine), so he wasn't hanging around his as much. Georgie and Ryan could chill out over his. They'd have the house to themselves anyway, as he worked at an insurance company on Saturdays. It was only answering the phone and putting invoices together or something, but it would look good on his CV apparently (cue eye roll). Izzy's parents had kindly agreed to have them over on Sundays, which I knew they were both secretly very happy about. Well, it was no secret with Georgie. He'd squealed in delight when I told him. I was concerned that Sammy or Charlie would start asking questions, but I had no other choice right now. I had to keep my brothers safe.

Part of me prayed that Big Mike *would* return. It had been over three weeks now and still no sign of him. I wanted him to walk through that door so I could beat the living shit out of him. I wanted it so bad I could taste it. He needed to pay. Deep down I knew I'd kill him if I saw him again, but who gives a fuck? He deserved to die. And I deserved to be punished for failing Georgie and Ryan in the first place. Win-win.

"Josh! Someone's at the door!" Georgie called from downstairs. I'd only gone upstairs to change into something more comfortable, but had ended up laying on my bed and staring up at the ceiling for God knows how long.

"Coming!" I tried to shake the failure and despair off me (yeah right, nice try) and plastered a neutral expression on my face. When I entered the kitchen, Ryan was heating some beans in the microwave and buttering toast. Not exactly an exotic dinner, but it was filling nonetheless. And cheap. I still haven't quite figured out how I'm going to make our money stretch even further on my reduced hours. I was avoiding thinking about it altogether, if I'm honest.

For the millionth time, I wished that we had a peep hole installed. My damn anxiety went through the roof every time I approached the door, fearful of who was on the other side. Yep, I know, pathetic.

"Mr Joshua Bugg?" There was a guy holding a piece of paper in a navy uniform, with the local supermarket name embroidered across his chest. I could see a large truck parked behind him at the side of the road, hazard lights flashing.

"Er, yeah."

"Great. I'll go grab the shopping," he smiled and darted back to his truck, opening up the back. He returned moments later with a big crate filled with food.

"Shall I take this inside for you or do you want to unpack it here?" he asked after I stared wordlessly at him for a few moments.

"Er...I think there's a mistake. I haven't ordered any shopping."

"Josh!" Ryan hissed from the kitchen. I had briefly contemplated taking the food and not saying anything, but it wasn't right. Not this much food. Ryan clearly didn't agree.

"Oh sorry, I forgot. I had very clear instructions for this delivery. Very unusual you know, for someone to call up and provide specific instructions for what to say, but there ya go. Hang on." He rooted through the pockets of his navy trousers until he located a scrap of paper. He unfolded it carefully, clearing his throat before reading.

"*This delivery has been paid for by Samantha Johnson. You will receive a similar delivery every Friday evening. If you have requests, let Samantha know. No arguments. Just accept the food, Josh.*" He turned the paper around so I could read the words for myself. What the *fuck*?

"But I can't..." The guy held his finger up, interrupting me and quite frankly, pissing me off. He searched his other pocket and pulled out another piece of paper.

"I said no arguments, Josh. You won't stop this. If you want to say thank you, yellow roses are Izzy's favourite." Stunned. I was ab-so-fucking-lutely stunned.

"So, shall I bring this in then?" the guy had the biggest shit-eating grin across his face.

"Hell yeah, bring it in!" Ryan shouted, barging me out of the doorway and gesturing for him to come inside.

"I er, need to go check something..." I made a run for it, dashing up the stairs and not stopping until I'd locked myself in the bathroom. *They don't need you anymore. You can't keep them safe anyway, so why are you bothering? They'd be better off without you. Maybe you should tell someone about what's going on so they can go find a nice family to settle down with instead. They'd be better off. You're a failure. A waste of space.*

I pressed my back to the door, sinking down until I was sitting on the cold, hard floor. I battled to push the negative thoughts away and sent a silent thank you to Izzy and her family. It was awkward, humiliating and mortifying, but I was so bloody grateful for their intervention. Maybe we'd be able to survive a bit longer after all. Maybe I could carry on living.

Chapter 27

Isabel

If you had asked me a year ago if there would ever come a point where I was *desperately* looking forward to walking through the doors of Gilleford Sixth Form each day, I would have laughed in your face. Like, hysterically. But here I was, hopelessly praying for Monday morning to hurry up and arrive. It was like this every weekend now. Sure, I loved hanging out with Ryan and Georgie on a Sunday, it was like having two little brothers of my own, but I wanted to spend more time with Josh too. I was turning into a bit of an obsessive weirdo actually, I thought about him all the time. When I went to bed, first thing in the morning, on the way to school…

I replayed our kisses over and over, wondering if I should have done something differently. OK, so the first kiss didn't really count. And the second one, he ended up running off after, so not great either. But I wanted to try again. Unfortunately, I only ever saw him at school, and I was not one of those students who was comfortable with public displays of affection in front of teachers. Unlike Sophie and Jack, who lately were inseparable and didn't seem to have any problems with PDA at all.

We've fallen into a comfortable routine; he waits for me at the bus stop before school, I walk with him and his brothers to drop Georgie off across the road, and then we walk to classes together. He and Ollie have started sitting with us at all at lunch too, then he walks me back to the bus stop again at the end of the day. I've asked him and his brothers over a few times during the week, but he always refuses, saying he feels like he's taking advantage of my family enough as it is. I'm not sure how he feels about the weekly shopping deliveries from my mum, but he hasn't mentioned them to me, so I haven't brought it up either. I know he's quite a proud person and other than *that* meltdown, I struggle to get him to open up. It was frustrating, to feel like you talk all the time, but you don't actually talk about anything substantial. To be honest, I was feeling like I had been friend-zoned and every day it continued, I felt my heart break a little bit more. But as pathetic as it sounds, I was grateful for any kind of interaction and relationship I could get with him. Even if it was only friendship. He had bigger things on his mind, after all.

"Earth to Izzy! Hello?!" Jess threw a grape at me and it rebounded off, rolling across the common room floor.

We were all in our usual spot in the common room before classes started, but I was struggling to stay focused. Jack and Ed were talking about some kind of football game that had happened over the weekend. Ollie was complaining about his mum's new boyfriend as Josh rolled his eyes, whilst Jess and Sophie nattered away. I was floating in and out of the conversations, wrapped up in my own thoughts.

"Sorry! What did you say?"

"I said, what are you doing for Christmas? At home or...?"

"Yeah, we usually spend every year at home, you know how amazing my dad's cooking is. I'm sure Nanny Steph will join us as usual too. Not sure what my uncle and his wife are doing, but we haven't seen them much lately, so probably just the four of us."

"What about you, Josh?" Sophie leaned forward so she could see him.

"Just me and my brothers as usual."

"What, no other family? What about your dad?" Josh shifted in his seat uncomfortably, his eyes flicking to me as he realised his mistake.

"Well Big...Dad...has to er, work Christmas Day. He gets triple pay, so..." he shrugged.

"You should spend it with us." *What?* Did I say that out loud? Josh tilted his head, a small smile playing on his lips as he watched me turn the brightest shade of red. Everyone else swivelled to stare at me.

"I mean, your brothers are practically family now anyway." Shit, that was the wrong thing to say judging by how Josh's face fell.

"I mean, er, you should all come over for Christmas Day and you shouldn't worry about it being weird because they're over all the time anyway." Josh's eyes grew wide, shifting to the rest of the group.

"Well, not all the time, I exaggerated…" God, this was a train wreck. I hadn't filled my friends in on the fact that Josh's brothers were over every Sunday, although I didn't go out of my way to hide it either. This was the first time either of us had acknowledged it out loud in front of other people.

"Forget it…" I muttered, avoiding eye contact with anyone.

"He'd love to, wouldn't you, Joshy?" Ollie slapped him on the back, his face cracking into a big grin. Josh frowned, not answering. Well, I felt like a complete moron. If Josh had ever thought of me as more than a friend before, he definitely did not now. He'd rather spend Christmas on his own with his brothers in his crappy little house than with me. Ouch.

"I'm going to pop to the library before class." I stood up, slinging my bag over my shoulder and making a hasty exit as my eyes blurred a little.

"Izzy!" Sophie called after me, but I hurried my footsteps, fraught with the need to escape. I ran into the main building and had the library in my sights, when I felt a hand grab my arm and spin me around.

"Did you mean it? You want us to come over yours for Christmas? You weren't just saying that?" Josh's eyes searched mine.

"Unlike you, I communicate my intentions clearly. So yes, I meant it. But if you don't want to, don't. It's no big deal." I tried to turn away, but his grip tightened, whirling me back to face him.

"What do you mean by that? We talk all the time…" he raised his eyebrows.

"Yes, we do, but about nothing important. I've seen you when you've been at your worst, Josh! I've seen the bruises and vomit and I know your secret. But none of that was *your* choice. If I hadn't walked Georgie home, I would never have seen you in such a state and you probably would never have had a reason to talk to me in the first place. If I hadn't followed you out the library that day, I would never have learned the truth. You don't *tell* me anything." The tears were threatening to over-spill. "And you kissed me. *Twice.* But if that didn't mean anything to you, then say so right now, so I can get over it and pretend nothing ever happened."

"Sunshine, I…"

"No! Do *not* call me that." This time I wrenched myself free and spun on my heels, fleeing to the girl's bathroom down the hall instead. He didn't try to follow.

~

Not feeling particularly enthusiastic about my education, I left school straight after lunch. I text Mum saying I wasn't feeling well, stomach cramps, and was home. If I had any more stomach issues, no doubt she'd book me in to see a gastroenterologist or something. I was going to have to come up with better excuses. Stupid boys. Stupid *Josh.*

I skipped dinner, preferring to stay upstairs with my

headphones on, blasting Bring Me the Horizon's latest album as loud as possible. Yeah, I could definitely relate to *Avalanche* right now. Movement in the corner of my eye caught my attention and I pulled my headphones down.

"Honey, there's someone downstairs for you," Mum popped her head around my door.

"Who is it? I'm not in the mood, to be honest."

"Josh." Great.

"I don't fancy talking to…"

"You should go down there. I already let him in." She grinned at me and then bounced out the door. Typical. I huffed, taking my frustration out on the stairs as I descended (OK, so you *could* describe it as stomping ungracefully down the stairs). Josh wasn't immediately by the door, so I headed to the living room, stopping in my tracks when I caught sight of him. He was holding the biggest bunch of yellow roses.

"I'm sorry," he rushed as soon as he saw me. His gaze shifted to the kitchen where Mum and Dad were standing with their backs to us, sipping tea and looking pointedly out of the window in front of them.

"I'm sorry I er, gave you mixed signals. I do like you. You're my sunshine." His cheeks coloured a little as Mum let out an 'awww.'

"Mum!"

"Sorry, sorry! We'll go upstairs and give you two some privacy." She shoved Dad out of the door.

"But I wanted to hear what he had to say…" my dad protested and I couldn't help but laugh. Josh walked closer to me and held the flowers out. I smiled and accepted them, walking into the kitchen to grab a vase.

"These must have cost a fortune, Josh. You shouldn't have…"

"And *that* is exactly why we can't be more than friends Izzy!" I whirled around at his raised voice, confused about why he was suddenly shouting at me.

"What…what do you…mean?"

"You *know* who I am. Who my family are. I don't have a pot to piss in. I hardly have enough to pay the bills. *Your mum* is buying our food shopping every week for fuck's sake. And thank fuck she is because I don't know how we'd manage otherwise. I can't give you anything, Izzy. I can't take you anywhere. I can't spoil you like you deserve. I can't even look after my own brothers properly…" He ran his hands through hair angrily, his breathing becoming more and more frantic. "I would like for nothing better than for you to be mine. But I don't deserve you. I *need* you, but I don't deserve you. You are my sunshine but all I'm going to do is bring you darkness and misery. You deserve better. I'm too selfish to not be friends with you, but I refuse to drag you into my life any more than you already are." He was panting now, fists clenched, face red. He'd never looked so bloody hot.

"Well, Josh Bugg, I have news for you…" I walked over to him, invading his personal space so my face was inches from his. He took a half-step back, shocked by my reaction, but I closed the distance again.

"You don't get to make decisions about what *I* deserve. About what *I* want. And I *want* to be in your life. I don't care about what money you do or don't have, or what you can or cannot buy me. I want *you*, Josh." I wrapped my hands around his neck, tugging him towards me. Third time lucky, right?

I felt my heart lurch as he resisted, preventing me from closing the last inch or two between us. He searched my eyes with his own and I couldn't quite read him.

"Are you sure?" he whispered. His face was completely neutral, as if he was carefully preparing himself to react in a certain way depending on my answer.

"Completely." I put a little more force into my grip, but I needn't have worried. He didn't resist this time. Our first kiss had been full of playfulness and lust. Our second kiss had been slow and gentle, apart from the abrupt end of course. This kiss was completely different. It was like I could feel Josh letting go. Letting go of his worries and his mistrust and his fear. Instead, he embraced it all. He embraced me. I felt something ignite within and it was like I couldn't get close enough to him. My fingers tangled in his hair and his hand slipped around the back of my neck. We pressed as close together as possible and our movements started to become more frantic. More desperate. Our tongues explored fiercely and I tilted my head to a different angle, needing to kiss him as deeply as possible. Josh growled low in his throat and I jolted, desire rippling through me.

"Woah," I pulled back, needing to slow things down and avoid my parents walking in on an entirely different scene to the one they left. I had never felt so attracted to someone, never wanted someone so badly. I was very inexperienced, probably embarrassingly so for a seventeen-year-old, but right then, I knew I could give myself to this boy. Completely.

Josh broke out into a genuine smile, his eyes shining as he tilted his forehead against my own. He wrapped his arms around me, squeezing and lifting me off the ground.

"Put me down!" I squealed, laughing. He held me up a second longer before dropping me gently back to my feet. I reached for his hand, squeezing a little.

"Josh! Can we come in yet? It's bloody freezing out here!" I frowned at Josh quizzically.

"Is that Ryan shouting through our letterbox?" I peered into the corridor and could see two silhouettes through the frosted glass of our front door.

"I er, didn't know if we'd be welcome or not, so told them to wait outside..." he was trying to play it cool with a lopsided grin, but I could see the slight blush colouring his cheeks.

"Mum! We have some extra guests for dinner!" I called behind me as I wrenched open the front door, smiling to see Ryan and Georgie waiting outside.

"You didn't kick his arse, then?" Ryan asked whilst Georgie shouted, "Told you she'd forgive him!" He ran past me, in search of my mum. He had grown quite attached to her, probably because she shamelessly rained near-constant attention on him.

"Hey man, want to help me prep dinner?" Dad high-fived Ryan as he and Mum came down the stairs, all of us heading back into the kitchen. I looked around and couldn't help but beam. All my favourite people in the world were here right now.

Chapter 28

Joshua

"MERRY CHRISTMAS!" Oh, sweet Jesus. How did I know that Izzy's family would be the type to go completely overboard at Christmas? My brothers and I had spent near enough the entire Christmas holidays over at Izzy's. I had picked up some extra shifts at the shop and stayed back at our house when I was working a late shift, but I don't think Ryan and Georgie have been home in almost two weeks.

I'd worked late last night but as the buses didn't run on Christmas Day, I'd gotten the last one back here and stayed up with Izzy's family watching Christmas movies until almost midnight. I'd finally gotten comfortable sleeping away from Ryan and Georgie, which is why my brothers, Izzy, and her parents were currently crowding into Sammy's office in the loft. They all had matching Christmas jumpers on over their pyjamas. I shit you not. Every single one of them had navy woolly jumpers with a snowy Christmas scene stitched through it. Even Ryan was laughing hysterically as he and Georgie jumped on the sofa bed, bundling on top of me.

"What the hell are you wearing?" I laughed, holding them both back from me so I could get a better look.

"Oh, don't get jealous Joshy, you have one too!" Georgie grabbed a garment from Izzy's arms, throwing it at my face whilst giggling. I groaned good-naturedly, pulling myself into a seated position and holding it up against me.

"Come on. I'll get breakfast on the go and then we can do presents before I leave to get my mum," Charlie gestured for everyone to follow him back down the stairs.

"I'll help," Ryan jumped off the bed and was the first to leave after him. He and Charlie had really bonded over the Christmas break, especially with Charlie teaching him how to cook a different dish every night. Ryan had turned into quite the chef. Sammy held her arms out to Georgie, who swiftly took off, jumping up into them. It looked a little ridiculous; a nine-year-old clinging to a grown woman. But who was I to judge? Georgie had been desperate for attention, for a mother's love, for so long now that it didn't surprise me that he was making the most of it from Sammy.

"Let's give these two some privacy," Sammy said, ruffling Georgie's hair whilst looking over her shoulder to wink at Izzy. "Only five minutes though." Her expression turned more serious as she raised her eyebrows, slowly disappearing from view as she descended the stairs.

"Merry Christmas, Josh." Izzy perched on the bed next to me, leaning in to give me a quick kiss on the lips. Although she was wearing the baggy, oversized Christmas jumper, she still looked sexy as hell. Mainly due to the tiny navy shorts she was wearing. Her legs went on forever. I had soon learned that the only problem with spending so much time with Izzy, was that it meant I was spending an agonising amount of time with a hard-on. Like right now. We had only managed to steal a few kisses, usually when I walked Izzy up to bed to say goodnight, but her parents were careful not to leave us alone for too long. I didn't blame them. If they knew what was running through my head most of the time, I wouldn't be surprised if they locked me out of the house altogether and never let me back in again.

"Morning Sunshine." I leaned in for another kiss, lingering a little, wanting more than just a peck. I felt my self-control slipping away a little each day. But we hadn't even talked about sex. Or if we were even in a proper relationship.

"Izzy! Breakfast!" Sammy called, making it clear that our time was up. I groaned in frustration as Izzy jumped off the bed, skipping towards the stairs.

"You know exactly what you do to me, don't you?" I laughed, not making a move until a certain part of me calmed down. She laughed, dancing down the stairs. I shook my head, amused by her sudden confidence.

She'd come out of her shell the past couple of weeks, getting more and more comfortable around me.

After several minutes, I shoved some clothes on (yes, including the hideous Christmas jumper) and followed everyone downstairs. There was hardly any room in the lounge due to the humongous Christmas tree and several piles of presents. I mean, seriously, it looked like Santa had thrown up in here! Mum used to put up one of those fake, perfectly symmetrical trees every year, but it was nothing like the real fir the Johnsons' had. The tree almost touched the ceiling and was decorated in the traditional red, green and white Christmas colours. There were candy canes, ornaments and brightly coloured baubles all over it. Not to mention the garish flashing lights woven through the branches. With the weight of all the decorations, it was lopsided and the branches stuck out at all sorts of angles, but I secretly loved it.

"Wowee," I wolf-whistled. "That is an impressive number of presents." Izzy was laying the table for breakfast, whilst Georgie and Ryan helped Charlie in the kitchen.

"Yours and your brothers' presents are stacked up over there," Izzy gestured with her head towards three piles by the sofa. I stared wide-eyed as I heard something clatter to the floor behind me. I turned and saw Ryan and Georgie both frozen and staring at the presents, a spatula lying on the floor at Georgie's feet.

"We...have presents?" He whispered.

"Of course you do! It's Christmas," Sammy laughed as she plucked the spatula from the floor and started washing it in the sink. Georgie immediately ran over to them, checking tags to see which were his.

"Joshy! Look! I have presents!" I tried to stop my eyes tearing up as I watched him gaze at a stack of at least ten presents. Even when Big Mike hadn't blown all our money on his shitty business, he and Mum had never made much effort. He'd buy her fancy jewellery and perfume, and she'd buy him expensive watches and suits. But when it came to us, they never paid much attention. Sure, we'd always been dressed in the best clothes to keep up appearances, but it was like we weren't worth the bother when there wasn't anyone important for us to show off in front of. When no one was around to see us open our gifts. Our presents would consist of clothes and vouchers. Half the time, they were the wrong sizes or for shops we'd never even heard of.

"Treat yourself," Big Mike would leer at us as we opened gift cards. There was zero thought put into it and whilst I didn't care about their crappy gifts, it killed me to see the disappointment in my brothers' eyes every year. So much so, I started saving up my own vouchers so I could buy them nice gifts at Christmas every year. We stopped getting anything for Christmas at all when Mum left.

"I tell you what, why don't we do presents now, and I'll warm breakfast up after we're done?" Charlie asked and Georgie squealed with delight. I felt Izzy slip her fingers around mine as I continued to watch Georgie bounce around excitedly.

"You didn't need to do this, you know," I whispered to her.

"We wanted to," she whispered back, leaning into me and kissing me on the cheek.

"Come on you two, go sit next to your presents so we can get started!" Sammy clapped her hands together, looking almost as giddy as Georgie. *Almost.*

"OK, go!" She clapped again and Georgie and Ryan began shredding paper, pieces flying everywhere. I couldn't help but observe quietly, taking in every smile, every cheer, every happy moment. Ryan had a couple of cookbooks, some DVDs, a new pair of jeans and several new t-shirts (I was relieved that I wouldn't have to buy him new clothes anytime soon), a fancy bottle of aftershave, a new football and a new backpack. Georgie had some new clothes too, a ton of different board games, three different lego sets, more DVDs, and a basketball hoop that could be mounted to the wall, as well as a basketball. They had both been spoiled rotten.

"Josh, you've not opened a single one yet. Go on, make a start," Sammy encouraged.

"Sorry. I was enjoying watching everyone else," I replied sheepishly. I turned over the first tag and saw *Merry Christmas, love Sammy and Charlie x* It was the same for all the presents in the pile, with the exception of three that were from Izzy.

"Save mine 'til last," she directed, a big grin on her face as I laughed. Sammy and Charlie had also gifted me aftershave, three new polo tops, even more DVDs (boy, we had a lot of films to watch), and a twenty-five-pound iTunes voucher. I tried to keep my face neutral as I put the voucher to one side, wondering if I would be able to exchange it for something else. They obviously didn't know that I had no way of using it and I didn't want to embarrass them.

"This one first!" Izzy handed me a heavy, rectangular box. Everyone stopped to watch me, making me feel very self-conscious as I started to tear the wrapping paper. It looked like some kind of wooden briefcase and I frowned, confused. Izzy gestured for me to open it, so I lifted the lid, pausing as I took in the contents.

"Do you like it? Jess said you're amazingly talented…" she trailed off, unsure of how I'd react.

"Wow." I didn't know what else to say. I had a complete artist's set in front of me, the case filled with oil paints, charcoal, pencils, watercolours and brushes. The next gift was a variety of different papers and pads to try them out on too. I had everything I could ever need to escape. It was perfect.

"Thank you," I kissed her softly on the cheek and she beamed.

"OK, I saved the best 'til the last," she smiled as she passed me a very neatly wrapped, small box.

"Oh Izzy…" It was an iPod. And now the voucher made perfect sense.

"This must have cost you a fortune, you shouldn't have…"

"Shhh!" She pressed a finger to my lips. "You deserve this Josh and I wanted to get you something nice. I've already uploaded my favourite songs to it, too." Not caring that everyone else was watching, I grabbed her chin and pulled her in for a quick kiss.

"You're amazing," I smiled at her, pushing down feelings of guilt, shame and embarrassment at not having been able to get her or her family something worthy. I was seriously doubting the pathetically underwhelming gifts I had stashed upstairs for them all, contemplating not giving them out at all. Ryan, Georgie and I had spent ages trying to think of gifts, but they looked fucking stupid compared to this lot. Nope, it was better to say we couldn't afford gifts and not give them anything.

"Josh, go get their presents from us!" Georgie called out. Great. I glanced at Izzy, Sammy and Charlie, cringing as I saw the happy surprise in their faces.

"Don't get your hopes up, they're nothing special…" I trudged upstairs, retrieving my backpack and bringing it back to the lounge with me. I sighed as I unzipped it, reluctantly pulling the gifts out. I handed Sammy and Charlie one gift each and then explained that the third one was a joint present for them. I gave Izzy a bag of little gifts, mostly picked out by Ryan and Georgie, with my gift at the bottom. I was actually feeling a little nauseous at the idea of them opening them.

"Aww, you remembered!" Sammy gushed as she hugged a small elephant ornament to her chest. "I pointed one out just like this to Georgie the other week when we were out shopping. They're my favourite animal." To be fair to her, she was putting on a pretty convincing happy face, but I was finding it hard to believe she'd genuinely be pleased with an ornament from a charity shop. It only cost a couple of quid.

"And this is just what I needed," Charlie smiled, holding up his knife-sharpening block.

"You kept saying how blunt your knives were and

259

that you were going to buy new ones, so I thought this might save you some money," Ryan shrugged.

"You're right, good thinking." Charlie was also great at faking facial expressions.

"Open the joint one, open the joint one! Joshy spent ages on it!" Georgie was bouncing with glee again as I felt myself shrink away in embarrassment. Why I had let my brothers convince me this was a good idea, I don't know. But I felt like an idiot now.

"Oh my…" Sammy put her hand up to her mouth and went quiet.

"It's silly, you don't have to keep it, I…"

"No, don't you dare! This is amazing, Josh. You did this?" Sammy interrupted and I nodded. "Breath-taking."

"You've got them spot on," Charlie added, nodding as he looked up.

"Let me see!" Izzy said, jumping up and rushing over, but Sammy held the gift to her chest.

"I have a feeling you have your own one and I don't want to spoil it," Sammy explained, winking at me. This was so embarrassing. Izzy sat back down, starting to rummage through her own bag. She laughed at all the chocolate bars Georgie had picked out, immediately slotted the bangles over her wrist that Ryan had chosen (costume jewellery from the charity shop again), and clapped happily when she saw some new DVDs.

"You said you hadn't seen it yet and we love it," Ryan nodded at the *Venom* DVD in her hand.

"I can't wait to watch it," she smiled. My heart jumped a little as she reached in and plucked out my gift. I was actually starting to sweat too. It was torture watching her slowly rip the paper off it. She gasped, raising her hand to cover her mouth in exactly the same way Sammy had.

"Josh..." To my horror, her eyes started filling up with tears. I leaned over to try and snatch the gift off her, but she pulled back, a deep frown pulling her eyebrows inwards.

"You don't like it, so give it...."

"Don't like it? Don't like it! I *love* it. Did you really draw this?" I nodded again. She stared at the framed drawing for what seemed like forever, before flinging her arms around my neck and burying her head in my shoulder.

"It's beautiful. How did you do it?"

"Your mum emailed me the photos from that day at the bowling alley, so I used a couple of them to copy from. I needed to practice them anyway."

"Practice?"

"Oh, nothing. Just practising my skills in general. So, you really don't mind that I only gave you a sketch for Christmas?" I asked, glancing at Sammy and Charlie as well to include them in the question.

"Are you for real? It's the most romantic, thoughtful gift I have ever received!"

"You are so talented, Josh," Sammy chimed in as she held out her sketch for Izzy to see.

"Oh jeez, this one is amazing too!" Izzy held both of them side by side and I looked over her shoulder, double-checking the accuracy of my sketches now that the subjects were all in the same room. Charlie and

Sammy had a sketch of Izzy with my two brothers. None of them were looking at the camera as Sammy had caught them unawares, so they were all looking at each other with genuine smiles on their faces. It was my favourite picture. Izzy's one was of the two of us. Again, neither of us were looking at the camera and in fact, most of my face was hidden. I had my arm wrapped around her shoulder, my face buried in her hair as I pressed a kiss to the side of her head. Izzy's head was tilted up as she tried to look at me, another smile on her lips. Sammy was great at capturing the best moments on camera.

"I didn't think it was possible, but I think I love you all a little bit more. What thoughtful, kind gifts!" Sammy started getting glassy-eyed as she took turns embracing me and my brothers.

"I couldn't have asked for a better...friend...for my daughter," Sammy said as she hugged me. It bothered me that she'd hesitated over what to call me.

"Actually, we're more than friends. Right, Sunshine?" I pulled back from Sammy, looking over to Izzy.

"We...we are?" Her eyes were wide as she stared at me.

"Well, I was hoping you'd be my girlfriend. If you want to, I mean?" Asking her in front of her parents wasn't my smartest idea, but I couldn't stand the idea of everyone thinking we were only friends anymore. She was so much more than that to me. I needed her as much as I needed to breathe. She was my sunshine, after all.

Izzy launched herself at me, throwing her arms

around me and wrapping her legs around my waist.

"Best Christmas present ever!" She whispered in my ear before kissing me roughly on the lips. Sammy laughed and clapped, but Charlie turned away, averting his eyes, making Izzy giggle. He cleared his throat.

"Right, who's hungry?"

Chapter 29

Isabel

This has, without a doubt, been the best Christmas for years. Usually it was only me, Mum, Dad and Nanny Steph. Sometimes my uncle and his wife would join us, but never anyone else my age. And whilst Mum and Dad were usually on good form and liked to play board games and stuff, I couldn't help but feel a little lonely every now and then. Nanny Steph was sharp-tongued and didn't like to get involved in games, even though she'd observe and offer unwanted advice at every possible opportunity. I loved her to bits and her sarcastic wit was very entertaining, but not exactly someone I could have a great conversation with. Although I did love introducing Josh to her as my boyfriend.

Boy, I hadn't been expecting that. Hoping, sure.

Praying and dreaming, you bet. But I didn't think he'd actually ask me. And don't even get me started on his sketches. I hadn't realised how good he was. He'd caught details that I hadn't expected; Georgie's freckles across his nose, Ryan's creases near his eyes as he laughed, and how my hair was always tucked behind my right ear. He was crazy talented, the life-likeness scary good. It literally looked like a black and white photo. He must have spent hours on them, and there was something so gratifying about knowing he spent all that time trying to make me and my parents happy. I knew he was special.

"So, did you have a good Christmas this year, honey?" Mum asked as she plopped down on the sofa next to me. I paused the film I was watching, tucking my legs up underneath me as I twisted to face her.

"It was brilliant, Mum." I embraced her tightly, yet again inwardly giving thanks for having such great parents.

"I loved having Josh and his brothers over. We've all grown quite close. But we wanted to just check-in with you about a couple of things...." She trailed off as Dad came into the room, taking a seat next to her. Oh great, where the hell was this going? Josh was working at the shop and his brothers had gone home to pack some more clothes before returning tonight. It looked like my parents were making the most of having me to themselves.

"You and Josh have grown pretty close too, haven't you?" Mum continued and I nodded cautiously.

"Well, you know we love having them over, we just

want to make sure you don't feel pressured into anything."

"What do you mean?" I was confused.

"What your mum is trying to say, is that you have clearly become some kind of role model to all three boys and that can be a lot of pressure for a young woman. We want to make sure you know that you don't have to be Josh's girlfriend because you think that's what he needs, or will make us happy, or his brothers happy, or…"

"No, no. I *want* to be with Josh. I do." I was starting to get annoyed at them implying I had anything other than genuine feelings for him.

"And that's great honey, really it is. We think he's a fantastic boy. But his family is obviously going through a tough time. I haven't heard him speak about his father or even make a phone call to him the entire time they've been staying here. We just want you to know that if things get tough or you don't want to be in a relationship anymore, it's perfectly fine to take a step back. You don't have to feel like you're responsible for them." Mum was smiling encouragingly at me, but all it did was piss me off.

"So, what you're saying is, is if things start getting too difficult or Josh needs too much help, I should just back off?" I folded my arms, raising my eyebrow as Dad sighed.

"No Izzy, that's not what we are saying, and you know it. We just want you to know that we will support you no matter what. And that we will support Josh and his brothers no matter what. Whether you are together as a couple or not."

"OK. I understand." Kind of.

"And he really is a great guy. Very sweet and he clearly cares a lot about you. It's like you've gone back to your old self this year and I couldn't ask for anymore," Dad explained, making me feel a little guilty about not telling them about the whole Ellie situation. But if they thought Josh was the reason I was 'back to myself,' then hey, I wasn't going to correct them. Well, I guess it was true at least in part. He *had* given me the confidence to be myself, be open and honest and not be afraid to voice my opinion, even if I disagreed with something.

"You're just saying that because you'd miss your sous chef if we ever broke up. Ryan never leaves the kitchen!" I said playfully, trying to lighten the mood and change the subject.

"That's true I suppose," Dad chuckled and nodded.

"So, what are we watching?" Mum asked, laying back into the sofa and hooking her legs over Dad's.

"I had *Venom* on, but it's only been on about ten minutes. I'll rewind from the beginning so you can watch it."

"Oooh, you know I love a bit of Tom Hardy," Mum laughed as Dad rolled his eyes. I was in the process of rewinding when Mum's phone started ringing. She jumped up, grabbing it off the side in the kitchen and lifting it to her ear.

"Hi Georgie, what's…" she paused, the colour draining from her face.

"Mum? What's wrong?" I sat up and Dad did the same, both of us alert. She gestured at us to be quiet as she listened intently.

"OK, OK, darling. I need you to go hide somewhere safe and we will be over straight away. OK, Georgie? Georgie? Are you there?" She stared at the phone in her hand.

"Car. Now. Something's wrong." Mum frantically started looking for her car keys, running for the front door. Dad and I leapt into action, scurrying after her as a sickening feeling churned in my stomach.

"Sammy, what's going on?" Dad jumped into the driver's seat as Mum turned around to face me.

"What's their address?" she asked and the serious expression on her face scared the hell out of me. I reeled it off as Dad repeated his question.

"Georgie is in trouble. He kept saying *he's back, he's back. He's going to kill him.* And then the line went dead."

"Who is back? That doesn't make any sense!" Dad floored the accelerator, flying around corners and charging down the road as fast as possible.

"He was crying, Charlie. He sounded terrified." Mum was sitting as far forward in her seat as possible, as if willing the car to go faster. She had a look of determination on her face, but I didn't understand how she could hold it together after that phone call. I tasted vomit at the back of my throat and I concentrated hard on keeping it at bay.

"This is all my fault," I sobbed, intense fear and shame threatening to overwhelm me. Why hadn't I just told them about Big Mike? Why hadn't I told anyone? It had to be him Georgie was referring to and now their lives were in danger. What if something serious happened to Georgie? To Ryan? To Josh? I couldn't breathe.

"Izzy, calm down or you are going to have a panic attack and we can't stop this car," Dad said calmly, catching my eye in the rear-view mirror. I focused on controlling my breathing, realising that Dad was right and that I couldn't fall to pieces right now.

"Izzy, what's going on? Do you know?" Mum twisted around in her seat and we locked eyes in an intense stare.

"The bruises...the ones you told me about...it was...their dad..." I tried to explain between sobs, but as I said the words out loud, terror started to vibrate through my body. I realised just how much I'd screwed up by not telling anyone what had been really going on. *Forgive me, Josh. Please be OK...*

Chapter 30

Joshua

Even though it was Boxing Day and I'd spent most of the day working, I couldn't help but have a spring in my step on the walk home. I was listening to my new iPod with All Time Low's *Something's Gotta Give* blaring as loud as possible. I felt great. Like the dog's bollocks. Izzy was now my girlfriend, her parents were amazing, and I'd eaten so much the past week or so that I had definitely put on some size. I had been doing push-ups religiously every day to keep up my upper body strength and I was pleased with the difference I had seen already.

I hadn't been hungry once and neither had Georgie or Ryan. This had been the best Christmas for a long time, maybe even ever. No, definitely the best Christmas we'd ever had. And it wasn't over yet. I was going to swing by the house, make sure Ryan and Georgie had packed their clothes, then we'd all head back to Izzy's for the rest of the Christmas break. Izzy and I had been invited to a New Year's Eve party over Sophie's and for once, I was looking forward to the New Year. Much like Christmas, we hadn't felt like celebrating the New Year much the past few years. Why celebrate the start of a New Year when it's going to be just as crappy as the previous one? But not next year. Next year was going to be a great year for us, I could *feel* it.

I could see the house in the distance and 30 Seconds to Mars' *Walk on Water* started up. I smiled, thinking how perfect that sounded. That was exactly how I felt right now, like I could walk on water. Usually I'd feel embarrassed or frustrated every time I saw our shitty street and our shitty house, but not today. Nothing was getting this good mood down.

"Ryan, Georgie, you ready?" I called as I turned my key in the lock, pushing the door inwards.

"Hello dickhead." I yanked my headphones out, letting them hang loose by my side, my eyes locking with the monster standing in the kitchen. It was like everything was in slow motion and my brain couldn't comprehend what was in front of me. Blood. So much blood.

"Ryan…" his name escaped from my lips in a whisper. Big Mike had bloody knuckles and Ryan was in a heap on the floor, unmoving. Unconscious. His face was a pulverised mess. I couldn't see his eyes or make out his nose or his mouth. It was a scene from a horror movie. I turned and vomited on the front doorstep, wiping my mouth with the back of my hand. My vision went blurry with tears. But then I felt it. The uncontrollable, unwavering, unforgiving rage. I clenched my fists, locking eyes with Big Mike again, taking deep breaths. In. And out. In. And Out.

And then I launched myself at him, my fingertips stretched wide as I aimed for his throat.

"You thought...you could break my nose...then live it up in here like kings?" We struggled as he grabbed my wrists, holding them an inch or two away from his neck. Our faces were so close I could smell the alcohol on his breath and see how wide his pupils were. The pulse in his neck was throbbing.

I jerked my hands back, slamming a fist into his stomach and bringing my knee up to his face as he crumpled. He twisted his face at the last minute, so my knee bounced off the side of his head.

"When they sacked me, I admit, I wasn't going to bother coming back to this shithole. And I don't give a crap what happens to you worthless bastards. But..." He swung at me and we were too close for me to move out of the way, his fist connecting with my jaw. The force flung my head backwards, my body soon following. I stumbled backwards into a kitchen chair, wiping blood from my mouth with my fingers.

"...When I heard you were getting food delivered every week and walking around town all smug, I knew I had to teach you a lesson." He advanced, homing in on his target. And that's when I knew that today was it. Only one of us was going to walk away from this. And I had a shit ton of things to fight for. *People* to fight for.

No, I wasn't going down without a fucking good fight.

I channelled every bad memory; every fight, every hunger pain, every ounce of fear I'd ever experienced, every last drop of resentment. It was like I could feel it all powering through my veins, coming to my aid.

"I. WILL. KILL. YOU!" I roared at him, grabbing the chair and swinging it like a baseball bat. He was caught off-guard and there was a satisfying crack as it collided with the side of his skull. He crumpled to the floor, grabbing a hold of the kitchen worktop to stop him from falling completely. He was on his knees, shaking his head to try and clear his vision. I launched a kick at his face, catching him across the jaw and causing him to drop to all fours, blood dripping from his mouth. I tried to kick again but he grabbed my foot at the last minute, forcing me away from him. I lost my balance, landing hard on my arse. It was a race to see who would get up first.

Chapter 31

Isabel

"What do you mean, it was their father!?"

"He...he was beating them…" I sobbed, my tears out of control now. I was imagining every horrible scenario possible, sickening scenes flashing through my head.

"When I found out, I wanted to tell you...but Josh made me promise...he didn't want...he didn't want…" I couldn't get the words out. I couldn't breathe. I really couldn't breathe.

"Sammy, calm her down!" Tires screeched as we went around another corner at a terrifying speed. I was vaguely aware of horns blaring, but it sounded distant. I couldn't see anything beyond what was in my head. Couldn't hear anything anymore. I only saw Josh's lifeless eyes staring at me.

I felt a sharp pain in my knee, pulling me out of the

darkness in my head. Mum's hand gripped it tightly. She was twisted so that half of her body was almost in the back of the car with me.

"Look at me." She let go of my knee, only to grip my jaw. Hard.

"We are going to fix this. We are going to *save* them. I am not going to let anything happen to them. OK, Izzy? Do you hear me? This is not your fault. Everything will be OK." There was no way she could know that. How could she know that? But the fire in her eyes was blaring in full force. I believed her. I did. They were going to be OK. They had to be OK.

Chapter 32

Joshua

He was a fraction quicker than me and he used his height to his advantage, jumping over Ryan's body on the floor to grab my head and slam it against the worktop. The pain was instant and almost unbearable. Almost. My vision was darkening, but then I saw Ryan's immobile form out the corner of my eye, and I roared back to life. He wasn't expecting my knuckles to connect with his nose and I felt a flash of satisfaction as I watched as, once again, blood spurted from it.

"You fucking shit...you..." his voice garbled as the blood sprayed into his mouth. I didn't hesitate. There would be no mercy tonight. I started raining punches on him, throwing all my weight into every. Single. One. There was a sharp pain in my left hand, but I kept going. I was winning. I could see it. He was faltering. He wasn't fighting back.

Chapter 33

Isabel

"Try calling Georgie again," Dad shouted above yet another car horn.

"I have been! He's not fucking answering! Shit!" Mum slammed her hand into the dashboard. She never swore. It was strange to hear her swear. This was bad.

"How much longer, Charlie? HOW MUCH LONGER?"

"Five minutes honey. Five minutes." *Five minutes Josh, hold on...*

Chapter 34

Joshua

Fuck. This was bad. I thought he was going down. He wasn't. He was just waiting for the right time. I thought that was it. I slowed down. A crucial mistake. Between my punches as I started to slow, feeling my energy traitorously starting to dissipate, he sprung forward and pushed me as hard as he could. I hit the back of my head on the hard, cold tiled floor, feeling the impact rattling through my brain. The open front door was swinging slightly in the wind. I was inches away from my vomit.

Big Mike turned his back to me, reaching for something on the side. I struggled to a sitting position, but the room was spinning. It was like trying to move through mud, I was so slow. I could see him creeping towards me, but there were five of him. And they were swaying, blurry. I frowned, concentrating as hard as I could to see what was in front of me. He was a foot or two away when my vision snapped into focus, a renewed punch of adrenaline kicking in as I saw what he was holding. A knife. A fucking big one.

"No…" I scrambled to my feet, stumbling and flinging my arms out to hold onto something. Anything. He started to laugh.

"It's over. It's always amused me that you thought you would ever beat me. Every time you fought, I could see the hope in your eyes. Pathetic. I am bigger. I am stronger. I am *better* than you, you worthless piece of shit." His face was a mask of red. It seemed like blood was dripping from every crease in his face. But I could still see his eyes. I could see the hatred. I glanced at the front door, briefly considering running. I caught sight of Ryan again and shame and guilt racked through me. I couldn't leave him. And where the fuck was Georgie? He couldn't have hurt him too, no way. Please God, no.

"Where's…Georgie…?" My voice sounded weak even to my own ears and I cringed, not wanting him to know how bad I was hurt. How weak I felt.

"Why do you care? You'll be dead soon," he laughed, spit flying from the corner of his mouth. He was closing in and I still couldn't see properly as I desperately tried to fend off unconsciousness. He sprung forward, jabbing the knife at my abdomen. I twisted, narrowly avoiding the blade. He stumbled, not prepared for the lack of impact. I tried to kick out at his wrist, but it wasn't good enough. My aim was off and it lacked power. I connected with his elbow but he barely flinched. He whirled, thrusting the knife again. This time I felt a sharp pain under my ribs. *No, no, no. Not like this.* I clutched my side, feeling liquid stream through my fingers. I wouldn't look, I couldn't. He expected me to go down, already smiling in triumph. In victory.

I pictured Izzy. Her smile. Her eyes. My sunshine. I demanded every last bit of strength to flow into my right arm and threw the hardest punch I possibly could. I felt bone crack under my knuckles, unsure if it was his cheek or my fingers. I heard the knife clatter to the floor. I fell to my knees, feeling my strength leave me again. *Get up. Get up, Josh.* I thought I could hear Izzy begging me to keep going.

"YOU'RE DEAD!" He growled, staggering towards me. He pushed me to my back, straddling me. His fingers wrapped around my neck. And he squeezed. And squeezed. *I'm sorry Ryan, forgive me.* The darkness was starting to take over and all I could do was stare at my brother's bloody, still body on the floor. He hadn't moved the entire time. *We'll be together soon, brother.*

Chapter 35

Isabel

"Get out of the way, you moron!" Dad leaned on the horn, shouting more abuse at the elderly lady in the tiny hatchback as we overtook her on the wrong side of the road.

"There, there! It's that road, Dad!" I pointed out *West View* and he swerved.

"STOP!" I shouted and Dad slammed on the brakes, the car screeching to a stop a couple of houses away from Josh's.

"Stay here, Izzy!" Mum shouted as she and Dad unclipped their seat belts, throwing them off them and launching out of the car. Sod that. I needed to see him. I needed to see he was OK.

Chapter 36

Joshua

"NO!" Was that Georgie? My eyes fluttered, trying to see whose voice it was. Suddenly air started filling my lungs again and the weight on my chest lifted. I couldn't move straight away. And my eyes wouldn't open. But I felt someone shaking me.

"Joshy...please...stay awake..." It *was* Georgie. I willed my eyes to open, feeling a surge of relief when I saw my little brother kneeling next to me. I was vaguely aware of Big Mike lying face down behind him, blood pooling. I blinked, seeing blood on Georgie's hands. I frowned, not understanding why he was holding the knife now. But wait, wasn't that the knife over there on the floor by Big Mike?

"I'm sorry...I should have come out sooner...but...I was...scared..." he was sobbing, raw pain racking through his little body, causing him to gasp and tremble.

"You'll be OK now." Could he hear me? Was I even speaking aloud? *I couldn't save him. I'm sorry. But you're safe now. Live. Live your life, Georgie. And look after Izzy for me, OK? I need you to be a big, strong boy and look after her for me.*

"Josh? Josh! Wake up!" *I should have done better. I should have tried harder. I failed you, Ryan. I am so sorry.*

"Please…please…Joshy. Don't go. Stay." *I don't deserve to live. I failed. He was right all along. I am worthless.*

I am unworthy.

JOSH AND IZZY'S STORY CONTINUES
IN…

I AM
UNBREAKABLE

WWW.ANGELAMACKWRITER.COM

ACKNOWLEDGEMENTS

A huge thank you to...

My husband, who has always encouraged me to follow my dreams, even if that meant sacrificing his own.

My mum, for reading the early draft of this book, brainstorming possible titles (even though I ignored your advice, sorry!) and for always believing I have what it takes to become a writer.

My best friend Nicola, for confessing that she cried whilst reading my draft for the first time - there's nothing a writer loves to hear more than that her characters created an emotional response in a reader!

My extremely talented cover designer Breanna Smith – your creative vision and patience is incredible!

You, the reader. I can't express my gratitude enough. I hope you love the story as much as I do.

You are all my everyday heroes.

ABOUT THE AUTHOR

Angela Mack lives in Suffolk with her husband, a mini Batman-wannabe, a troll princess and two dogs. She likes to blast pop punk when writing, much to the disdain of her neighbours. She can't swear in front of her kids, but she sure makes up for it in her books. She never thought she'd have the courage to publish her innermost daydreams, yet here we are!

'I Am Unworthy' is her debut novel.

To keep up to date with Angela's upcoming releases, please visit www.angelamackwriter.com or follow her on Instagram, @WriterAngieM.

Printed in Great Britain
by Amazon